HIGH IN THE STREETS

High in the Streets is by turns hilarious, moving, and raw. A gritty tour de force that takes the best aspects of James Salter, Norman Mailer, and Bret Easton Ellis to heart, Binder's novel is an accomplished debut by a writer with a singular, animated voice, attuned to the strange rhythms and desperation of latter-day Los Angeles and the people who live there.
Michael Abolafia, New York Review Books

Binder is a born storyteller, and his novel is as philosophically astute as it is hilariously funny. We can expect great things from this wild new voice.
Clancy Martin, a Guggenheim Fellow and the Pushcart Prize-winning author of the books *How to Sell* (FSG), *Love & Lies* (FSG), *Bad Sex* (Tyrant)

High in the Streets is pure narrative, one sublimely strange event after another. My favorite parts are the stories within the story, those plump nuggets of secondary or tertiary narrative, rendered with seeming ease and worn so lightly. In the right hands—i.e., in hands like Matthew Binder's—they could each spin off and become narratives of their own. Binder's talent for invention is real, and it is substantial.
Lary Wallace, Features editor of Bangkok Post: The Magazine and regular contributor to Aeon, the Los Angeles Review of Books, Library of America's Reader's Almanac, and The Paris Review

High in
the Streets

High in
the Streets

Matthew Binder

Winchester, UK
Washington, USA

First published by Roundfire Books, 2016
Roundfire Books is an imprint of John Hunt Publishing Ltd., Laurel House, Station Approach,
Alresford, Hants, SO24 9JH, UK
office1@jhpbooks.net
www.johnhuntpublishing.com
www.roundfire-books.com

For distributor details and how to order please visit the 'Ordering' section on our website.

Text copyright: Matthew Binder 2015

ISBN: 978 1 78535 283 6
Library of Congress Control Number: 2015949728

A CIP catalogue record for this book is available from the British Library.

Design: Stuart Davies

Printed and bound by CPI Group (UK) Ltd, Croydon, CR0 4YY, UK

We operate a distinctive and ethical publishing philosophy in all
areas of our business, from our global network of authors to
production and worldwide distribution.

A big Thank You to my best helpers:
Ryan Morse
Clancy Martin
Kent Nelson
Lary Wallace
Michael Abolafia

Matthew Binder is a former wastrel of the highest order. A cold list of his past behaviors would qualify him as a bastard in anybody's book. *High in the Streets* is his first novel.

Chapter

I've just moved my work desk into the master bathroom of my house. This is the last room in my home in which I haven't yet failed to accomplish work. Every other space has proven hopeless for me—too plush, too serene, too full of distractions. I'm feeling like the bathroom might just be the austere setting I need to buckle down and manifest more of my brilliance.

Unfortunately, it seems I've strained my back in the process. Every time I twist or bend left, it feels like someone is sticking me with a blazing-hot dagger. I'll have to remember to make an appointment to see my orthopedist, Dr. Hosseini. He'll fix me right up. Regardless of my ailment, the move to the bathroom needed to take place—just had to occur. When inspiration calls, you must answer. Getting my desk up that flight of stairs was an imperative.

Sitting in my bathroom office, I type the opening line: *God and everything was overthrown—everyone raging in a wild, deranged dance of life.* This feels like a great sentence. Such powerful, terse language, and so profound, too—future readers will be instantly smitten, critics will pile on the accolades, the sales numbers will shatter all records. The words are that exquisite!

Upon typing the sentence, I look up and am struck by the reflection of myself in the bathroom mirror. There I am, the amazing crafter of sentences, the virtuoso behind the most compelling first line in the history of literature. My God, I feel proud, never better. Also, I can't help but be overwhelmed by the sheer magnetism of my face. There is something about the natural light streaming in through the window that makes me look positively elegant. Not since Hemingway has an author exuded such physical charm. I wonder if I should go get my camera and take a picture. The shot would look fantastic on the book jacket. What a combination: a first line of prose so genteel and subtle it could only have been divinely inspired, and the most perfectly distinguished author photo on record.

An unbelievable formula for success.

It's an hour later, and I haven't typed another word. I'm stuck. Paralyzed. Terrified. How the fuck am I supposed to write a second book? A second book is nothing like a first book. A first book is simple. There is nothing to it really: one just writes about oneself. Chapter after chapter the words spew forth from your fingers and onto the page. It's as easy as breathing. As natural as fucking. The material is all there, nothing labored at all. Just sit down and type. It comes like a gift mounted on the backs of angels' wings.

Okay, sure, there is a bit of embellishing in the parts that need embellishing, but that's to be expected. Besides, the whole thing is written under a veil of fiction. Nobody actually thinks I did all those things I wrote about. If they did, I'd be brought up on charges for a litany of crimes. For instance, there's a bit in the book about how Donald, the protagonist, has a friend who suffers a terrible motorcycle accident.

The poor man is interned in a hospital for months on end. The prognosis is paralysis. He'll never walk, never play his guitar, never wipe his own ass or make love to a woman again. However, the man comes from a large family and is burdened with the love and support of countless friends. They tell him he's an inspiration, that he needs to keep fighting, and that they're holding out for a miracle. He smiles through all of this, puts on his bravest face—he doesn't want to disappoint them, break their hearts. After four months, the doctors move him into a rehabilitation clinic to begin intensive therapy.

Day after day, he's put through terribly painful exercises—torture, really. The best-case scenario is that with a lot of hard work and some luck, his ability to speak will continue to improve and someday he'll be able to swallow solid foods again.

Donald, as often as he can, takes the bus across town after the graveyard shift at his job stocking shelves at the local grocery and then waits at a nearby McDonald's for the clinic to open for visiting hours. There he sits with his friend, reading to him, telling him stories, doing whatever he can to make his friend's life a little bit more bearable.

One day, Donald arrives for his visit and his friend confesses that he truly wants to die. He says that he's not angry and that he's not afraid, but that he can't do it alone and that there is nobody else he can ask. Donald listens to his friend's pleas and is torn about what's the right thing to do. Finally, he tells his friend that he will continue to visit him every day for the next week but that he doesn't want to hear any more about the man's desire to die. Donald only wants to discuss other things on these visits, happy things, and if the friend manages this for an entire week and at the end of it still wants to die, Donald will help him.

So for a week Donald makes the trip across town every morning after work and waits patiently at the McDonald's for the clinic to open for visitors. The two friends discuss past adventures, women, books, film, and God. It's a wonderfully rewarding experience for Donald, and he believes it is for his friend, too. On the last day of the week, Donald returns to the clinic. He is convinced that the time he's spent with his friend will bring about a change of heart. When Donald enters the room, the friend is lying in bed smiling. He looks more peaceful than Donald has seen him at any time during one of his visits over the past months.

"You look great, pal," Donald says to his friend. "You must have some good news to share."

Donald leans in very close to hear the response, as his friend's voice is softer and quieter than the sound of a blade of grass blowing in the wind. "I'm so grateful for this past week," the friend says. "I know what an effort it is for you to be here with me. So thank you. And you're right: I do feel good, and why shouldn't I? I've been given a tremendous gift. I get to die today with the comfort of knowing my best friend is by my side."

Donald can tell by the look in his friend's eyes that there is no talking him out of it and so he doesn't try. The two friends exchange heartfelt goodbyes and then Donald places a pillow over his friend's nose and mouth and applies the required pressure. Donald makes every effort not to cry throughout this terribly difficult ordeal. He doesn't want the sound of his grief to be the last thing his friend hears on this earth. Instead Donald tells his friend that he loves him and that he's going to a better place and that soon he'll never feel pain again. It takes only a single minute for the friend to pass, but in that minute Donald experiences more feelings of love, fear, gratitude, sadness, and joy than in the entire rest of his life combined. Afterward, Donald sneaks off the clinic's campus to elude any suspicion of wrong-doing, goes home, packs, and hitchhikes up to Big Sur to chill in silence at the New Camaldoli Monastery.

Shortly after the book's release, an interviewer asked me whether any of this scenario was autobiographical. I said, "Of course not. Doing something like that is grounds for sending a man to jail for murder." I then winked my eye at the interviewer. "You think I'd risk something like that?"

Anyhow, that first book struck a chord with the public, loud enough and hard enough to pay for this house I'm living in. And it bought me my first new foreign car too—a BMW. I can hardly believe it— a big black BMW!

It has recently come to my attention however, that I've been living a bit outside my means. I let things get a little loose—financially, that is. Sebastian, my agent, has informed me I'm nearly penniless. I've run through close to four million bucks since I took up with my fiancé, Frannie, just two short years ago. When I bought the house, Sebastian went berserk. "What the fuck do you need a three-million-dollar house for?" he asked. I assured him it was completely necessary. "My temple of love," as I put it. "Your temple of love?" he asked. "What the hell has gotten into you?" I went onto regurgitate some nonsense Frannie had filled my head with about modern architecture—about how "form follows function," and about the emphasis that architects such as Le Corbusier and Walter Gropius put on geometric shapes and simple lines, "a significant departure from the style of previous eras."

Sebastian was so angry he didn't even make an appearance at the house-warming party. How someone could miss a private performance from Stephen Malkmus of Pavement is beyond comprehension. That was my one request of Frannie for our little shindig—that I get to choose the music. Turns out, even this small wish to pick the tunes was too much. Instead, we ended up compromising, if you can call it that. Frannie hired a DJ to spin Eurotrash electro, and I booked Malkmus (I'd met him at the premier for the movie adaptation of my manuscript) to play some old favorites on his acoustic guitar. Problem was, Frannie banished Malkmus and his guitar to the garage. She didn't think it would mix well with the more sophisticated and chic atmosphere she had worked so hard to cultivate in the main house.

Truth is, I never even wanted the place. Frannie forced it on me. I was perfectly content living in the same 600-hundred-square foot, one-bedroom apartment I'd been living in before the success of the book. But when I fell in love, I fell hard, and I was ready to spend every last dollar I had to win over this lady of mine. And, as it turns out, I have. That's why it's so damn important I churn out another manuscript. Sebastian assures me it doesn't even have to be any good. He says my name on the spine alone is worth a million.

And as much as I'd like to write another masterpiece, I don't think I have it in me. The guy who wrote *That's Why I Drink Every Night* wouldn't even recognize this new Lou, this man of comfort, this sloth, this weakling, this privileged little piss-ant. The guy who wrote *That's Why I Drink Every Night* had a lust for life, a thirst for drugs and booze and women and violence. The guy who wrote that book was high on cocaine and mushrooms and wine and whiskey. He wrote it in bathroom stalls and in bars, on park benches and under them, too; he wrote it in filth and squalor, covered in sex and reeking of sweat and blood and piss.

But not this new guy—this new me, he's got no fire in his belly. He doesn't know what it is to be hungry, to be destitute and depraved, to have the urge to murder, and cravings to die. He's content, complacent, satisfied. A man like that has no business writing a book.

I mean, fuck, what would it even be about? It certainly couldn't be about *me*. I've completely fallen out of love with myself, and you can't write about what you don't love. Instead of vim and vigor, I've been wallowing in security, and nobody wants to read about security.

My telephone rings.

"Hello, Frannie."

"Hello, darling. How'd it go today?"

"I wrote a magnificent first sentence. Very literary."

"Yes, and then?"

"Then nothing." I go to light a cigarette and realize I've tried to fire up the wrong end. On the second try I get it right. "Oh yes, one more thing. I injured my back moving my writing desk into our bathroom."

"You've moved your desk into our bathroom?"

"It was the only room in the house I was yet to try."

"You're not obstructing access to my sink or personal effects, are you?"

"It's a very big desk."

"Don't get down, darling. Things will come together. You're a brilliant man. But I can't allow you to keep your desk in our bathroom."

"Maybe I'll try the hot tub."

"Why don't you come meet me and some friends for dinner?"

"What friends?"

"My friend Olivia and her husband."

"Who's Olivia?"

"Lou, come on, you've met Olivia several times. She's my college friend—the lawyer. She's a junior associate at the firm that represented you in that mix-up over when you pawned all the furnishings of that beach house we rented last summer."

"The woman with a cast on her arm?"

"No," she says. "Don't you remember her from my birthday party? She explained to you the difference between English and Western riding styles."

"Bicycles?"

"Horses, Lou, horses."

"No recollection."

"Lou!"

"I don't think I'm up for it. Not tonight."

"Of course you are, darling. It'll do you good. Meet us at Chaya Venice at eight."

At 7:30, I go to the liquor cabinet and open a bottle of *Don Julio Real*. I got turned onto the stuff from the company's founder, Don Julio. He gave me my first bottle as a gift for making a reference to the tequila in *That's Why I Drink Every Night*. In the book, Donald steals a bottle from behind the bar of a yacht where he's been hired to cater. He ends up locking himself in the bathroom, polishing off the whole thing. When he returns to work, the party's host confronts him about the missing bottle, and Donald throws himself overboard to evade capture.

Apparently, due to the mention, sales of *Don Julio* spiked. It's a $400 bottle, and I've gone through at least one a month for the past two years. My God, how money has changed me! Five years ago, I wouldn't have thought twice about licking Jose Cuervo off the floor.

I stand at the bar in the den and take three shots in succession while reading the news on my iPad. A story about a man from Albuquerque, New Mexico, catches my eye. This man was driving down the street in his car, in the middle of the day, having sex with a girl. He couldn't see because she was straddling him, and he hopped the curb and hit a telephone pole. The girl was ejected from the vehicle and sustained serious injuries. The driver fled the scene on foot but was chased down by two witnesses. They found him hiding behind a cactus, naked except a cowboy hat.

This story gets me feeling all right, and I drink two more shots in this man's honor.

I pull up to the restaurant at 8:20. I'm late, but Frannie knows that's to be expected, so I'm not concerned. It wouldn't surprise me if dinner was really at 8:30 and she just told me 8 to get me there on time. When I walk in I ask the hostess if my party has already been seated, and it has. Frannie is not as clever as I have given her credit for.

The dining room of the restaurant is large and open, with high wood ceilings from which whimsical paper lanterns dangle, the motif a hybrid of country-western and Asian. I ask the hostess about the theme and she says it's "Rustic Festive."

As I approach, Olivia and her husband are smiling. Frannie is not. The husband stands up to shake my hand and introduces himself as Doug. He's a large, well-built man with a soft, light-brown mustache and innocent-looking grey eyes. Sizing him up, I wonder if I could take him in a scrap.

I sit down next to Frannie, pick up her glass of wine, and take a big swig. "Sorry I'm late," I say. "Big accident on the 5. Traffic was backed up for a mile, so I took side streets. But that was murder too. So many lights. You know how it is."

"So, Lou," Olivia begins, "Frannie says you've begun a new novel."

I try to recall if I've met this woman before. I can't place her. She's certainly very pretty—thin figure, well-proportioned face, high cheekbones, green buttons for eyes—but I can't remember having ever met her.

"Hard to say, for certain. I might get out of that racket. Been considering some other ventures."

Frannie puts her hand on my forearm and gives me a puzzled look.

"Really, like what?" Olivia asks.

"I'm thinking of taking up arms with the Jews against the Arabs. Either that or I'll side with the Arabs against the Jews."

"Excuse me?" Doug says.

"War. I'm thinking of going to war."

"I don't understand," Olivia says.

"It's nothing," I say. "Something I'm considering."

Doug picks up his water glass, averts his eyes, and takes a sip. Olivia tears a piece of bread in two, and drops it on her plate.

"He's kidding," Frannie says. "He's not really considering going to war—are you, darling?"

"Why not?" I say. "It doesn't sound like such a bad idea. It would certainly liven things up a bit. War is not nearly the detriment to one's existence that boredom is. I mean, what else am I going to do, spend all my time driving around L.A. in my fancy car, going to restaurants, take up golf?"

"I think it would make a hell of a book," Doug says.

"Right," I remark, "my great war novel."

"Hell, I wouldn't mind seeing one of these skirmishes escalate into another full-on war," Doug says. "I've been bullish on the domestic natural-gas market for some time. A good war in the Middle East would send the price of oil skyrocketing and we'd make a fortune."

Olivia and Doug exchange loving smiles.

"I like you, Doug," I say. "You got a lot of spirit—can see an opportunity in even the most ominous of situations."

Doug furrows his brow and glances back in Olivia's direction for assurance.

Frannie reaches under the table, squeezes my thigh, and whispers, "Be nice!"

I continue: "I'm serious, Doug, you're the best part of America. You don't know defeat."

Doug's eyes gleam with pride and my mind is filled with fresh horrors about the future of the world.

Chapter

Frannie is next to me in bed sleeping. I hear sounds coming from her. There is the sound of her stomach. I press my ear close enough to hear it growling. Frannie never eats after 9 p.m., even if she stays late at the office and misses dinner. She claims it might wreak havoc on her metabolism, and she can't risk it. Also, there is the sound of what I assume is her dreaming. When she dreams, she says not words exactly, but half-words, half-words and sighs—lots of sighs. I wonder if she's fantasizing about fucking and if so, who? Surely it couldn't be me. It's sweet to think so, but I'm not so naïve. She's fucked me enough times for her subconscious to know there's no use wasting perfectly good dreams on me. That said, it's got to be someone, probably somebody from work or the gym.

Prior to settling into our routine, Frannie really used to be quite the sexual maven, and I should know. Before she came along I had more than my share of women, but she was the best of the lot. It's not even close. In fact, more than just being damn good at the act, I'd go as far as to say that Frannie was a sexual innovator. One of only maybe two or three I've come across in my experience.

For instance, there is this one position she introduced me to where I lie on my side and she lies flat on her back and we twist our legs into a queer pretzel shape and I slide a finger, or sometimes two, into her backside, and then she screams out, "Oh, Lou, you're the best fuck ever! I swear it, the best fuck ever!" And then she comes after about thirty seconds of hard thrusting and, of course, the fingers in the rear help too—but the kicker is, she doesn't let me stop after she climaxes. No, she makes me keep going, even when I barely can, and then she comes again, sometimes twice more.

Thinking about this sideways position makes my cock stir,

11

and I move my hand down to check on it and it's about two-thirds hard. I give it a few pets, and it's nearly all the way now. What to do now about it? There are some factors I need to consider.

First and foremost, Frannie hates morning sex. Wasn't always that way, but has been for about six months' time. Just last week when I tried for some morning congress, she rolled over in bed and clinched the sheets tightly around her body and said, "Darling, not now, I'm tired. I must get some sleep. Try again later." Then I bit down on her butt, and she turned and hit me upside the head and said, "I said not right now!" I slinked off the bed without a peep, and then she felt bad and said, "Oh darling, come back. I'm sorry." But it was too late, and I went downstairs and watched last night's baseball highlights on the TV.

On a more emotional level, also, things between us lately seem strained. I think she's slowly coming to the conclusion we may be incompatible. I'm in complete disagreement, of course. This is the most solid relationship I've ever been a part of. She's never once punched me or kicked me, thrown boiling hot water at me, or set any of my clothes on fire. Not like any of the other girls I've dated. And, in return, I've never committed any of those injustices against her.

But I think my initial appeal is beginning to wear thin. Now that she's seen underneath the surface of things, perhaps it's not so terrific. Truth is, she never signed up for falling in love with me. She signed up for what I represent. I've seen it a hundred times since my book got published. Women always think that falling in love with a successful novelist will be the ultimate romantic happenstance. The befalling appeals to their vanity. They'll never admit it but what they long for is to serve as the muse in a love story for the ages. And I suppose it's true—a man's best work usually comes as a byproduct of his feelings for a woman. However, it must be said, this work is not usually produced during the rapturous grips of love; rather, it comes in the aftermath and carnage of an affair gone sour.

But for the very best of women, simply *inspiring* art is not enough. No, the very best of women are actually masterpieces themselves. No good could ever come of any art created in their image, for it would be nothing in comparison to their own existence. The very best of women have already ascertained the pinnacle of perfect form—an embodiment an artist can only futilely strive for. It can be in the way she holds her head while smoking a cigarette, or in the way her hips and ass swing as she walks, or, perhaps, in the soft coos she emits while making love—for these are the most exquisite constructions of this world, something a painting, a poem, or a photograph could never capture.

Before I came along, Frannie had been engaged to a chemist-turned-entrepreneur named Seth—he had made a ridiculous sum of money curing seemingly impossible ailments and diseases—as wonderful a guy as you'd ever want to meet. I'm told that by everyone—Frannie's mother, her friends, even her hairdresser, who once mentioned it in passing. Frannie once said to me: "You know, Lou, one good chemist is more valuable in this world than a thousand writers." I must admit that stung a bit, but I'm not such an egoist I can't see the logic in such a statement. And I know I'm not always so cordial or easy to get along with, but can I really be so lousy that all her closest friends and family believe they're warranted in telling me how fantastic her ex is?

All this thinking about my relationship is bumming me out, but there is nothing to be done about it now. There are more pressing issues, namely this protuberance throbbing in my underpants. I pull the sheet away as quietly as I can manage, so as to not wake Frannie, and I slip into the bathroom and start the shower. The boxers slip off gingerly over the throbber, and quickly I'm under the water, doing work on myself. There was a time when a morning ritual like this would've seemed regrettable or shameful, but that time has passed.

When I'm done in the shower, I go back out to the bedroom. Frannie is just rising.

"You're up early," she says.

"I was feeling inspired. Hoping to get a jump on the day."

"That's good, darling. What do you have planned?"

Frannie refers to me as "darling" whenever things are well. If she doesn't refer to me as "darling," I know I'm in for it. This is a habit she picked up abroad. Frannie is in fashion, and months ago she spent three weeks in London working on the spring Versace line. Ever since, it's "darling" this and "darling" that. When I mentioned this new proclivity, she insisted that she had always used the word, and when I told her that wasn't true, that she had never called me "darling" in the past, she got hurt feelings and acted as if I had done her a great injustice.

"I'm meeting Sebastian for lunch, and this afternoon I'm taking Cliff to a doctor's appointment."

"Doesn't he have anyone else to shuttle him around?"

"Last time he took the bus and got lost. Ended up in Chinatown and missed his appointment."

"I don't like it one bit."

"There's nothing to worry about." I lean in and give her a kiss and a cuddle. "Let me make you some eggs."

"I've got to get going," she says. "I'm meeting Mila Kunis and her team this morning. We're dressing her for the Globes."

"I'm not sure what any of that means."

"Of course you don't, darling. Why would you?"

She enters the bathroom, and closes the door behind her.

Sebastian insists I drive all the way across town to meet him for lunch—he always does—something about it being close to his office and my not having a job.

"But I'm the talent, and you're the agent," I remind him.

"You haven't been the talent for some time," he says over the telephone.

So here I am, sitting on the sidewalk patio of a restaurant off Sunset, sweating because I'm wearing jeans and a long-sleeve shirt, and the umbrella over my table does nothing to block the sun. I've already gone through three Coronas and a basket of chips and guacamole, and when I light up a cigarette, the waitress tells me to put it out, and there is still no sign of Sebastian anywhere.

"Fucking asshole!" I say, loud enough for all the surrounding tables to take notice.

The waitress comes by with the most annoyed look on her face. "Sir, you can't shout obscenities in the restaurant. My manager told me to tell you that if it happens again, we'll have to ask you to leave."

Finally Sebastian shows up. He's wearing white pants with a tan belt and a slim, grey two-button blazer. Underneath the jacket is a blue shirt with a pattern of tiny white anchors on it. The top three buttons of the shirt are undone. In one hand he's carrying a coffee and in the other, a juice smoothie. If I didn't know better, I'd swear he was a homosexual.

"I've been here for a half hour already."

"Bikram yoga ran late, and I needed to shower, hit the juice bar, and pick up a latté."

"You fucking realize that you're meeting me at a restaurant, right?"

"Whatever," he says, sitting down across from me. "So how are things progressing?"

"Progressing?" I finish a Corona and flag down the waitress to put in an order for some tacos. "The pages are starting to flow. Just finding my rhythm. It's a process—you know how it is."

"I'd like to see a draft by the end of the month."

"I don't think so, Sebastian. It's not ready, and I don't show anybody my work until it's ready."

Sebastian takes a long pull from the straw protruding from the juice cup. When he removes the straw from his mouth, there is a piece of orange rind stuck in his designer-stubble beard. I reach out and give it a flick.

"I want to read it. I can help you. I really can. It's what I do."

"Listen, Sebastian, I didn't have any help on the last book, and it took all right. So if you don't mind, I think I'll just go about it myself"

"You're wasting my time, as usual."

He gets up from the table.

"Where are you going? You're supposed to buy me lunch."

"I don't want to be late for my next meeting."

He's already got his back to me, and is halfway to the door.

"You didn't seem too concerned about showing up late to *our* meeting!" I shout across the patio. He doesn't reply and I scream out, "Asshole!"

The waitress reappears and informs me I need to leave.

Chapter

I've made exactly one new friend since my fortunes changed. I used to have dozens of friends. Maybe not dozens, but at least there were people I could talk to, people who could relate. Those people, for the most part, are gone now. Our paths diverged, and what we shared is no longer.

I met this new friend a few months back at an airport bar. I was flying somewhere, I don't remember where exactly, maybe New York, possibly Chicago. Anyhow, I was at the bar trying to get my head together, and I looked over and saw this guy who looked just like this ballplayer I used to love to watch play. This ballplayer, back in the day, could really cover some ground out in centerfield and could stretch a single into a double better than anyone since Pete Rose. Hell of a player, a real hustler, ballsy as hell! So I was checking this guy out, and he looked just like him, only he was a real fat fuck, and his hair was grown down to his shoulders, and he was wearing a floral-print Hawaiian shirt and shorts. When he glanced in my direction, his eyes were red-rimmed and cooked all the way through.

Now I'm not the sort who goes around making conversation with strangers, but I really love baseball, and the resemblance between this bum at the bar and my favorite ballplayer was uncanny.

I finished three whiskeys before I finally worked up the stones to say to him: "Hey, excuse me, you Cliff Adams?"

And he went, "Depends—what the fuck do you want?"

"Holy shit," I said to myself, "it *is* Cliff Adams," and then I got all excited like I was meeting God himself.

"Fucking hell, Cliff, I just want to buy you a drink."

"Nobody's gonna try and stop you," he replied.

Turns out that Cliff had been having a rough go of it lately. His baseball career ended ten years earlier after a one-year suspension for steroids, followed by a broken back he suffered charging full-on into the centerfield wall to make a play. One of the best efforts anyone's ever made on a ball. And I told him as much, straight away. But I'm sure everyone has.

"It was my job to catch the damn ball," he said when I brought it up. "What else was I supposed to do?"

After retirement, he fell victim to an unscrupulous money manager who got him involved in pyramid schemes, bad real-estate deals, and a chain of car washes. Poor Cliffy lost millions— tens of millions, in fact. Eventually, he ended up doing four years in prison for tax evasion. Now he's been out of jail for two years and is nearly penniless.

This morning I've agreed to pick Cliff up and take him to the doctor. He's not legally allowed to drive due to a suspended license—something involving a mix-up over driving under the influence. What a joke! This is a guy who has more eye-hand coordination than 99.99% of the population, and the state is worried he's endangering the populace because he's had a few beers? The only reason the cop pulled him over was because somebody had smashed out his back window. Happened after a bar fight, minutes before.

Cliff had been watching the game at his local when two drunk loudmouths started in on him. "Hey, Cliff, you fat fuck, how was prison? They treat you real nice in there? Different sort of locker-room experience, huh, you fucking has-been!"

What's a guy to do? A man can't let that sort of talk pass unpunished. So he walked over to the two guys and slammed their heads together. A full-scale bar brawl ensued, spilling out into the street. Cliff knocked one of the guys clean out with a haymaker punch. The other fled on foot. When Cliff heard sirens, he jumped in his car, and as he sped off someone threw a brick through his back window.

But now Cliff is having health problems, and he needs rides to and from the doctor. Earlier this year he had a heart attack that nearly killed him. He had a smaller one the year before, too. Now there are complications with his liver—could be from the steroids, maybe the booze?

I show up at his place at 2 p.m. He's standing on the curb, surrounded by a rag-tag group of children. Each of them is waving a baseball cap or a ball in his face to sign. He takes the time to scribble out a personalized message to each eager kid. Cliff is wearing another floral-print Hawaiian shirt, a red one with blue flowers, and his hair is pulled back into a ponytail. The bags under his eyes are deep and horseshoe-shaped, and his cheeks and forehead are the color of crimson. Seeing him standing out in front of his house, looking all indigent and broken, it's nearly impossible to imagine that this man once hit two home runs in a single World Series game.

I get out of the car and join him on the sidewalk.

"Hey, kids, you should get this guy's autograph, too," Cliff says.

"They don't want my autograph," I say.

"Who the hell are you, mister?" one of the kids asks

"That's Lou Brown," Cliff says. "He's a world-famous writer."

"A writer?" a different kid asks.

"I wrote one book, that's all."

"That's nothing," the same kid says. "Why would I want your autograph?"

I light up a smoke. "I didn't say you would."

"It was a hell of a book," Cliff says.

The kids quickly lose interest in me, and when Cliff is done signing their memorabilia, they run off without giving me another look.

Cliff lights up his own cigarette.

"So what is it this time?" I ask. "Your heart, your head, or something new."

"I got to get a waiver signed."

He opens the passenger-side door and climbs in. Standing on the curb, I watch as nearly an inch of ash dangles from the end of his cigarette before falling onto my leather seat. He calls out to me, "Get in the damn car, Lou, we're already running late."

I get in, start the car, and put us in motion

"So what sort of medical waiver do you need?"

"It's not a big deal. I'm doing a boxing match, and the promoters won't sanction it unless I get cleared."

"A boxing match?"

"I'm broke and I need to pay child support."

"You have kids?"

"I got one."

"You never told me that."

"You never asked."

"You know how to box?"

"I can hold my own."

"Who are you fighting?"

"It doesn't matter."

"How did you even get involved in something like this?"

"The promoter thinks people will pay to see a washed-up old ballplayer duke it out."

"But look at you, you look like hell. You're in no condition to fight."

"Just drive the car, jerk."

He's late enough for his appointment that I drop him off before I go looking for parking. By the time I get to the lobby, he's been taken back. I sit down and pick up an issue of *Sports Illustrated*. LeBron James is on the cover. His eyes are full of pride and contentment. I remember long ago seeing a similar look on my own face. In the next seat over is a small pale girl with a narrow face and sunken eyes. She looks more mouse than human. Her mother is playing with the girl's limp brown hair with one hand, and filling out paperwork with the other. I lock eyes with the mom and notice she is crying. I nod and give her a reassuring smile, and she finds the courage to do the same. When I lean over to replace the *Sports Illustrated* on the coffee table, I catch a glimpse of the paperwork. It says the little mousy girl has something called Renal Carcinoma. I pull out my cellphone and google it. It means she has kidney cancer.

I text myself the following sentences: *I'm finding it harder and harder to imagine a God, but I've never been more certain about the presence of the Devil. He is everywhere, not just in shadows, but standing in plain light.*

After a few minutes, Cliff lumbers out a door and into the waiting room.

"What's your afternoon looking like?" he asks.

"I was going to try and commit some words to paper."

"You want to skip it and go to a casino?"

"The doctor going to clear you for the fight?"

"I'm fine."

"I'm not driving all the way to Vegas."

"Something around here, then. Come on, Lou, I need this."

"I'll have to call Frannie."

Twenty minutes later we're driving east on the 10-freeway, heading toward The Rolling Hills Casino. Frannie isn't at all pleased that I'm going gambling with Cliff. Not only because she doesn't like Cliff, but because she thinks playing cards is low-class. Frannie is highbrow all the way. It's what attracted me to her in the first place. Before her, I'd never been with a lady of sophistication and culture. My former lovers tended to be of a different sort—dropouts, addicts, sadists, loons.

Frannie comes from a good family—Jews. Her father, Noah, is a well-respected doctor in Los Angeles—a cardiologist, I believe—a sober and solemn man who isn't prone to vice or folly. Her mother, Dianne, is a retired college linguistics professor who now fills her days with pilates, shopping trips, and long afternoons at the tennis club. That's Dianne's passion—tennis. Apparently, before turning to the linguistic arts, she had briefly played as a professional. Supposedly, she was on her way to winning championships, but had had her career derailed by motherhood. I learned of her tennis achievements during my first visit to Frannie's parents' home. The walls of their not-so-humble abode are cluttered with photos from Dianne's sporting days.

"Did Frannie ever tell you about the time I beat Chris Evert in straight sets?" she asked me.

"It's odd," I said, sounding as sincere as possible, "but she never has."

The woman then broke down into tears as she recounted all the biggest matches of her career. The whole time she spoke to me, I was nearly convinced I had been made the butt of a grand joke.

I said to Frannie afterward, "Your mother is a lucky woman if not being able to play pro tennis is truly the worst thing that has ever happened to her."

"You don't know what you're talking about," Frannie replied to me that day.

It wasn't until months later that I learned that Frannie's family actually had been the victim of great tragedy and suffering. It turns out Frannie had an older brother, David, who had perished from disease.

The story goes that David had been suffering stomach pains for several weeks before he was taken for a checkup. Frannie's father, the doctor, was sure it was nothing—a minor trifle. "Growing pains, my good boy," he had said to his son.

In my time, I've learned that there are two different kinds of doctors when it comes to treating their own families. The first type is terribly overbearing and handles every minor ailment as if without the fullest attention it will lead to an early grave. These doctors' homes are stocked full of remedies, potions, and elixirs. I know this from experience.

I once held a job as a house painter for a season, and that summer I spread color on many physicians' walls throughout the greater Malibu area. One hungover July morning, I took a nasty spill from a ladder and fell ten feet onto my back. I didn't have insurance so I never received an X-ray, but I'm certain I suffered at least a few broken ribs. From that day on, I always made it a point to find my way into the medicine cabinets of all the homes I worked. If it weren't for the stolen painkillers, I wouldn't have been able to continue.

The second type of doctor treats his family as if they are invincible. The homes of these healers contain nary an aspirin, not so much as a bottle of cold medicine. Unfortunately for Frannie's brother, their father was this type. I can't begin to imagine the guilt Frannie's father has had to endure. A doctor of medicine allowing his own son's cancer to go untreated is the cruelest irony I've ever heard. Anyhow, once diagnosed, it didn't take long. The tumors had already spread all around his stomach and were completely inoperable. Months of chemotherapy and drugs did nothing for him. He passed away the day before Frannie's thirteenth birthday. To this day, we've only ever discussed it the one time. It's her private pain, too much for her to revisit.

And as much as it saddened me to hear of her loss, in a way, I believe it brought us closer together. Up until she shared with me the story of her brother's cancer, I could never really see her as a whole person. Her life was more like an outlandish fairytale—too charmed, too neat, unblemished. A person who has never had to overcome adversity, never really experiences anything. Even his victories appear hollow and unsubstantial, for without pain, pleasure is a mundane baseline.

Perhaps because of David's early death, Frannie's parents saw to it that she was catered to in every manner imaginable. In her was bound up all the joy and hope the family had remaining. Furthermore, she was the sole future of the bloodline. Due to this fact, she was denied nothing in her youth: prep schools, private tutors, horseback-riding lessons, European summer backpacking trips. Frannie uses the term *well-bred* in reference to her upbringing. That's one way of putting it. For her sixteenth birthday, she received a brand-new Audi 5 convertible, and six months later when she totaled it, her parents replaced it with a Lexus SUV. When it was time for college, her parents footed the bill for a fancy private liberal arts university to the tune of $50,000 a year. David Foster Wallace, who Bret Easton Ellis correctly identified as the most pretentious and overrated writer of a generation, was her English teacher. There, Frannie was made editor of the school's newspaper and dated an heir to an oil fortune. Her junior year she studied abroad in Paris, staying in a chateau owned by a distant uncle. While there, Frannie took an internship with Chanel, where her boss took notice of a dress she had hand-stitched for herself, and made her an offer of full-time employment. She stayed on for only six months, returning to California due to homesickness, but cementing her future in the fashion industry.

In contrast, that same year I turned thirty-three and was fired from my job as a gravedigger, and spent three months sleeping under the Santa Monica pier. That winter I contracted shingles and was found unconscious floating in the water when the tide came in. I spent a week in the hospital recovering.

"Lou, a casino, really?" Frannie says to me when I call her. "And with Cliff of all people?"

"Cliff needs me," I whisper into the phone, trying to spare Cliff my words. "He's having a real rough time."

"And how is a casino going to help?"

"Life is full of missed opportunities, and a guy like Cliff may not get too many more."

She hangs up without saying goodbye.

"Your lady doesn't like me too much, does she?" Cliff asks.

"It's not you, it's me. She just hasn't figured it out yet."

"And when she does, it'll be ugly. I know it well."

"What happened with your wife and kid?"

"What do you think happened? Meghan and I got married when I was rich and famous, and she divorced me when I wasn't."

"What's your kid like?"

Cliff fumbles through his pocket searching for his cigarettes. "He lives with his mother and her new husband in Palm Springs."

"He play ball?"

Cliff stares out the window. "He quit when I went to prison. But Charles is a good kid: real smart, not like me at all."

I look out my own window as traffic slows to a halt. In the next car over is a man with the top three buttons of his shirt undone, shouting into his cellphone.

"I'm sure he's a good kid," I say

"It's funny, I never even wanted kids, was totally freaked when we found out Meghan was pregnant," Cliff says. "I had this buddy in the minors who told me when he looked into his kid's eyes he didn't feel a thing. Nothing. No connection at all. That's what I worried about."

"So was that the case?"

"Fuck no," he says, smiling brightly. "As soon as I saw my kid I was in love. The day he was born was the best day of my life."

"Better than hitting two home runs in the same World Series game?"

"Shit, Lou...not even close!"

An hour and a half later, Cliff and I are sitting at a blackjack table. We've each already had four Crown and Cokes, and with each drink Cliff inches closer to coming completely undone.

"You want to get some blow?" Cliff asks me.

"I can't, pal. I had to quit getting high when I took up with Frannie. I promised her I wouldn't. She'd kill me."

"How long's it been?"

"Close to two years."

"Two years, no drugs at all! How's does that feel?"

"You kidding me? I miss it like hell. I can't remember the last time I howled at the moon."

"You're probably better off," Cliff says, tossing his cards after losing his third hand in a row. He increases his bet from forty dollars to one hundred dollars. "I got to make up for these bullshit hands."

I don't say anything as I watch him place his bet. I'm busy concentrating on my own cards. I've won four of the last six hands and I'm up fourteen hundred. I'm feeling pretty good about things. Feeling like I'm in control, for once. Not at the mercy of the writing gods or fighting to stay in Frannie's good graces. So often I feel as if I'm not even myself these days—that I'm hiding my impulses and thoughts. And what do I have without those? Nothing—that's what! No wonder I can't write another book.

I'm dealt nineteen, and the dealer is showing a six. Cliff has sixteen. I stay, of course, and so should he. Cliff eyes his cards and then glances at the dealer. This croupier's got one of those long black mustaches that twirl up at the ends. After waiting a few more seconds for Cliff to make up his mind, the dealer says, "Make a decision, sir."

Cliff hits, and busts.

"What the fuck are you doing?" I ask him.

"Play your own damn cards."

The next hand he doubles his bet again.

"Seriously, pal, what are you doing? You can't afford these hands," I say, lighting a cigarette.

"If people only gambled what they could afford, it wouldn't be very interesting, now would it?"

The next round is dealt. I show seventeen and the dealer is showing a nine. I stay. Cliff has two eights, and he splits. A maniacal grin consumes his whole face. The dealer gives him two more cards: a nine and a Queen. Cliff tips his head back and swallows an entire Crown and Coke, ice and all, in one huge gulp. The dealer deals himself a four, followed by a Jack, and busts.

"See, asshole!" Cliff says to me in a hoarse growl, as he collects the nearly four hundred bucks he won on the hand. "Life is finally opening up to me again!"

For the next two hours, Cliff has a tremendous run of good cards, and he goes up nearly twelve hundred, but then hits another losing streak, and ends the night three hundred dollars down.

I'm down too, nearly five hundred.

At five in the morning we start the journey home. Cliff smokes cigarette after cigarette on the drive. There is the faint glow of morning sun rising in the east. The freeways are not yet littered with morning commuters on their way to desk-jobs. We pass a Dodgers' baseball billboard and I mention that we should catch a game sometime. Cliff mumbles something under his breath about not wanting to line the pockets of crooks. I turn the radio on and Tom Petty's "Free Fallin'" comes blasting out of the speakers. After the first chorus, Cliff turns it off. I drop him off as the sun peeks over the horizon. As he gets out of the car, he says, "I'm sorry I've been such a shit all night."

"Get some sleep," I say.

He checks his wristwatch. "I got training in two hours."

"When's the fight?"

"Next Thursday."

"You think you're ready?"

"I just need the money."

Cliff turns toward his apartment and lumbers away.

Back at my house, Frannie has locked the door to our bedroom. I go out to the living room, lie down on the couch, and stare at the grand piano Frannie purchased a few weeks earlier. I reach into my pocket, retrieve my phone, and type out the following message for myself: *It's nearly impossible to live the life one was intended for here in America.*

Chapter

When I awake in the morning, Frannie is nowhere to be found. I go to the kitchen, start the coffee, and dig around the fridge. There is a carton of eggs and a bag of turkey bacon. I let out a sigh of disappointment as I examine the fatless meat. It seems odd to me which aspects of Judaism she chooses to follow.

"You don't eat pork?" I once asked her.

"Of course not, I'm Jewish."

"But you eat lobster and shrimp."

"So what?"

"They're not kosher either."

"Jesus Christ, darling! What do you want from me?"

"Nothing. I'm just trying to understand."

But the thing is, there isn't anything to understand. The rationale is completely nonsensical. It's a losing proposition trying to get to the root of it. Anyhow, that doesn't change the fact that we only have turkey bacon in the house. I throw a bagel into the toaster and pull out the frying pan and go to work on the fraudulent breakfast meat and the egg.

When it's ready I go out to the patio to enjoy the mid-morning sun. Frannie is out there in a pair of cutoff jean shorts and my old Guided by Voices T-shirt that she's halved in order to expose her belly. A surge of furious anger courses through my blood. It's bad enough she's ruined a shirt that's been with me for over twenty years, but she doesn't even like the band. Months ago I played their seminal album *Bee Thousand* for her and she said, "Darling, it's charming but it's not for me," —and now she's co-opted the shirt as her own.

"What's with the shirt?" I ask. "You said you didn't like GBV."

"I don't—not really, at least."

"So why did you destroy my shirt?"

"What do you care? You never wear it."

"Only because you told me I couldn't. You said it was childish for a man of thirty-eight to be wearing a band T-shirt!"

"It looked silly on you, darling. But it looks hot on me, don't you think?"

What Frannie is doing outside is painting. She likes to do landscapes with watercolors. From our patio there is a view of the hills surrounding Laurel Canyon. She's actually quite skilled as a draftsman, but she lacks vision, and doesn't practice enough. She'll start a painting and get halfway through it, and then let it sit for months on end. The one she's laboring on now has been in the works since I can remember. Frannie says she gets frustrated when she can't get the sun's light right. I marvel at how many shades of blue she has in her paint set—perhaps twelve or more in all. All the moods of the sky and ocean, she says.

"What time did you and Cliff finally make it home last night?" she asks.

"Not too late."

"Really? Because I woke up at five in the morning, and you still weren't back."

"I don't know, Frannie, I guess it was late, then. By the way, thanks for locking me out of the bedroom."

"I didn't want you to wake me up."

"Okay, I get the picture."

I go back inside, take a beer from the fridge, slam it down as fast as I can, and then pop the top off another and head back out to the patio. Frannie is looking at me with a pensive face—eyebrows arched, brow furrowed, mouth tight. As a consequence of her anguished expression, I feel a pain in my head. A look like the one she's giving me demands acknowledgment, words, an apology, at least a gesture, and I don't have one to give.

"I'm worried about Cliff," I say.

I can tell this is not what she wants to hear. She wants to be reassured that she's my number-one priority—that all my other emotions and allegiances pale in comparison to what I feel for her. And sometimes that's true. Sometimes I feel as long as I have her I could lose everything else and still be all right.

For instance, two weeks ago I got a telephone call that a friend from my former life had been shot and killed by a police officer during a botched robbery attempt. And sure, it was his own damn fault he got killed—what do you expect is going to happen when you pull a gun on an army of police officers? But still, my heart broke.

The dead guy, Danny, had been a great pal. One time, when I was about twenty, I needed to borrow a car, and he lent me his and I crashed it and didn't have the money to pay him back. Instead of being an asshole about it, he got me a second job at the restaurant he managed so I could raise the funds. And another time, we were at a party, and I had gotten real drunk and made the moves on a girl who I knew had a boyfriend. Later that night, this girl's boyfriend and a gang of his friends caught me and her in a most compromising position in the party apartment's master-bedroom closet. They all rushed in on me while I was stark-naked and started beating me nearly to death. When Danny heard the ruckus, he jumped in the fray and took a real ass-kicking on my behalf. He didn't have to do that, but he was loyal as hell.

Anyhow, we had lost touch, and I didn't even know that Danny was having problems, and I fucking lost it when I heard he had been killed. If Frannie hadn't been there to stay up through the night saying the right things to me, rubbing my head, and wiping away my tears, I don't know what might've happened.

"Cliff? You're worried about Cliff?" she says. "What about me? Don't you even care about my feelings? You know I don't like Cliff and I asked you not to go gambling with him, and what do you do? You go off anyhow and then don't come back until the next morning."

"What do you want me to say? He's a pal."

"You're marrying me, not Cliff," Frannie says. "Speaking of, my parents are on their way over to discuss the wedding."

"Now?"

"Yes, now. They'll be here any minute."

As if scripted in a movie, the doorbell chimes. Frannie goes to the door to let them in. The mother, Dianne, looks to have had work done since the last time I saw her. Her face is too tight and smooth for a woman of her age. As she turns her head to kiss Frannie on the cheek, I can see the skin under her chin reaching its elastic limit. When she forces herself on me for my requisite kiss, I lean in close, and she retracts.

"Drinking already, Lou. It's not even noon."

"Easing myself into the day."

"What a luxury to be able to sit around at all hours drinking. Must be part of your process."

"It's not bad work if you can get it."

The father, Noah, nudges past Dianne and holds out his hand. I give it a good shake. The man has grown out a damn fine beard. It's silver and thick, very distinguished-looking. The sort of beard I wish for myself when I'm his age. Also, he looks trim, the body of an athlete.

"Retirement's treating you well," I say. "You look like a million bucks."

"She's hired me a trainer," he says, pointing to Dianne, "and talked me into running a half-marathon."

"Yes yes, he looks very fit," Dianne says. "Let's talk about this wedding."

Dianne and Noah move toward the couch. It's still a mess from my having slept there. Noah sits down without hesitation, but Dianne just stares at it as if it were the scene of a gruesome crime. Frannie rushes in to fix the pillow under Dianne's watchful eye. After Frannie performs a good fluffing and straightening, Dianne sits. Frannie takes a place on the loveseat across from her parents. I sit down on the piano bench, too far off for Frannie's liking. She says, "Come on, darling, join me over here."

"Anyone care for a drink?" I offer.

"Ice-tea, non-sweetened," Dianne says.

"Water, please," Noah replies.

"Babe?" I say to Frannie.

"Water too, please," she says.

I pour the waters and the tea, grab the last beer from the fridge for myself, reconsider, put it back, and pour myself a water, too. But when I try to pick up all four drinks at once I drop one, shattering the glass. Frannie's hoarse shout beckons from the living room: "Is everything all right in there?"

"Yes, just wonderful," I say to myself.

I place the three remaining drinks on the counter, bend over, and begin picking up the broken pieces of glass. Frannie appears in the doorway as I'm about to dry the floor with a dishtowel.

"Mom and Dad are waiting," she says.

"I'm moving as fast as I can here," I say from my knees.

Frannie disappears back into the living room. When I finish I toss the towel into the sink, and then go back to the fridge. I take the last beer, twist off the top, and suck it back as fast as I can. I then deliver the three beverages and join Frannie on the loveseat. Noah has a pen and paper out and is taking dictation from Dianne.

"I've spoken to Rabbi Braunstein and he said he'd be honored to perform the ceremony," Dianne says.

"That's fine," Frannie says, "but let's keep it light on the religion. Lou isn't too comfortable with it."

"Is that true, Lou?" Dianne asks. "I've heard from some of my friends that your book has some very interesting things to say regarding spirituality. However, I haven't read your work myself. But, I'm curious. Tell me, did you have a religious upbringing?"

"Not really," I say.

Frannie takes my hand in hers. "You don't have to get into

this if you don't want to," she says.

"Oh, shoosh, Frannie," Dianne says. "Go on, Lou. I'd like to hear about the spiritual guidance you received as a child."

"There's not much to tell," I say. "My parents paid lip service to Catholicism when I was a little kid, but after my father left my mother basically gave it up."

"That's too bad," Dianne says. "A child should have a sense of faith instilled in him."

"You think so?" I ask.

"Yes, very much. It's hard enough to negotiate this world as it is—I can't imagine not having my faith to provide me with strength."

Noah puts down the notebook and interjects. "Dianne, leave the man alone. We're here to plan a wedding, not discuss theology."

"I just wonder: if Lou had some faith, maybe he wouldn't have experienced some of the troubles he's had."

"Mother!" Frannie says.

"You know, Dianne, I've thought about it a lot. You're right, life is hard, and many times I've found myself at the breaking point. But that doesn't mean I should submit to illusions or delusions to ameliorate my suffering."

"Okay, darling, we get it," Frannie says to me. "And, Mom, lets drop the religious talk."

"No, no, no, it's fine, we're all adults here," Dianne says. "We can have a civil discussion. So, Lou, tell me, are you one of these people who attributes man's salvation to the accumulation of knowledge?"

"Can we please stick to discussing the wedding?" Noah asks.

"Yes, mother—the wedding, remember?"

"You two shouldn't get so sensitive," Dianne replies.

"Fine, I'll say it." I take a cigarette from my pack and twirl it between my fingers. "Yes, I give credence to reason over super-stition." Dianne laughs as if I've said something wildly funny.

"But don't get me wrong. I don't think further innovation and scientific progress are improving anyone's lives. If anything, I think we're becoming an increasingly lonely and unhappy species."

"You do?" Frannie asks.

"Of course I do," I say. "Technology will be our undoing, I'm certain of it."

"I'm changing the subject," Frannie says with a severe tone of frustration. "Let's discuss food. I've spoken to the chefs at several restaurants, and I think it would be really fun to do something totally different and unexpected. What do you guys think of serving all East African cuisine?"

Noah scratches his head and then writes something on the pad of paper.

"Honey," Dianne says, "be serious."

Frannie squeezes the fabric of her shirt so tightly her knuckles turn white.

My phone rings. It's Sebastian, my agent. I excuse myself and retreat to the kitchen.

"You remember you have a reading on campus today, right?"

"What campus?" I ask.

"Come on, Lou. Don't do this to me."

"Cut the shit, Sebastian, I'm sort of in the middle of something. What campus—UCLA, USC, where?"

"Loyola Marymount,"

"Loyola what?"

"Marymount," he says, a hint of anger seeping into his voice.

"Never heard of it."

"Goddamn it, Lou."

"All right, all right, what time do I need to be there?"

"The reading is at 3:30 in Hannon Library. Do I need to come get you to ensure you'll be there?"

"I'll manage."

When I return to the living room, Noah and Frannie are

hugging. I'm nearly certain I see a tear rolling down her cheek. Noah is whispering what I imagine are consoling words into his daughter's ear. Dianne is standing by the front door, tapping her foot, rooting through her purse.

"Thanks for having us over," Noah says, "but we have to go. Dianne's got us on a tight schedule."

I shake his hand once more and wave goodbye to Dianne. When they leave, Frannie insists that she needs a nap.

I go to the closet to select my clothing and decide to class it up a bit for the reading—attempt to play the part of the esteemed author. But the good slacks don't fit. Can't get the zipper to climb or the button to cinch. Maybe they shrunk in the wash. I try another pair. Same thing. I can't get the button in place. I move to the mirror for an inspection. Immediately I notice the problem. It's my belly. There are mounds of soft doughy flesh where before there was only ribs. When did this happen? I give myself a few pats on the stomach with my hand, and creases of fat roll across my midsection like soft waves gently lapping onto a beach. My God, I think, I've become a monster!

With trepidation, I decide to give myself further examination. I start at the top, with the hair. It's turning gray and dusty, but it still has its good shape and length—disheveled and overdue for a haircut. This brings a reassuring smile to my face, which in turn brings attention to the teeth, which are starting to darken a bit, no longer glistening like the white ivory teeth of my youth. However, they are good teeth. They have character: a bit misaligned and a chip or two, but nothing off-putting. Next, I move north, to the nose. It's long and slender except for the bridge, where there is a bump on the right side from when Frank Mendenhall punched me in high school. I can live with that. Continuing my exploration north, there is a series of deeply imbedded cracks and canyons protruding out from the corner of each eye. Frannie calls them my *wisdom lines*. Staring at them, I'm reminded of my grandfather, standing in the driveway, bent over the hood of my mom's Oldsmobile station wagon, assessing engine trouble, grease on his face, a cigarette between the teeth— a man who died at forty-three of a heart attack—only five years older than I am now. The rest of the face seems to be in working order. The stubble on my cheeks is rugged and masculine—dark like the hair on my head, with patches of grey. And the skin is sufficient too: tanned and a bit leathery, but no unsightly growths or defects. All in all, despite the minor imperfections, I still find myself handsome.

Eventually I settle on my everyday Chambray blue-cotton pants with a brown belt, a tucked-in white button-down shirt, and my desert boots. Taking one final look at myself in the mirror, I cut a fine figure indeed.

At 2:45 I pile into my big black BMW and step down hard on the accelerator. This thing can really move, and I maneuver in and out of traffic with tremendous finesse. Car after car I pass on the freeway, squeezing through the tightest of gaps, taking chances a lesser driver would never consider. Marina del Rey is the next exit. I head west, aiming for the Pacific Coast Highway. In the distance, high up on a bluff overlooking the marina, the university sits perched like a modern-day castle. I pull into the far-right lane to get the view of the ocean. The last holdouts of morning fog float over the emerald-green sea. Hundreds of yachts and fishing boats scurry in and out of the port like frenzied ants. So taken with the scenery, my pace slows to a crawl. The driver of the car behind me lays on the horn. A red convertible pulls up next to me. It's Charlize Theron. I give her a wave, and she responds by flipping me the bird, before speeding off.

I arrive on campus at 3:37 and park my car. I have no idea where the library is, and I begin to wander. At 3:45 I ask a young Asian man with shiny black hair and acne where I'm going. He points to a building with a towering mass of steps in front it. I thank him for the courtesy and break into a light jog toward the library. Halfway up the steps, I stop to catch my breath, make a promise to myself to soon begin an exercise regimen, light a cigarette, and climb the second half at a much more leisurely pace. Once inside I immediately see Sebastian.

"There you are, dammit."

"Here I am, just like I said I'd be."

"You're late."

"Am I?"

"Twenty minutes."

"Not so bad, then."

Sebastian leads me into a small auditorium where about two hundred people are waiting patiently for my arrival. I scan the room. It's nearly all college kids—an even split between boys and girls. This is reaffirming to me. Appealing to the youth is the most important thing. Older people are dead inside. There is no use in writing for an older audience. Their minds are already made—fixed in stone. Nothing I or anybody else will write can make a damn bit of difference to them. The best one can hope for with an older crowd is to entertain them, but I have no interest in that. There are plenty of others out there who can better amuse. I write to comfort and to scare.

The eccentrics and the deranged should know they're not alone—that what they are feeling is natural and should be embraced. Don't be ashamed of your impulses, desires, and sicknesses, I want to scream at them.

And on the flip side, I want the straight kids—the future real-estate agents and insurance salesmen to know what lengths a maniac will go to in this world. I want them to read in shock and horror about what lurks around the corner, what their future children might turn out to be. They should learn about addiction, hate, fear and obsession. Even though they will never experience these sensations, they should know an alternative exists to their world of complacency, stability and boredom.

I sit down at a table at the front of the room, stationed high on an elevated stage. There is a microphone on the table and I say, "Hello" into it. The crowd responds by standing and applauding loudly. My face blushes and my arms and legs go shaky. I put my hand over the microphone and turn to Sebastian. "Bring me a drink," I say. He quickly scurries off. After a few moments the clapping stops and everyone sits back down. It suddenly dawns on me that I'm completely alone, and everyone is waiting for me to do something.

"I've forgotten to bring a copy of my book," I say into the microphone. "Does anyone have one I can borrow?"

Nearly every hand in the room shoots up into the air holding a book.

"You there," I say to an emaciated red-haired boy in the third row wearing a Dinosaur Jr. T-shirt, "yours will do. Bring it here, please."

The boy lumbers up to the stage to give me his copy. His hand is quivering. "*You're Living All Over Me* is one of my favorite records," I say to him. He smiles weakly and wobbles back to his seat.

I open the book to a random page and begin reading from a sentence mid-paragraph, halfway down the page.

"*On the bus, I'm forced to sit between an overweight black man with patches of missing pigmentation on his face and neck and a bookish white woman who clutches at her purse and is mistrustful of her surroundings. As I squeeze between them, the noisome combination of his sweat and her perfume overwhelms me, and I nearly wretch. Unaware I'm doing it, I hum a song I can't place, and I draw the stares of those around me.*"

A minute into my reading Sebastian appears by my side and sets down two bottles of Budweiser on the table. I crack one of the beers and peer out into the audience. Everyone is at rapt attention. My eyes catch sight of a girl sitting in the front row with a skirt on and her legs spread just enough. When I look up to her face, she is chewing on a pen, and when I look back down she crosses her legs. As I begin to read again, my mind can't push the girl out of my thoughts, and I start to stutter. The blood that hasn't rushed into my face is now down below, and I readjust myself to make room for it in my pants.

Thirty minutes later, I finish my reading and everyone stands once more and claps even louder than before. I climb to my feet to take a bow and notice my erection is still clearly visible within the confines of my pants—an undesired consequence of a tucked-in shirt. A man from the crowd screams out: "Whip it out, Lou!" I cover my groin with my hands and then retake my seat behind the lectern. Sebastian descends onto the stage and takes the microphone.

"Now if everyone will sit back down, we'll begin the question-and-answer portion of this evening's festivities."

The people's butts go down, and their hands go up. A man with a long ponytail and glasses meanders the room with a microphone, waiting for me to choose someone to ask a question. Instead, I signal for Sebastian to bring me more beer. I'm stalling as long as I can manage. I hate this part of it. I'm not a talker. I'm a writer. I need time to consider what I put out into the world. My spoken words are never any good. They always come across as crass, sending the people home thinking I'm a bore. There's no use in asking me questions. Everything I have to say in this world is in the damn book.

For the first question, I pick a well-muscled and tan-looking surfer boy from the back of the room. He stands up and in his affected beach-bum accent says, "We're having a party at my house tonight. Would you like to come?" Upon posing his question, he breaks down into a fit of nervous laughter.

"What's the address?" I ask into the microphone.

"You want me to announce it to the whole room?"

"Yes."

"To everyone?"

"It's a party, isn't it?" Even from the far distance of the stage, I can see that the boy is blushing violently. He whispers something into the ear of the boy next to him. "Out with it already," I say. He proceeds to publicize the address. "Everyone got that?" I ask the audience. There are shouts of "One more time!" so I tell the boy to repeat himself, and he does. "Thank you," I say. "Perhaps I can stop by."

I point to a dark-skinned chubby woman with creases in her jowls, sitting toward the middle of the room. She points to herself and mouths the word "Me?" and I say, "Yes, you. What would you like to know?"

She struggles to her feet and stammers out: "Mr. Brown, I come from India and have only been in the United States for two years. I came here to study biology and my plan is to attend medical school after graduation."

"Good for you," I say, attempting to sound earnest. "What is your question?"

"In your novel, the protagonist states after the union at his factory job disbands that 'America is the incarnation of disaster' and that 'she will sink the whole world down into an abyss'. Well, I disagree. India has undertaken a tremendous Americanization process, and I think it's for the better. Can you please comment?"

Sebastian arrives with more beer, and I open one and begin chugging.

"Well," I say. "As far as I understand, India is a country of sects and schisms, and religious, political, and racial antagonisms—a country full of strife and chaos. But so is America. Don't be contaminated by America's cheap idealism—it's phony—America is run by a single political party, the 'Business Party,' and they have but one item on their agenda: increase consumption and profits. That can't be a model for the whole damn world. If you can't see where it's all headed, then you're in for a rude awakening, sweetheart."

The girl sits down without a response, and I'm grateful for it. The last thing I want is a discussion on politics.

After a series of monotonous inquiries regarding craft and influences, Sebastian takes the microphone and says, "One final question."

The girl in the front row who earlier had her legs spread raises her hand, and I look at her and say, "Go ahead."

She stands up, and she must be at least six feet tall, and she has long straight blond hair and blond eyebrows. Her lips are plump and the shine from her gloss glistens when she speaks. "As far as I know, you never published anything before your novel, not even a short story. What made you decide to write a book, and how did you get started?"

I take a deep breath, reach for my cigarettes, and light one. "One day I came home from my shitty job and realized I had nothing to live for and decided to kill myself. So I sat down and started to type out my thoughts into a suicide letter, and the simple act of committing words to the page was like opening up a window to my mind, and all of a sudden the whole world shone in."

The air in the room feels electric. One can feel the different atomic particles buzzing back and forth.

"Is that a true story?" the girl asks.

I shrug and say, "Maybe".

The truth is, during the months I wrote my novel, I had a strict suicide routine. Each morning, first thing when I rose, I used to put the barrel of a loaded gun into my mouth and put my thumb on the trigger and pull back as far as I dared. My hands trembled as I did this, and my heart raced. But the closer I came to death each morning, the more it filled me with courage, and the better I wrote.

Sebastian takes the microphone once more and gives instructions to the people who want their books signed. He has the audience line up by section. Nobody in the room leaves. They all have books. This is going to be a long ordeal, and I have Sebastian fetch me a coffee.

Signature after signature, I'm forced to endure all sorts of abuse. The worst variety comes from the aspiring writer, of which there are many. Each of these ambitious young wordsmiths comes equipped with copies of their own manuscripts, which they try to force upon me as if part of the job description of writer is to help and instruct. I inform each and every one of them that I'm sorry, but I'm simply too busy to read any of their work. This is met with hurt feelings and disdain and has probably cost me future readers of any further work I may or may not be able to accomplish.

Following the book signing, Sebastian informs me we're having dinner with members of Loyola's English department at a sushi restaurant. The meal is allegedly in my honor, but I was never consulted about what I'd like to eat. I actually despise sushi—always have, ever since Frannie introduced me to it. The smell of raw fish makes me retch, and white rice reminds me of elementary-school cafeterias. Besides, I lack the finger dexterity to manage the chopsticks. Had I a choice, I would've picked barbecue.

The restaurant is swank—dim, *dutey*, and fresh, as Frannie would say. The place is crowded with the young and affluent. We have a reservation for one of the teak booths that line the windowless, teal-paneled walls. I overhear someone in my group say the place is "intimate and clubby," but to me it feels suffocating and synthetic. The group includes Sebastian, a man I only know as the head of Loyola's English department, and one of his graduate students, the girl from the front row. She introduces herself as Sally.

In the booth, I'm seated next to Sebastian and directly across from Sally. She's really quite stunning: neon-green eyes, fair ivory skin, and a sullen, vacant stare. I'm instantly taken with her, and my instinct is to crawl back into myself like a tortoise.

"Interesting reading today, Mr. Brown," the unnamed professor says. "You have some fascinating ideas, but I'm wondering how serious you are about them."

He is a spindly and twitchy man with glasses and a thin mouth.

"How so?" I ask.

"I don't see them as realistic. I can't imagine a man living that way with any enduring success."

"I don't follow," I say. "Give me an example."

"For instance, there is a scene where the protagonist and his girlfriend are completely destitute, not a nickel between them, and are as desperate and vulnerable as newborn babies. So desperate, in fact, that Donald, your protagonist, decides to rob a drug dealer, which he barely manages to do, nearly getting himself shot in the process. His take was close to a thousand dollars, if I remember correctly—a tremendous score for a man in his position. However, when he returns to his girlfriend that evening to tell her the good news, he doesn't find her. Instead, she has left him a note stating she's gone off with another man. He is so heartbroken by this he goes out into the street, finds a trashcan, and burns the money."

"So what's your problem?"

"He needed the money to live. He should've kept it. The man has no self-preservation instinct."

"He only cared about the money to make life better for her."

"It's a nice idea, but no one could actually live that way."

"You're wrong. The only ideas that have any value are the ones we really live. Otherwise, it's simply theory. And I have no use for theory." My voice cracks while delivering my impassioned plea.

"All the same, I don't see it."

"It might be too much for a man of your stripe."

A tense silence follows my personal attack.

I look up at Sally to gauge her reaction to the exchange. She provides me with a coy smile, and my self-worth is replenished.

"How about you, Sally, what do you think of Lou's book?" Sebastian asks.

"What I believe Lou doesn't understand is that feelings of religious conviction do not need to fall under any sort of reasoning."

Sally's face indicates no sign of discomfort as she makes her remark and, in this moment, I regret the entire premise of my novel.

"You might be right about that," I say. She flashes me another smile, and I feel more alive than I have at any time in recent memory.

"So, tell me, Lou," the professor says, "do you really believe your readers will find any answers to life's questions in your writing?"

We sit there, holding the longest silence—so long I can hear the ringing in the air.

"I'm not certain I have any answers, but I believe there is value in my meaningfully fumbling with it."

"I suppose that's a matter of opinion," the professor says.

When I return home in the evening, Frannie is lying across the black leather sofa in the living room with the lights off and reality television blaring. She's wearing a low-cut, white three-quarter length sleep shirt and her long billowy hair drapes down in front of her shoulders, framing her breasts.

"Hello, darling, how was your reading tonight?"

"Fine," I say.

"Just fine? Not wonderful, not atrocious? It's not like you to be so terse."

I sit down on the couch, and Frannie lays her head in my lap. "I think my book may be too cynical."

"Oh, darling, you were such an angry young man. Aren't you glad you've put all that angst behind you? Things are so much better for you now."

"I guess so."

"I'd say you're in a million times' better position than you used to be. You used to have nothing. Don't you remember?"

"It wasn't always bad. There were good times too."

"You're happy with me, aren't you?"

"Don't ask me questions like that. Of course I'm happy with you."

"Well, good, you should be. I practically saved you."

I pick her head up off my lap. "Saved me?" I say. "What do you mean by that?"

She sits up straight and eyes me skeptically. "When I met you, you were living like an animal. Remember that awful little apartment in Lincoln Heights? The place had roaches everywhere, and the neighborhood streets were patrolled by gang members, and you could hear shooting in the nighttime. But look where you are now, look at what you have. Like I said, I saved you."

"Frannie, you didn't give me this. I already had the money when we met."

She laughs abruptly. "Yes, you had the money, but you certainly didn't know what to do with it. If anything, I saved you from yourself."

I stand up, flick on the lights, go to the bar, and pour myself a scotch, neat. "Well, you certainly know how to help me spend what I've made."

Frannie comes over to the bar and throws her arms around me. "Don't be upset with me, darling. You know how much I appreciate you, don't you?"

I smile brightly and paw at her behind.

She kisses me softly on the mouth. "Let me finish watching the last few minutes of my show, and then I'll meet you upstairs. How does that sound?"

"Why don't you skip the show and let me romance you right

now?"

She shakes her head. "It's only a couple of minutes. I'll be right up."

I trod up the stairs and lie down on the bed, in all my clothes. Next thing I know it's three hours later, the lights are off, I'm still fully dressed, and I'm nearly dangling off the edge of the bed. Frannie is next to me sleeping, and she is spread out like a human letter X. I get out of bed, go to the bathroom, brush my teeth, take off my clothes, and then try to scoot Frannie back to her side of the bed. Unable to do so, I reclaim my tiny corner of space, and attempt to fall back to sleep.

Chapter

My whole life I've thought myself defective or at least peculiar. As a boy, I could do what the others did—with some effort I managed algebra, chemistry experiments, and reading Conrad. In this way I was not strange. However, there was one thing I simply could not suffer—foreseeing a future for myself, an attainable goal, something to strive for—as all my friends and classmates did. They saw themselves becoming doctors, teachers, engineers, and judges, and planned accordingly. Take this set of courses, get this certification, intern for this many years, keep your head down, work hard, and you'll reach your aims.

Sometimes, as a kid, I used to get jealous. I thought it must've been thrilling to know what hopes the future held—the luxury of salary and raises, of finding a wife and building a family, saving for vacation and retirement.

And despite all evidence to the contrary, I always did believe myself destined for great things—saw myself to be of an elevated status. Perhaps that's what gave me permission to act as I have. But after years and years of waiting for an event to come along and change everything, it finally has, and nothing is better; perhaps things are worse. I feel totally hopeless, but in that despair comes some relief. The burden has been lifted, the need to succeed banished, the desire to fulfill some latent potential no more. No longer do I have to envy my colleagues and compatriots because success is of little value in life.

But this is a troubling realization. What now, if the realization of the American dream is no good?

Oh how I miss being a poor and miserable failure—I was so free then!

It's morning now and I'm lying in bed with Frannie, her back to me. With the start of a new day, the rising of the sun, the sound of the birds chirping, the garbage men collecting their cans, the thoughts in my mind have been turned upside down. I can't stop thinking about time—rather the passing of time—and how it is my enemy. Every month, week, day, hour, minute, and second I don't do something is a small defeat. I'm crying out for a disaster, a calamity, a grand failure to rob me of my possessions and bring me back to my humble beginnings to start anew. And as I lay there considering how I'd like to see the whole world thrown into chaos, watch as the people claw out their own eyes or disappear into the mountains or sea, I feel Frannie press her bottom up against my penis. At first I figure this must be accidental, but as she wiggles more and more, it becomes clear she is doing so with intent.

So I reach my hand under her nightgown and massage her breasts. Both nipples go hard and after a few moments she guides my hand down between her legs. I notice immediately she is hairless.

"What have you done to yourself?"

"Huh?" she asks between throaty sighs.

"Down there, what have you gone and done?"

"Oh—I got a wax."

"But why?"

"What do you mean, *why*? Don't you like it?"

I can't say what I'm thinking. No, I'd be killed if I were to reveal that. What I'm thinking is this: A waxed cunt looks like a dead clam.

"Of course I do," I say. "I just prefer a bit of hair, that's all."

"Really?"

"Yes, it's the bit of hair that gives it its mystery and allure."

"You must be kidding."

"Yes, of course, I'm kidding," I recant.

She throws off the Egyptian-cotton sheets she purchased for more than the cost of some used cars, and straddles me. Frannie really does have a magnificent body, and I've got the best view in the house. I place my hands behind my head and lie back and watch the whole production unfold. Her tits bounce up and down in perfect rhythm, and her tight stomach stretches and unfolds like an accordion in the hands of a master polka musician. But Frannie's eyes are closed, and she looks as if she's off in a distant galaxy—lost in a world of passion in which I scarcely exist. At no point during the act does she acknowledge my presence. I might as well be a piece of machinery or a robot. In this moment, I suspect that everything we once shared has evaporated into molecules and spread out across space. In a desperate attempt, I try to force a façade of intimacy by first placing my hands on her breasts and then on her ass, but when she makes no indication of noticing, I cease my efforts and allow myself to come without warning.

"You came?"

"I did."

"Ugh," she says, climbing off of me. "You don't make any effort at all, anymore."

"An *effort*, I don't make an effort? What about you? Where were you throughout all of that? You certainly weren't here with me."

"Oh please, don't get all emotional. What kind of man are you?"

The urge to grab her by her hair and throw her to the ground and beat her surges through me, but instead I climb out of bed and go to the bathroom. My intention is to take a shower—to rinse myself clean. I refuse to spend my day covered in her influence. But my shower is unrecognizable to me—it's gone digital. Frannie has had it upgraded in the past twenty-four hours, since my last wash. Where there were once handles marked "Hot" and "Cold," there is now a keyboard. I poke around at it with no success. It is beyond my comprehension.

I abandon my effort and go back to the bedroom.

"I can't get the shower to work."

"Surely you're not that inept."

"You underestimate my incompetence," I say. "Now come show me how to use this damn thing."

"I need a minute to finish up here."

"Finish what up?"

She pulls back the sheet covering her lower half, and holds up a vibrator.

I slink out of the bedroom and go find another shower.

When I'm done rinsing off, I decide to head down to Venice Beach. There is no parking anywhere. Finally I spot a woman coming out of her house to walk the dog. I offer her twenty bucks to let me park in her driveway, and she agrees. The boardwalk is packed with bikini babes, tourists, misfits and freaks. Two bicycle cops have a teenage boy pushed up against a palm tree and are searching his pockets. When they find nothing, they let him go, and as the boy is walking away, he screams an obscenity at them. The cops jump on their bikes and pedal after him. After a short chase, they tackle him to the ground and put him in handcuffs. All the people stand around and watch as if it is theater.

I buy a coffee from a Mexican man pushing a cart. He's got an enormous, bulbous nose and emits a hearty but unwarranted laugh after everything he says. "What size do you want? Ha ha ha!" "Do you want room for cream? Ha ha ha!" "Have a nice day. Ha ha ha!"

I sit along the seawall, facing out toward the ocean. The head-high waves are populated with rubber-limbed, long-haired surfers. Each new set sends them jockeying for position. The same three or four guys are always in the right spot and catch all the good waves, while the rest of the pack sits on the shoulder waiting for scraps. Whenever one of the lesser surfers tries to break rank, a better surfer always dives in at the last second, forcing the inferior waterman off the wave. Too many infractions of this kind and the novice is forced to the beach.

A man with no legs at all, a human torso, cruises along the bike-path on a skateboard, using his arms to propel him forward. He's got a steady rhythm, like a master kayaker, negotiating his way in an out of beach traffic. The man wears the long black hair of an Indian Chief tucked up under a cap with a picture of a yellow smiley face on it. His skin is the color of soft baby shit and a long scar runs across his neck. He's taped a paper Burger King cup to the front of his skateboard. Periodically he stops and the kind folks within a close proximity reach into their pockets to see what they can spare. When the cup is nearly overflowing, he takes out the bills, wraps them in a rubber band, and places them in his jacket pocket. The jacket is forest-green and military-issue with a collection of gleaming medals and decorous ribbons pinned to the chest. The bottom of the jacket is held together by safety pins, creating a diaper effect.

"Hey, crackerjack, help a wounded veteran out?"

I hand him three singles from my wallet.

"That the best you can do, crackerjack? I lost my legs fighting for this country so you could have your freedom." I pull out a twenty and he snatches it before I make the effort to hand it to him. "Thanks, crackerjack, that's real generous of you."

"Thanks for your service," I say, reaching for my cigarettes.

"You spare one of those, too?"

I hand him one and bend down to light it. There is the heavy stink of whiskey on his breath.

"You want to grab a drink, soldier?" I say. "It's on me."

He agrees, and we start down the boardwalk together. Random boardwalk passer-bys offer him hi-fives and words of encouragement. Whenever there is a pretty girl nearby he steers himself over, and grazes his hand against her legs and ass. Some of them shout reproaches at him, but most are too shocked to say anything.

We come to a bar just off the sand called Lahaina Beach Club.

It's more like a wooden shack with a patio, but it's popular, and the place is packed. The white exterior paint on the building has been corroded off by the salty sea air. The railing is covered in seagull shit, and the three wooden steps leading up to the deck are wobbly and splintered. I stand back to see how the invalid attempts to manage the stairs, but he doesn't try at all. Instead he shouts at me: "Goddamn it, crackerjack, don't just stand there, pick me up! I'm a veteran, for Christ's sake!"

Most of the bar's patrons have turned their attention toward us. The half-man grabs his skateboard, and I pick him up from under his armpits. His shirt is covered with sweat; sinking my fingers into him feels like squeezing a wet sponge. I hold him out away from my body, careful not to make any unnecessary physical contact. He's surprisingly heavy and I feel a twinge of pain in my lower back.

He points to a table by the railing. "Put me in that chair," he says.

I set him down gingerly and lift my hands to my face and sniff them. They smell like a tire fire. I excuse myself and go to the bathroom, where I scrub them until the skin nearly peels from the bone. When I return to the table, there are already two empty shot glasses, an empty beer bottle, and a second beer bottle, nearly empty, as well.

"I ordered us some drinks, crackerjack. But you took too long so I drank them."

"Why don't you call me Lou?" I say, looking away from him, signaling the waitress.

"Alright, Lou, call me Vic." The waitress arrives, and we order three tequila shots and three more beers. "He needs to catch up to me," Vic says, reaching out to caress her arm.

I intercept his wandering reach and force his hand back to the table.

"He's harmless," I say.

"Vic is anything but harmless," the waitress says before

walking away.

"They really know you around here."

He smiles broadly.

"So you're a veteran. Where'd you serve?" I ask.

He finishes what's left of the second beer.

"Operation Desert Storm. Daddy Bush's war, not baby Bush's. I worked a checkpoint at the Kuwaiti border. Two months in, I got caught on the wrong end of an IED."

The waitress delivers the drinks. I lift a tequila shot and Vic does the same.

"Here's to you, pal," I say, and we both take back our drinks.

Vic coughs violently, a chest full of phlegm comes up, and he spits the lugie onto the ground.

"You ever come close to death, Lou?"

"I've tempted it a time or two, but nothing like you."

"And how did that feel to you?"

"I used to tell myself I was ready for it, but now I think I might be more afraid than anyone I know."

"Did you know there is a time when each of us is scheduled to go? It's true, it's pre-destined. On that day, the heavens are waiting for you, and when you die, you're shepherded to paradise. However, it's possible to miss your appointment. That's what happened to me. Something went wrong and only half of me died: my soul. My body clinged to life when it shouldn't have. Now my soul is locked out of Heaven, because it doesn't have a body. That's part of the deal—your body has to go with the soul in order for it to find peace, otherwise it's lost. And now I'm stuck down here without it. The death of the soul while the body still lives is worse than Hell."

"So how do you go on?"

Vic forces a smile. "I live for the pleasures the Devil gives me. I know I can't go to Heaven, so I'm free to do as I please. I'm the freest man in the whole world."

"That's something."

"You don't believe me, do you? Let me tell you something. I once killed a man for no reason at all. It was the middle of the night, and I was wheeling my skateboard around the outer edge of skid row. It's something I do when I can't sleep due to my nightmares. But on this night I decided to venture past the perimeter of the row and into this old, abandoned industrial park. I found a man passed out atop a pile of old tires, and I started rooting through his pockets. But then something came over me. I can't really explain it—something primal, something visceral, something almost erotic or sexual. I took out my knife and stabbed the man in the neck. He woke up immediately as the blood sprayed out of him like a fountain. There was a moment when the two of us locked eyes—a shared mutual recognition. I'm telling you it lasted only a split second, but it was the most alive I've ever felt. It's hard to describe, other than to say, I felt more God than man. Afterwards, I felt terrible, but not because I had killed him. No, I cried for a different reason. I was jealous of his death. I knew that both his body and his soul were together in Heaven." Vic picks up his beer bottle, and when he realizes it's empty he places it back on the table, picks up mine, and takes a long pull. "So what do you think of that story?"

"I think that after sex, murder might be the most natural instinct in the world."

"You really think so?"

"I do, I really do."

Vic reaches out, taking my hand. "Can I tell you something else? Something I haven't told anyone?"

"You've already confessed to a murder. I don't know why you'd hold back now."

"I didn't lose my legs in the war."

I yank my hand from his grip. "What the fuck are you talking about? You weren't in Iraq?"

Vic finishes the last drops of my beer. "I was there, all right, but I got sent home because of my diabetes. That's how I lost my legs."

"Diabetes?" I say. "I'd say that's ten times as tragic as having them blown off in war!"

"After the doctors took my legs I couldn't get a job, and the military didn't give me shit, so I went out and bought a bunch of war medals and ribbons and pinned them to my shirt. And when I did that, people started treating me real different. All of a sudden I was some sort of hero, and not just some guy whose body doesn't produce enough insulin. And after telling my story enough times, I actually convinced myself the story was the truth. I really believed it, through and through. I thought I'd done all those things I'd claimed to. And even when I did remember that I was only telling lies, I'd tell myself it was okay because I really think I would've been a fine soldier and could've done all the things I said I did, if only I'd been given a chance. So if you ask me if I feel bad about being an impostor, I'll tell you no, I don't feel bad about it, not at all."

The tears spring up in my eyes. I'm horribly ashamed by my own cynicism. What right do I have to be angry at the world? I should drop to my knees and thank the heavens for my good fortune. I'm the luckiest man on Earth. I should walk the streets with a happy smile on my face and a bounce in my step, greeting everyone I see with well wishes, spreading my joy around to those less fortunate.

As I'm about to reach over and take Vic in an embrace of brotherhood and camaraderie, he screams out, "I gotta have a fucking piss!"

"What?"

"I need to empty my fucking bladder."

"So what do you want me to do about it?"

He unfastens the safety pin that holds the bottom of his shirt together.

"I need you to lift me up over the urinal. That's what I need you to do."

I pick him up, and this time, inspired by my newfound fellowship, hold him securely to my body, as if he were my own child. He clings tightly around my neck. His sour breath is in my nose and mouth, and his sweaty torso is pressed up against my chest. I can feel the wetness clinging to my shirt. All around us, people try to look away, but there are whispers, laughs, and cries.

Once inside the bathroom I hold Vic up in front of the urinal, and he pulls it out and starts to go. I'm tempted to have myself a peek, but I'm afraid I'll be scarred for life. Years of comfort and excess have developed in me a weak constitution for human frailty and suffering. But a little voice in my head tells me that I need to look, that it'll remind me once again of what sort of true cruelties exist in this world—the kind I used to be able to describe so well in my writing, not these third-rate cruelties I've been obsessing over now for so many years. Vic has a good, steady stream, and he makes carnal, pleasurable grunts. Finally I work up the courage, and I casually crane my neck over his shoulder to get a glimpse. It's fixed to the very end of his body, appearing to float below him, all twisted and battered, scabbed over from rubbing against the deck of his skateboard. When he's done, he shakes it out and says, "Sorry, Lou, got some on your shoes."

I look down to see that the toes of my boots are dotted in little pools of urine.

"Let's get another drink," he says.

"Why don't I take you home instead?"

"One more for the road?"

"Okay," I say. "One more for the road."

I wake up to dawn-patrol surfers running past me down to the surf. I hear one of them call me a bum as he runs by. A half a piece of sausage pizza lies a few feet from my face, and a seagull is stalking it like prey. My head is heavy and throbbing, and there is sand sticking to my sweaty cheeks and forehead. Vic is lying next to me, his army jacket under his head, used as a pillow. He is snoring loudly. I try to shake him awake, but he is too deep in slumber. In his dream he calls out, "I'm the fastest runner on the block." I light up a cigarette, remove my socks and shoes, and walk down to the water's edge. There are large piles of seaweed washing ashore. Hordes of flies buzz around them. The cold water stings my feet and ankles. I try to work up the nerve to dive in, but the will isn't there and I return to the sand. I check my phone. There are three voicemails and six text messages from Frannie. She is convinced I'm either dead from an accident, drugs, or violence—or that I'm cheating. From the tone of the messages, it's clear she prefers the former.

Vic opens his eyes, and first thing reaches into his pocket, removes a flask, and takes a hit. He holds it out to me and I pour the whiskey into my mouth, swish it around, and swallow. It burns my throat and I give a small cough.

I hand the flask back to him. "Can I drop you off somewhere?"

"Nah, I'm good," he says, shaking the flask. "I'm going to head over to the 7-Eleven for a burrito and a refill."

"It was good to meet you," I say as I put on my shoes.

"Good to meet you, too, Lou."

Trudging back across the sand to the boardwalk, I stop and lean into the opening of a trashcan and vomit. A jogger runs past me, and I wish him a good morning. He gives me a dirty scowl and accelerates his pace. I trudge back to my car and head home.

Frannie has already left for work when I get there. I go to the freezer and retrieve the vodka and the Bloody Mary mix from the fridge. I pour myself a tall glass. The newspaper is sitting on the counter. The front-page headline is about the soaring unemployment rate. I look up from the paper and glance around the kitchen: brand-new stainless-steel appliances, granite counters, handcrafted cabinets, rusted oak-wood flooring.

I flip to a different article. The title reads: "Those with Jobs are

Working Longer Hours than Ever." I pick up a pen and write on the envelope of the mortgage bill: *The high cost of security in modern America.*

I dial the phone.

"Where the hell have you been?" Frannie says.

"I'm sorry."

"Go on, explain yourself—if you can."

"I wasn't feeling very well last night and I had a few too many drinks." I can hear myself slurring, and I double my efforts to straighten out my speech. "And things just sort of unraveled from there."

"It's because of the vibrator, isn't it? I'm sorry I was so cruel. That was awful of me."

"It's not just that, it's the book, too."

"I feel rotten about it."

"It really wasn't all you."

"Can you forgive me?"

I fix myself another Bloody Mary.

"If you can forgive me, I can forgive you."

"Under one condition."

"What's that?"

"You have to come with my friends and me to this concert tonight."

"What concert?"

"Sander Van Doorn is DJing at Create?"

"But you know how I hate these things."

"Do this for me, please, darling."

At eleven, we're standing in front of the club. Frannie tells me her friends are running late and won't be there for another hour. The line is at least one-hundred people long. Scanning the crowd, I'm amazed by the bodies on these women. Every single one of them looks as if it's been engineered in a lab.

The men, too—not an ounce of body fat anywhere, it's all

swollen muscle stuffed into too tight T-shirts, and pants that'll require the Jaws of Life to remove. And the fucking tans on these guys! To attain this aesthetic would require, daily, at least two hours of gym time, followed by an hour in one of those human ovens.

"Do we have to do this?" I ask.

"Come on, don't be like that. This is going to be fun!"

"I'm thirty-eight, ten years too old for this place."

She's hardly listening, too overwhelmed with all the energy buzzing around her. I catch her staring at two guys I recognize from TV.

"You know—there is an inverse relationship between the size of their muscles and the size of some other important anatomy."

"I think it's hot and you're just jealous."

Frannie is always trying to persuade me to go to the gym. She thinks I need to bulk up—muscles are her thing. God only knows how she can stand the sight of my naked physique.

"Yeah, I'm fucking dying of envy."

We skip to the front of the line because Frannie is on the guest list. The guy with the clipboard—a young male model, to be sure: chiseled features, strong chin, perfectly coiffed hair—says, "Frannie! How are you tonight, girl?"

I light a cigarette.

The doorman and Frannie exchange kisses on the cheeks. "Hi, darling," Frannie says, "it's so good to see you."

He looks at me dismissively. "How many do you have with you tonight?"

"Mikey, this is Lou." Frannie pats me on the shoulder as if I'm some orphan she's brought along as charity. "It's just the two of us for now. My friends are coming later."

He opens the velvet rope, and as we slip past, I casually flick my lit cigarette in his direction, it landing at his feet.

Inside the club is a teeming mass of posturing hipsters, drugged-out club kids, and furious dancers. I can sense something dreadful in the air. This is not the first time Frannie has dragged me to one of these places, and each time she has, the night has ended in catastrophe. The scene always unfolds predictably: she surrounds us with her terrible friends and, under their influence, Frannie transforms into a most insipid of creatures. The mindless banter centers on diets, tawdry romantic scandals, reality television, and fashion. In order to assuage my anxiety, I withdraw and drink heavily. At first, Frannie hardly notices. She's content with my lack of participation. But there always comes a point in the night when things turn. It's usually around the time she has had her third or fourth drink that she loses her grace and poise. Her speech becomes erratic and slurred, her movements clumsy and unencumbered. Everything I am is wrong and ugly—a disappointment and an embarrassment. I'm accused of being "no fun" and "dull." It's strange how time changes one's perception of things.

Two years before, on one of our very first dates, I took Frannie to a karaoke bar. She sang the tunes off the radio sung by the pop princesses of the day. She couldn't hit the high notes, but she had drunken enthusiasm and danced well. All the men in attendance clapped loudly for her efforts.

Not to be outdone, I serenaded her with "Stuck in the Middle with You." My rendition was so spirited that it earned me a free round of shots from the bartender. As I went to claim my whiskey, I noticed a man who exuded an aura of danger unmatched by any I'd ever seen. I was so impressed by this pervasive quality he possessed, I insisted he drink with me, and he did with no resistance at all. Turns out this man was an Army Ranger sharpshooter who had recently returned from overseas action. After much prodding, I convinced him to duet with me on "Take a Walk on the Wild Side." This led to a fast friendship, followed by an endless succession of tequila shots.

That night, poor Frannie bore witness to a cokefueled game of Life or Death. This sniper had dared me to allow him to shoot a can of beer off the top of my skull. And, of course, I had the utmost faith in him, and permitted him to do so. His aim was true, and a single bullet passed over my head, tearing the can in two. This brought Frannie to tears, and she begged me never to do something so foolish again. Ever since, I've worked diligently at curtailing my more unhinged tendencies.

Frannie grabs my hand and leads me through the throngs of sweaty bodies. "Let's get a drink," she shouts over the pulsating rhythms exploding from the club's speakers.

We push our way up a flight of stairs, into a smaller room. The line for the bar is endless, and I can see the disappointment sweeping over Frannie's face.

"What do you want to drink?" I ask.

"What?"

"Drinks! What do you want?"

"Vodka-Red Bull."

I shove my way past all the punks and poseurs already in line. They respond with sulky looks and quiet protests, but I push forward without hesitation, until I find myself up against the bar.

"A vodka-Red Bull and a Maker's on rocks," I holler at the bartender, a man with unnatural good looks and a vapid, empty gleam in his eyes—another aspiring star of the silver screen, I'm certain.

"Thirty-two dollars," he says, placing the drinks on the bar.

"Fuck you, thirty-two dollars!" I say. "Seriously?"

"It is what it is."

I pay in cash, leaving too generous of a tip.

"Voila," I say to Frannie, upon finding her leaning against a cocktail table.

"How did you do that?" she asks.

She gives me a tender kiss on the cheek. I respond by grabbing her head and pulling it in close, parting her lips with mine, slipping her a bit of tongue. She pulls away, disgusted, leaving my mouth ajar.

A booming voice bellows through the air. A behemoth of a drag queen is standing on the stage with a microphone. She must stand six foot six flat-footed, and nearly seven foot in heels. Her face is caked in white make-up, except for her candy-apple red cheeks and electric-blue eye shadow. The yellow-sequined dress she's managed to squeeze herself into barely contains her prosthetic tits and is cut impossibly short.

"She must be tucking, right?" I say into Frannie's ear.

"I think she looks amazing!"

Her thunderous baritone continues over the backdrop of a soft beat: "You bitches are in for a real show tonight!" And then the music stops, and she strikes a provocative pose. She stays frozen in this position, tits pushed out, ass popped—until a new and more aggressive beat starts thumping, and she erupts into a series of spastic and graceless dance moves.

I redirect my attention back to my drink. Frannie, on the other hand, is enraptured. Her eyes are glued to the stage and she dances in place, screaming out nonsensical come-ons. She continues watching this vulgar display for another five minutes, until she receives a text from her friend.

"I'm going to go meet Violet downstairs. Why don't you wait here, and we'll come right back up."

Burdened by the undulating bodies pressing in all around me, I move to the relative safety of the railing. Peering out across the dancefloor, the flashing reds, blues, and yellows of the lightshow nearly induce in me an epileptic seizure. From the corner of my eye I manage to catch Frannie greeting her friend Violet, and the group Violet has brought with her— another girl and two guys. They are all wearing the gender-appropriate Hollywood uniform. Frannie hugs each of them enthusiastically. I watch the pleasantries unfold. But instead of turning back toward the stairs, one of the guys throws an arm around Frannie, and the whole group disappears into the crowd. For several minutes I stand at my perch. But it's no use—they are gone, lost in the sea of partygoers.

I go back to the bar and order several shots and take them in succession. When I try to order a fourth, the bartender says with a smug and stupid face, "Sorry, pops."

"You got to be fucking kidding me."

"E-e-e-xcuse me...," he replies.

I reach across the bar and grab ahold of the collar of his shirt. "Stop stuttering, you moron. It does nothing for you."

The bartender turns his head from side to side looking for someone to come to his rescue. I suddenly feel a sense of empowerment I'd long forgotten existed. But my reverie dissipates as I'm grabbed around the neck by what I'm certain is a giant. The blood my heart is supposed to be pumping toward my brain gets turned around and sent back to my toes. Suddenly my vision betrays me and all I see is a black abyss, dotted with tiny flecks of shimmering light. Before I give way to impending death, my reflexes kick in, and I let go of the bartender's collar and swing my elbows back in a violent jerking manner. They connect with what feels like a brick wall. That is the last thing I remember before waking up on the floor.

"What happened?" I ask, rubbing my eyes with my fists.

"You're a damn fool," the man says, "that's what happened."

I sense that a group of people is standing around in a circle, looking down at me. I look up to meet their gazes, but everyone appears blurry and distorted, like specters or hallucinations. "What did I do now?" I ask.

"You attacked my bartender," the giant says.

"Your bartender?" I say, suddenly remembering. "That fucking tyrant, that goddamn fascist, that malevolent despot."

"You better cool down, my man, before you get yourself really hurt."

I continue to rub my eyes with my fists, and finally my vision returns. With my newfound sight I gaze up to see the man that nearly killed me. He's a man of African descent with deep-set squinty eyes, and a broad square head from which a long braided goatee dangles. He's got a menacing grimace—his two front teeth gapped enough to slide three stacked quarters through. "Christ, pal!" I say, as I struggle to stand. The man holds my elbow to steady me, entirely swallowing my arm in his grip. Once on my feet, I continue, "Don't you think that was a bit excessive? I was only having a small chat with him."

"Pull that shit again and you're 86'd. You understand me?"

I stumble my way to the stairs, still not fully recovered. The stairwell is lined with mirrors from floor to ceiling. I can see myself from myriad angles. My neck and throat are red, and there is already blue-black bruising forming. I look like a self-asphyxiating masturbator. By the time I reach the bottom of the stairs my neck is so cramped I fear I'll soon reach terminal paralysis.

I limp from one end of the club to the other searching for Frannie. It's nearly impossible for me to maneuver, as I can barely stand. The music is too loud, causing disorientation, and I nearly lose my way. After I struggle through a second lap across the dancefloor, I collapse into a booth already occupied by what appears to be a bachelorette party. The kind women can see that I'm in trouble and offer me water, which one of them carefully pours down my throat while another steadies my head.

"Do you need us to call you an ambulance?" the bride-to-be asks.

"That might not be a bad idea," I say.

The woman tells the dispatcher on the phone all my symptoms: compromised motor skills, slurred speech, strangulation marks on the neck, bloodshot eyes, ringing ears, profuse sweating, extreme nausea. There is a great deal of urgency and care in the words they exchange. It's very comforting to know that I'll be well looked after. My troubles begin to melt away.

But then I spot Frannie on the dance floor. She's engaged in the sort of filthy behavior one sees in rap videos. She's with the same guy who had put his arm around her before she disappeared into the crowd. He's dancing behind her, hands on her waist, grinding his pelvis into her backside, nuzzling his face into her neck. A course of adrenaline surges through my body. I no longer feel stifled by a stiff neck or any fears of impending impairment to my voluntary body movement. In fact, it's just opposite. I feel equipped with the strength of an entire army brigade, imbued with the rage of a mob of pro-lifers protesting the opening of a new Planned Parenthood clinic.

I set my feet on the ground and maneuver through the crowd, shoving people out of my way. I stop directly in front of Frannie. She's dancing so hard it nears religious fervor. Eyes closed, she's committed herself entirely to the act—a baptism, for lack of a better word. She does not take any notice of me. The man pressing himself against her does.

"What the fuck are you looking at?" he says.

I swing wildly and connect with his nose. The man staggers backward into a crowd of dancers, holding his face in his hands, blood seeping through his fingers.

"What the fuck are you doing?" I say to Frannie.

She stares at me wild-eyed, as if in a voodoo trance. I seize her by the arm and drag her toward the club's exit. From behind I hear a loud howl and the rumbling of stomping feet. I turn to see the man I've punched making a charge at me. I push Frannie out of the way just in time to take the full force of his attack. The man lands on top of me and we exchange blows. I take one to the mouth and wonder if I've lost a tooth. A second one catches me in the ribs, and I gasp for breath. I grab the man by his ear and give it a firm yank. He rolls off of me and shrieks in pain. I catch him with a haymaker that strikes him in the eye. The force of the punch sends me careening backward, and I land flat on my back. I look across at the man and he is down on his knees, pressing the sleeve of his shirt against his bleeding eye. I can barely maintain my balance, let alone stand up and finish him. Instead I wobble to my feet. Frannie finds her way to my side. She wears a dazed and ecstatic expression on her face.

"What the hell was that?" she says. "You're some kind of animal." She reaches down and picks up my trembling hand. All the skin on my knuckles is ripped open, exposing bone. "Chris is my friend." She drops my hand to my side.

I see security hustling towards me and I abandon Frannie and stumble through the crowd, making my way to the bathroom. I run the water and lean over the sink, rinsing the blood from my mouth. The man at the next sink over says, "Rough night, ehh?"

"Not the best."

"Maybe I can help."

He takes a paper towel from the dispenser and hands it to me. I look him over: tight button-down shirt, square jaw, soft lips, experimental hairstyle, eager eyes.

"You're not my type," I say.

He laughs a girlish laugh and bits of spittle hit me in the face. "No," he says. "Not sex, drugs. Do you want any drugs?"

I consider my promise to Frannie to stay drug-free. "You have blow?" I ask.

He takes me by the arm and leads me to an open stall.

"You have cash?"

I retrieve two hundred-dollar bills from my wallet and exchange them for two plastic baggies of white powder. The man gives me a small pat on the ass as he exits the stall. I stare down at the drugs, and it's almost as if I can hear them beckoning. They say, "Come home, Lou, we've missed you!" I pull my Beamer key from my pocket and use it as a spoon, shoveling heaping piles up my nose. That good burn in the sinuses strikes like a lightning bolt from Heaven. I feel reborn, this time as a bullfighter or a jet pilot. I scream out, "I feel like a million dollars! Maybe even two million!" I finish the first bag and start on the second. Halfway through, I look up to see the security guard who had accosted me earlier, leaning over the door of the stall.

"You just don't learn, do you?" he says.

"Oh please, not now!" I shout back.

His massive hand reaches out and throttles me by the throat. I struggle and shake like a freshly caught fish floundering on the deck of a boat.

"You want to open that door now?" he asks.

I reach for the door's lock with my last bit of strength. He lets go and I collapse on top of the toilet. The door opens and he lifts me from under the arm, pulls me to my feet, and drags me through the crowd. Outside I'm met by a police car and taken to the station. I'm fingerprinted, stripped naked and checked for contraband, issued official prison attire, and thrown into a tiny cell with a drunken Indian who can't stop having diarrhea. The next morning I'm brought before the judge and arraigned. I'm wearing handcuffs and an orange jumpsuit. The official charge is possession. Bail is set at ten-thousand dollars. Sebastian, my agent, pays it on my behalf.

He's waiting for me on the steps in front of the county jail when I'm released. He's holding a copy of today's newspaper.

"You made page six," he says.

"Not bad," I say, lighting a cigarette.

"Where do you want to go?" he asks.

"A hotel, I suppose."

I get into Sebastian's car—a new Porsche—with my cigarette still in mouth. His eyes fill with righteous indignation. "Not in the car, Lou, not in the fucking car!"

I flick the cigarette out the window and, in the doing, catch a whiff of my underarm. I smell like a maggot-ridden corpse. "Flop sweat," I say to Sebastian. "It's the absolute worst."

Sebastian scrunches up his face in genuine disgust. "Try not to get any on the leather." He reaches into the tiny backseat and locates a towel. "I was going to use this for yoga today, but this is an emergency."

I lay the towel across the seat. "Thanks for bailing me out."

"So what happened?"

I look down at my hands, both covered in bandages. "I was exercising a protest against life."

We stop at a red light in the heart of Hollywood. A white Rolls-Royce convertible idles next to us. We both turn to look. A bald man with a paunch that rests against the steering wheel is sitting next to the most exquisite Asian woman. He's pawing at her neck and breasts. She throws her head back and laughs at whatever it is he is saying. Sebastian returns his attention to me. "I'm going to drop you off at the Standard on Sunset."

Ten minutes later I'm standing in the lobby of the hotel, with nothing but the clothes on my back. The place is a nod to retro-chic, with its all-over white shag carpet, turbo-suede sectional couches, and Andy Warhol-inspired cladded walls. Behind the front desk is a glass cage, in which a topless girl crawls around on all fours.

I book a room for the night. The front-desk clerk charges me two hundred and sixty dollars. He's a tall and wiry thing with a thin face and no cheekbones or chin. I hold out my credit card, and he looks down at my heavily bandaged hands, saturated in dry brown blood.

"Have room service bring me up a roast-beef sandwich and a twelve pack of beer," I say.

"What kind, sir?"

"What kind what?"

"Of beer, sir."

"It doesn't matter."

"No?"

"I go for it all."

"Understood, sir."

He carefully extracts the card from my hand, making sure not to touch my wounds. After running the card he leaves it on the counter, along with the credit-card slip for me to sign. "Are you okay, sir?" he asks.

"Dandy," I say.

I ride the elevator up to my floor with two girls dressed nearly identically in oversized sunglasses, skinny jeans, and tube-tops. They have a Mexican bellhop with them. The poor fellow is strapped with shopping bags the girls have hung on him like ornaments from a Christmas tree. His arms are shaking under the weight of their retail therapy, and beads of sweat drip off his cap.

The taller of the two girls is telling the shorter one that last week she had accompanied her boyfriend on a business trip to New York, and that he had paid for her to have a spa day while he worked. She confesses to having had sex with her masseuse on the massage table.

"Oh my God, really?" the shorter girl asks.

"He was hot—huge muscles, big dick!" the taller one replies.

"And what about Ben?"

"Ben doesn't have huge muscles or a big dick."

Both girls giggle.

I say to the Mexican bellhop, "*Perras locas blancas.*" He tries to stifle a laugh, but fails to do so, and drops a bag labeled *Prada*.

"Excuse me," the tall, philandering girl says to me.

"Yes?" I say.

"What did you say to him?"

"I said you're rotten."

"Excuse me..."

"I don't think so."

"Can you please stay out of our conversation?"

"You realize you're shouting your infidelities into the ears of complete strangers, right?"

A lump forms in the girl's throat and her voice cracks. "I'd hardly say I was shouting."

"Poor Ben," I say.

The girl points a nervous finger at me. "You don't know anything about Ben or me."

I dig into my pockets looking for cigarettes, coming up empty-handed. "The next thing you're going to tell me is that you're in love."

"Screw you. We are in love."

The bellhop and I both laugh again. "No one could love you any better than they could love a bug or a rat," I say.

The elevator stops and the door opens. Each girl takes a turn calling me an asshole, before pouring out into the hall. The bellhop flashes a hearty grin at me and then chases after them. I watch them turn left and disappear around the corner.

The wrap around my hands has compromised my finger dexterity, and I fumble with the key, dropping it several times to the floor before I manage to get the door open. Once inside I peel off my clothes. The stink of the county jail has entered my pores and contaminated every fiber of my body. I take the plastic garbage bags out of two of the room's trashcans, place my hands in them, and tie them off around my forearms. I turn the hot-water handle of the shower all the way and climb in. The water burns, and I take the soap and scrub, trying to peel off at least one layer of skin. After several minutes the shower fills with steam, and I can't see a thing. I hunch over and feel around for the knob to turn off the water, but miss and fall into the shower curtain, tearing it off the rod. I go head-first over the edge of the bathtub and onto the floor below. A thick cloud of steam, the color of expired milk, billows out, and I open the bathroom door to make my escape.

Someone is beating on the door to my room. It sounds like a brutal and chaotic affair. I look down at the contemptible pile of clothing on the floor, kick it across the room, and stride naked to the door.

"What is it?" I say.

"Room service. I have your beer and sandwich."

"Thank God, I'm starving!"

"I've been out here for ten minutes, already." I open the door open enough for a pale, freckly arm to slip the items through.

"What's going on in there?" he asks. "I heard screaming."

"Screaming?" I say. "You heard screaming?"

"Yes. Is everything all right? Do you need help?"

"It's nothing. I can handle it."

He pushes a clipboard and pen through the cracked door. "Please sign this, sir."

I scribble out a tip, sign, and slam the door shut. Underfoot the white shag carpeting has transformed into a marshy bog. From the bathroom there is a river of shower water flowing out into the main room. I toss my food and beer onto the bed and tear and thrash at the plastic bags on my hands, ripping them from my limbs, as I rush into the bathroom. The blue-and-white-checkered linoleum floor is covered in two inches of moving water. I dive to my knees and lunge for the shower handle to cease the relentless flow of floodwater, then collapse prostrate onto my back.

I get the unshakeable sensation that the Devil himself is doing work on me. A haunting image of him at Sabbath dinner sucking the marrow of a darkened bone coalesces in my mind. He speaks to me in an infernal whisper. "You've finally reenlisted me to contest your vision."

"I hoped I could be faithful to a new master," I say trembling.

"Your hope had no footing because you weren't ready to face the doom."

I close my eyes and say a silent prayer. But before long, I'm shrieking and hollering, splashing water about the room with my flailing arms and legs. Tears spring from my eyes and roll down my cheeks onto my tongue. My anguish gives way to mirth, and I find myself in a fit of laughter. Finally, after several minutes, I stand up and catch my reflection in the mirror. My eyes possess a strange combative glow. They seem alive somehow. Staring at the image, I make my finger into a gun and fire a shot at myself. "Bang!" I say aloud.

I put on the cozy hotel robe, lie on the bed, and pop my first beer. The clock reads 4:37p.m. By 6:15, I've finished all but two of the beers and fall asleep.

Just past midnight, I wake up and call the front desk. "I need a taxi," I say.

"No problem," an amiable voice replies.

"Now," I say. "I need a taxi now."

"We'll have one for you in five minutes, sir."

"I'm going to be back in a couple of hours, and I'll need another room. This one is flooded."

"Flooded, sir? What happened?"

I twist the cap off the second-to-last beer in my twelve-pack. "The place is soaked. Could've been bandits in the night, but who knows for sure? I was sleeping."

"We'll check it out."

I ride the elevator down to the lobby wearing my cozy robe and nothing else. I have the last two beers in my hands. In the elevator with me is a man with pale-blue, watery eyes, a long sun-kissed ponytail, and the thin mustache of a high-school kid.

"Late-night sauna?" he asks.

"Who?"

"You, man. Heading to the sauna?" he says, smiling, his big white teeth glowing in the dimly lit elevator.

"Hunting."

"What?"

I guzzle the remainder of the second-to-last beer. "Hunting."

The elevator reaches the lobby, and I amble my way outside. The taxi is waiting for me and a chubby bellhop with greasy hair pressed flat against his forehead is holding open the car door. He glances down at my bare feet, visibly perplexed.

"Take this," I say, handing him the empty beer bottle.

I get in the cab. There is the shifty dark-eyed glare of a man watching me in the rearview mirror. He has rap music playing quietly on the stereo, and he's tapping along to the beat with his fingers on the steering wheel. I open the last of my beers and take a steady pull. The cab driver cranes his neck to face me. He's got a healthy thicket of silver and black facial hair, and raised cheekbones.

"No beer in the taxi," he says in his accented way.

I pound the remainder of the beer in one long go, open the window, and toss it out the window to the bellhop. The bottle passes through the ruddy-faced boy's hands and shatters at his feet. He throws his arms up in despair.

"Where to?" the cab driver asks.

I give him the address to my house, and ask if I can smoke.

"No smoking," he says, and then turns up the rap music to discourage any further conversation.

Twenty minutes on and we're deep into Laurel Canyon. Up ahead, framed perfectly by the palm trees on either side, is the Hollywood sign, and behind us, the view stretches out across downtown. It's dark now, but in the daylight the serenely green, manicured lawns of the houses look like foreign oddities against the backdrop of the water-starved brown and dusty hills.

We turn left onto a smaller, more secluded road and navigate its windy arcs, dips and climbs until we reach a second, even more private road that bisects the first and turn right, following it to the end of the line. "Stop here," I say, in front of my house.

"Thirty-nine dollars," the cab driver says.

It dawns on me that my car is still at the club. That is, if it hasn't already been towed.

"Wait here. I'm just going to run up and grab some clothes."

"Meter's running."

Following the flagstone path up along the driveway, I set off the motion detectors. Yellow ribbons of oppressive light beat down on me, burning my eyes, upending my cover of darkness. Moving past the garden of red and pink cottage roses, I can't remember having ever noticed their presence before. I wonder to myself if all my perceptions of the world and memories of past events are distorted.

Through the upstairs bedroom window, I see the light turn on. I slide my key into the door, turn the knob and slip inside. Soundlessly, I slip across the foyer and into the living room. I feel like an intruder entering someone else's world, tainting its pristine manner with my very presence—the white leather sofa, the grand piano, the obtuse paintings of cones and cylinders that line the walls, evoking memories of high-school geometry.

I carefully place each step as I ascend the stairs. The soft wood creaks beneath my weight, and at the top of the steps I turn right and negotiate the hallway. Finally reaching my bedroom door, I give a knock. No answer. I knock again.

"Frannie, it's me."

Again, no answer.

I open it and go inside. Frannie is standing next to the bed in her nightgown, the skin on her face flushed, her electric green eyes burning fearful and hostile. She's gripping a baseball bat in her hands.

"What are you doing?" I ask.

She drops the bat and collapses onto the bed. "You jerk!" she says. "I thought you were a burglar."

I trudge over to the bed and pick up the bat.

"I can't stand this anymore," she says. "Last night was the third night this week you haven't come home!"

I hold the handle of the bat with my right hand and pat the barrel into my left. "I've been in jail, thanks to you."

"You've been in jail?"

"It was in the goddamn papers this morning!"

She takes two long strides, sidling up next to me, reaches out and touches my cheek with the palm of her hand. "Because of the fight? You disappeared so quickly."

"Don't try to handle me, woman."

I turn for the closet, locate my suitcase, and toss it to the floor. I snatch handfuls of shirts and pants off their hangers, and pack them away.

"Where do you think you're going?"

"You think I'm going to stick around after that sort of humiliation?"

"You're overreacting. Don't be crazy. Please."

Frannie throws herself at me, clinging to my body, pressing her chest and face against my back and neck, holding on as if letting go meant the loss of everything.

"There is a cab waiting for me downstairs."

"You can't leave. We have to talk about this. I'm not letting you leave."

I get right up on her, only inches away. I raise my wounded fist in the air, holding it in front of her eyes. "Stay the fuck away from me, you understand? I don't believe anything you say to me."

Frannie collapses to the ground, holding herself in her arms, hot tears streaming down her face, desperate cries of grievous anguish seeping from her mouth, her body shaking like it's attached to strings with an invisible puppeteer standing above her, playing terrible tricks on her. "Why are you doing this?" she pleads. "I don't understand."

I head down the stairs, and out the front door. I stop again in front of the roses, giving them a sniff. A single tear falls from my eye, and I wipe it away. I take three steps toward the cab, turn around, pluck a single pink bud, and place it in my bag.

The taxi driver is smoking a cigarette as I climb inside.

"Back to the hotel," I say.

He starts up the engine and presses a heavy foot to the accelerator, propelling the vehicle forward, its spinning wheels kicking up rocks, debris, and a cloud of dust. When the taxi reaches the hotel, I grab my bag from the seat and step out onto the curb. I owe the driver ninety-seven dollars, and I give him one hundred.

"You cheapskate!" he shouts.

I kick the door of his cab. "You should've let me smoke!"

The cabbie shouts expletives in his foreign tongue and drives off. The chubby bellhop races to my side. I drop the bag at my feet. He picks it up and follows me. There is a different man at the front desk. This one is older, maybe forty, the skin on his face sagging a bit around the jowls, and his hair is too thin for how long he wears it.

"I called down earlier about a flood in my room," I say.

The front-desk clerk types away at his terminal. "Mr. Brown, it seems there is a small problem."

I place my forearms on the desk and lean forward. "Yeah, the room is soaked."

His eyes and mouth are full of nervous twitches, violent blinks, and involuntary lip curls. "Did you have some sort of accident with your shower?"

I stand up tall, straighten my robe, presenting myself in the most dignified fashion possible. "What kind of accident?"

"We sent a member of our staff up to the room and it appears someone tore the shower curtain off the rod and then pointed the showerhead over the rim of the tub and simply let the water flow."

"You're kidding me."

"Do you know anything about that, sir?"

"Like I said before, I was sleeping."

He looks down at my hands, covered in the bandages, now bloodied and tattered. "I'm afraid we're not going to be able to place you in another room tonight. We've gathered your belongings for you." The man reaches under the desk and with only two fingers picks up a bag that contains my stinking clothes, and sets it in front of me. "Can I call you another cab, sir?"

I bang my bloodied stump onto the desk. "This is an outrage," I shout. "I demand another room."

"Sir, please, don't make me call the police."

The wounds in my hand open up, and the blood flows. I bury the hand deep into my cozy robe. The fabric surrounding my chest quickly turns from white to red, and the crimson tide spreads south as my hand seeks out fresh refuge. "Oh, all right," I say, "call me a cab."

"And, sir, we're going to have to charge your card for the damage."

I leave the bag of prison-soiled clothing on the desk. The bellhop trails behind me, lugging my suitcase. There is already a cab waiting for me outside. I bid farewell to the bellhop and hand him a fiver.

The driver takes me to the club where I left my car the night before. There are two tickets on the windshield. I light a cigarette and start the car. Waylon Jennings is on the radio. I drive past the outskirts of Hollywood, head south down the 405, reconsider, then head east on the 10, ending up in Boyle Heights, at a place that can aptly only be characterized as a flophouse. The neon sign out front reads, "The Frontier Motel," but most of the light bulbs are out, so from a distance it actually reads, "h Fr t r Mo el". There are two motorcycles and a tan, late-nineties mini-van in the parking lot. My black BMW looks entirely out of place here. I park it under the only functioning light in the lot.

I check in, and on the walk to my room, I'm confronted by a blonde woman in hot pants. She looks Norwegian, if anything—about forty, in a low-cut red halter top that exposes the stretch marks on her belly. Before she can proposition me, I ask, "Can I bum a smoke?"

She flinches. "Excuse me?"

"Do you have a cigarette?"

"Sure, honey, you can have a cigarette," she says in a wheezing, paltry voice. She digs through her oversized, red purse. "I like your robe."

"Parting gift from my last place of residence."

She looks out across the lot. "I like your car, too."

"Transmission's shot. Barely gets me from A to B."

"My name's Emma. What's yours?"

"Lou."

"I'm glad we found each other, Lou. I think it's both our lucky night."

"I don't think so."

"Why not?"

"I've recently been put off women."

Emma's scarlet lipstick looks as though it's been applied by a small child with a crayon. The color's smeared all over her front teeth and past the borders of her lips. "That's because you haven't tried *me*, honey. You don't know how beautiful I am underneath all these clothes. I have the most beautiful body in all the world."

"I can see that," I say, making a thorough examination with my eyes. "Looks to me like you must've been an athlete. Let me guess: gymnastics?"

"Honey, you nailed it," she says. "I'm the greatest gymnast you've ever seen." She assumes some sort of athletic position that seems to me closer to wrestling than gymnastics. "I can do one hundred flips in a row with no problem at all." Everything she says is tinged with a classical Scandinavian pitch, making even the most outrageous talk about gymnastics sound formal and stilted.

"Before we get down to all this flipping business," I say. "I'm going to need a drink."

"This really is your lucky night."

Emma reaches into her purse to reveal a bottle of Jim Beam.

"You always carry booze in your purse?"

"Always when I'm working. Only sometimes when I'm not."

"I guess you're right. I'm lucky to have met you when I did."

She opens her mouth wide, exposing a gummy smile. "You're too much, Lou, just too much."

My room is on the second floor. I lead Emma up the chipped

and cracking concrete stairs. Halfway up, she gets one of her heels stuck and falls forward onto her hands and knees, skinning them. "Goddamn it," she shouts. I help her to her feet, and she tells me I'm a perfect gentleman.

Inside I pour us both glasses of whiskey—neither of us takes ice. The room smells of stale cigarette smoke. The drywall repair job in the ceiling has sprung a leak, and drops of moisture fall from it, collecting in a small puddle on the carpet. Emma spreads out across the bed and I sit in a chair, on the other side of the room. She fidgets, constantly readjusting herself—first lying on her side, supporting her head in her hand, cupped behind the ear, then rolling onto her belly with her arms folded in front of her, chin resting on the tops of her arms. Finally she sits up, back against the headboard, her legs in front of her like a teepee, knees adjoined and feet spread. The hot pants are creeping up the backs of her legs, revealing dimpled flesh. I turn my head, unable to look without grimacing.

"Don't you think I'm beautiful?"

"You have a certain charm."

She spins her motel-provided plastic cup in her hands. "Don't you want to come sit with me?"

We both take long sips, finishing our drinks. I stand up, reach for the bottle, and make my approach. I sit down on the edge of the bed, and she gets on all fours and crawls over to meet me. I top off both of our glasses. She places her free hand inside of my robe, on my bare thigh, and massages.

"Why so tense, honey? Nothing bad can happen here." She moves her hand further up my leg and the bottom of my robe comes open. I look down to watch her work. She's got the hands of a strangler—cracked nails and a deep scar running from the base of her thumb to her wrist. "A man in a robe like this should have no worries at all."

"It's the weight of the world, it's crushing me."

"No crushing weight, not here."

I stand up and start pacing back and forth, mumbling to myself.

"Sit back down, honey," she says. "I'm just getting warmed up."

I ignore her, continuing to lap from one side of the room to the other, always looking straight down, only considering the very next step—one foot in front of the other.

"Ideas have to be wedded to action," I say.

She lies down onto her back and places a finger into her mouth, striking a most clumsy pose. "That's what we're here for, honey—action!"

"There can't be any discrepancy between the ideas and the living."

She takes the finger out of her mouth and scratches her behind. "What discrepancy?"

"As I told the professor, 'The only ideas that have any value are the ones we truly live. Otherwise, it's simply theory.'"

"What ideas?"

"Never mind," I say. "What about your gymnastics?"

"You'd like to see my moves?"

"Yes, of course." I rush to her side, take her hand, and pull her to her feet. "Come on, do some somersaults for me."

She stands awkwardly, her hands held out in front of her, knees bent, feet together. She pushes off the ground, her momentum driving her forward, tucking her head at the last possible second before crashing into the floor. Splayed out on her back, she asks, "Like that? That's good, yeah?"

"Terrific," I say. "I want to see more."

She climbs to her feet and hops up and down, her legs bowing in and out, open and shut.

"That's so good," I say. "I thought you were Scandinavian, but now I'm sure you must be from the Eastern Bloc."

She stands on her toes and spins, losing her balance, stumbling into the bed and against the wall. All the while, she is singing a song that is all melody, no words. "Dee, dee, dee, da, de, da, la, la, la, la..." Her eyes roll back into her head, her face displaying the serene joy of a child lost in play.

Feeling inspired, I spring to my feet and dive into a headstand. All the blood rushes to my brain, and my eyes fill with tears, compromising my vision. My ears feel like I'm deep underwater with all the pressures of the ocean bearing down on me. I'm near fainting, and I collapse to the floor.

Emma topples over, landing on top of me. My face is in her armpit. There is a light stubble to it, feels like sandpaper against my forehead, and the smell is of sour milk.

"I bet you've never had pussy as good as mine," she says.

I roll away from her, finding myself in the soggy pit of carpet, under the hole in the ceiling. "I already told you: I'm off women."

She uses the corner of the bed to prop herself up onto her knees. She is breathing hard, her chest heaving up and down, her words sounding labored and slurred. "You a fag or something? I didn't take you for a fag, but no straight man turns down pussy this good."

I stand up and place the trashcan under the leaky ceiling. Each drop makes a maddening *plop*. "I'm sure you have a magnificent pussy," I say. "But it's like I told you, I've lost the taste for it."

She flops onto the bed, lying on her back. Her belly is lined with stretch marks—a virtual kid factory. "So what'd you bring me up here for?" she asks.

"You looked like good company."

She pulls two cigarettes from her purse and hands me one. "My company costs, honey."

I reach into my wallet, take out a hundred and twenty dollars, and toss it onto the bed.

She fingers the money and shoves it into her purse. "So, honey, what's got you so upset?"

I pour two more drinks. "Lately I've been thinking about how, as time passes, things seem to be getting worse and worse."

"They are?"

"Yes, definitely, but now I realize that's essentially meaningless. Things aren't getting worse. They're just becoming more like the future."

"You shouldn't spend too much time thinking about all this," she says, taking her drink from me. "It'll only cause you grief."

I toss my drink back in one fluid motion. "The future belongs to the machines and the robots, anyhow."

"To the loss of humanity," she says, holding up her cup in a salute.

I hold up my own cup. "To the robots."

I finish my drink and lie down next to her on the bed.

"It's not so bad," she says.

I turn out the lights, and the two of us smoke cigarettes in the dark until we fall asleep.

Chapter

I wake the next day. Emma is gone. She's left a note. It reads: *You left your keys on the floor. I thought about stealing your car but didn't. I didn't even take anything out of your suitcase. Hope to see you again soon. XOXO Emma.* At the bottom of the page she drew a crude picture of a robot holding a man under water.

I go outside to make an inspection of my car. A vandal has keyed the passenger door, but there is no sign of forced entry. I retrieve my suitcase from the trunk, return to the room, and get dressed—Levi's 501s, desert boots, and a blue-and-white vertical-striped, tailor-fit, casual button-down shirt. I go to the mirror to make my once-daily inquiry into my physical wellbeing. The face reflected back at me is more weathered than I remember it. The crow's feet, deepened. The sagging eyelids look more like saddlebags. The cheekbones, hollowed.

I dial up Cliff. He tells me he's late for his sparring session with his trainer, that he's really coming along, fantastic power, but that he's got to work on his combinations and footwork.

"Feeling pretty good, then?" I say.

"Good? No, I wouldn't say that. I'm scared as hell."

"Of this guy you're fighting?"

"Of course not," he says. "Of losing my son."

"Fear comes in all shapes and sizes."

"Pick me up at noon. I want to take you someplace."

"Where to?"

"I don't want to ruin the surprise."

Cliff is standing in front of an ice-cream truck, along with a handful of Latino and black kids, devouring the last few bites of a bomb pop. The truck is parked on the curb in front of Cliff's apartment building—two stories, gray cedar shingles, badly in need of paint, bars on the windows. The sound of the truck's tuneful summertime jingle fills the air.

Cliff is wearing another Hawaiian shirt. This one is black with pictures of pineapples all over it. He's got it buttoned all the way to the top—his formal look. His face is even puffier and redder than the last time I saw it, and he's got a blackened right eye.

While the formality of his dress and the battered face are of some alarm, it's not what really gets me. No, it's the hair. He's gone and lopped it all off. The ponytail is no more.

He climbs inside the vehicle.

"Nice new 'do," I say.

"You like it?"

"You look shiny and new."

Cliff shakes out two cigarettes from the pack he's retrieved from his shirt's chest pocket, hands me one, lights it for me, then lights his own. "I went to this Asian barber down the street. He didn't speak a lick of English. The guy butchered me. I mean, look at the back." He turns to show me the rear of his head. The barber has shaved away four inches past the hairline.

"They call that the Thai fade," I say.

"I'm like Sampson. My strength lies in my locks."

"I think you look good. More like you did during your playing days."

"Younger?"

"More dignified."

Cliff rubs the sheared area on the back of his head.

"So what's with all the mystery this morning?" I ask.

He begins picking at a thread of his luau shirt. "When was the last time you went to mass?"

A terrible shudder passes through me, catching me off-guard, and I break hard, bringing us to a jolting stop. Turning to him, I say, "I've always gone to great lengths to avoid such places."

"What places?"

"Churches, the zoo, slaughterhouses, weddings, shopping malls."

"You going to take me or not?"

The thought of being surrounded by all those dejected beggars with their minds closed to the realities of our collective moral predicament, making their ineffectual appeals to someone who ceases to exist, who never existed, fills me with a stinging agitation. "You're being serious, aren't you?" I ask.

"I like the sound of Latin."

"Yeah?"

"The mystery is a comforting thing."

I wonder to myself what it'd be like to be able to suspend all disbelief and allow the blessings of the priests, those sexless merchants of goodwill and spirit, to fill me with the type of strength it takes for the faceless masses that comprise the core of the respectable citizenry to wake up each day and go out and sell used cars, answer phones in call-center cubicles, and push brooms across marble floors.

"If you think a two-thousand-year-old solution is going to solve your modern problems, then you're in worse shape than I thought," I say.

Cliff doesn't say anything. He looks like a wounded hero returned from war, a broken bastard that the world has no further use for.

"I'm sorry, pal," I say, "Let's check it out. I could go for some pipe-organ music this morning."

We take our seats in the third row from the back of the nave. A hunchbacked priest shrouded in black robes stands at the altar, flanked by angelic choir boys dressed in long skirts, swinging a big silver censer, filling the room with its frankincense vapor.

The prayers begin. The words flow off of Cliff's tongue and through his lips in a thin, reedy warble. I gaze vacantly across the sanctum. It strikes me that all around the world these same rituals take place every day, and that for as long as history has been recorded wars have been fought over them. I'm simultaneously fascinated and stupefied by the unintelligible absurdity.

Looking up, the stained-glass images of Mary and baby Jesus, blazing brightly in all shades of red and blue and gold, come alive, and a feeling of peacefulness sneaks up on me and settles into my bones. I tap Cliff on the shoulder and he turns to me, his eyes moist and threatening to unleash tears.

"You doing all right, pal?" I ask.

He ignores me, nodding his head to the rhythm of the prayer—a most devout member of the flock getting his tending.

Halfway through the service, I stand up to leave. Cliff follows close behind. Walking down the aisle, I spot an old cripple, in the last row, smiling warmly. Before pushing open the big oak doors, to the waiting world outside, the cripple hobbles from his seat and gives chase after us.

Eyeing us with anxious anticipation, he asks, "Would you like to make a donation to the church?"

Cliff takes a five-dollar bill from his wallet—all he has—and drops it into a timber box with a cross etched into it. He makes an indication with his eyes that I should make my own contribution. Instead, I pat the cripple on the shoulder and say, "Keep up the heavenly work," and push through the doors, making my escape.

A light rain is falling from the sickly pallid, yellow sky. My good feelings dissipate and I feel all alone with my thoughts—a dreadful feeling. The sweat is dripping through my shirt, and my skin feels prickly and hot like during the onset of a psychedelic drug trip.

Cliff looks at me as if I'm the enemy of mankind. "You can't humiliate me like that in my church. It's all I've got."

"It's all you got?"

"It's all I got."

I lower my head and slink back into the church, but catch my foot on the carpet and stumble into a pew, spilling the baptismal bowl, making a ruckus, causing all the heads of the kneeling, candle-lighting congregation to take notice. I drop a twenty into the box and an old woman in a scarf and heavy jacket throws her arms in the air, making a divine benediction. The cripple makes the sign of the cross and I flash him the peace sign before slipping back out into the stifling Los Angeles summer air. Looking up to the sky, hoping to catch a sign from God, a ray of sunlight hits the leaves of an errant cedar tree and sparkles like green jewelry.

Cliff unbuttons his pineapple printed church outfit, revealing a wife-beater undershirt and a thick mess of wiry and tangled chest hair. He points up to the heavens with a mumbling prayer on his lips, and doubles over next to some bushes. I light a cigarette as he wretches. When he's done forcing up a bellyful, he collapses onto his back.

I look up to the sky and a hawk flies overhead with a snake in its talons. I turn back toward Cliff. He's crawled under a cluster of shrubs, and only his head is poking out. The usual red hue of his skin is gone, now his face is completely colorless, looks like wet clay.

"I'm suffering a crisis of faith."

"That's a good place to start," I say, helping him to his feet.

We set off for a park two blocks down the street from the church. A farmer's market is in full swing. Booth after booth of fresh-picked peaches, artisan tomatoes, and obscurely named greens of countless variety. Men and women in cutoff jean-shorts and T-shirts with altruistic slogans plastered across their fronts negotiate the prices of homemade soaps, cleverly constructed wine racks, and crystals containing peculiar healing powers. Bands of heavily bearded musicians, in tattered clothing, armed with acoustic guitars and banjos, sing inane folk songs about love and hope.

A woman with a purple flower tucked into her wavy, blond ringlets insists we sample her homemade lemonade made with hibiscus and lemons from her family's orchard. She's wearing a sheer white sleeveless top with no bra underneath. Her nipples, taut as nails, can be seen as clearly as the upturned button-nose fixed across the middle of her face.

I take a sip from the type of paper cup used to dispense pills at the psych ward. "Tasty," I say.

"It should be. I made it myself."

She attempts to hand a cup to Cliff. "How about you, would you like to give it a try?"

Cliff simply walks away.

"What's with him?" she asks.

"He's worried the problems that torment him in life will follow him into his death."

"Sounds serious."

"The crisis of modern man."

She points to him, mixed amongst a crowd of suburbanites convinced that buying locally grown onions qualifies them as stewards of the Earth. "What are you still doing here? Go to him. He needs you."

There is not a man alive who doesn't fall in love with every beautiful woman he meets, however briefly. In each one, there is the hope that she'll draw something out of you you've never before understood existed. It's a desire to be reborn or at least recalibrated, to be made whole and right, to finally find some lasting contentment in this world.

This lemonade maker offers me exactly this. She is a shining light sent from Heaven to shield me from the vast chasm of darkness. In her presence I'm prepared to renounce my contemptuous mistrust of this world, cast off this dark cloud of belligerence, derision, and scorn, and start fresh as a new man prone to optimism and fits of fancy. I can't help but hope this is the woman who'll never turn petty, small, and mean. That she'll be the one who'll inspire me to always be generous, honest, and forthcoming. How can a man not become fixed on such a prospect?

"Before I go, tell me your name," I say.

"It's Lana, now go—now!"

She turns her attention to another customer. I linger for another moment, hoping she'll speak to me again, but she never does. I silently curse myself for being so vulnerable.

A man and his wife walk past me and he is berating her for buying mealy tomatoes. The wife covers her face with her hands to shield herself from the embarrassing onslaught. I look back at the lemonade woman and am made glad for my emotions, even if they have no hope of fulfillment.

I find Cliff sitting on a bench, chewing his fingernails, spitting the clippings at a pack of squirrels who've clamored together to feast on spilled kettle corn and pieces of shredded pita bread.

He breaks from his trance and peers out into the distance.

"I met a girl," he says

I give him a firm pat on the back. "That's great," I say, "nothing wrong with that."

"It's not that simple."

"Of course it is. Men need the company of women. It's biology."

A man with a thin, greasy beard and a hemp necklace stops in front of us. He's holding onto a clipboard. When he smiles I see his two front teeth are chipped and rotten. "Do you have a minute to talk about the rainforests?" he asks.

Without a word, Cliff snatches the clipboard from the man's grasp and sends it sailing, Frisbee-style, into the leafy canopy of a tree. It gets hung-up in the branches and only a few loose sheets of paper come floating to the ground.

"You bastard!" the man shouts.

Cliff stands up. At six feet two inches tall, two hundred and forty pounds, he cuts an imposing figure. The wandering altruist apologizes profusely. "Get out of here," Cliff says. The man collects what papers he can salvage.

"She's sixteen," Cliff continues. "I'd seen her around the neighborhood for months but we never met. Yesterday she was walking home from the store, carrying her baby brother in one arm, and a big paper bag full of groceries in the other. She looked so beautiful, the most perfect angel I've ever seen: long black hair, thick and glossy, a wide brown face, the color of coffee with cream, eyes, black like a Mayan's. And those lips, those amazing lips—she's Mexican, but she's got the lips of a black girl."

I've never seen Cliff speak with so much passion.

"So what happened?"

"My intention was to only help her with her groceries. But, you know how it is," he says, shaking his head. "She knew I was a ballplayer. I think her father must've told her. We ended up back at my place."

"These things can't be helped."

"Afterwards, I told her she had to go but she wouldn't. I begged her, I really did. She got hysterical and started crying like a child. I'm telling you, she was really wailing. Then, laying there in the sheets, she told me she loved me."

"You've got to put a stop to it."

"I know I should, but I don't think I can."

"So what are you going to do?"

"I don't know."

All around our feet a flock of pigeons join the squirrels. They stand around flapping their wings, and pecking their heads at morsels of food. Cliff picks up scraps of garbage, and offers it to the vermin. One by one the filthy little beasts bob their heads against the flesh of his palm, picking out the tidbits of refuse.

"You really think you might love this girl?"

He stands up, shaking out his hands, wiping the remnants off on his shirt. "Love her... What does that even mean?"

"I mean, do you see yourself with her?"

"Be serious, I can't imagine anything worse. Not for me, of course, but for her. What kind of future would she have?"

"I see."

"But she's got such a youthful energy."

"Yes, that makes sense."

"I'm addicted."

"I can imagine."

He furrows his brow at me and gives a lopsided grin, exposing his bottom row of teeth. They are stained yellow, and the gums look to be receding. "In an odd way, it feels...how can I say this? Decent."

"That might be a stretch."

His eyes roll back and all I can see are the whites, as if he were blind. "You don't know what it's like. You're on top of the world. You have it all—the house, the money, the fame, the career, the Jew heiress—but I've fallen from grace. I'm a nothing, a joke."

"Things aren't always as they seem."

A man with soft white hair and a wrinkled face, clutching a cane, and a woman with papery-thin skin, sunspots, and a hunch between the shoulders stop in front of us and kiss on the mouth. Their lips hardly move, not enough moisture, two parched mouths pressed against each another. Both Cliff and I recoil, staring, lost in the moment.

"I'm sorry," I say. "If you love her, you love her. That's good enough for me."

Cliff shrugs his shoulders. "I shouldn't even be thinking about this sort of thing anyway. I should be concentrating on the fight."

My vision catches sight of a young eccentric exhibiting his paintings, and I walk away from Cliff. The artist has a thick red beard, badly in need of a trim. His eyes are set too close together and appear disproportionately small for his broad face.

I stand in front of a painting on the wall of his booth. It's clear that this artisan is not a man of exceptional vision or talent. Six paintings, hung side by side, all of the sunset, each equally undistinguished.

"Sir," he says, "is there nothing here that interests you? I can make you a very good price."

I force myself to offer a kindly smile. "Not today."

With a disdainfully proud tone, he says, "You don't understand. These are very special paintings, the best you'll find anywhere. Someday, I assure you, I'll be recognized as a magnificent artist."

I think to myself how every man of this younger generation thinks he is special, worthy of being singled out from the masses. It's due to the cultural zeitgeist they were raised in. But none of it's true. If everyone were special, the word would lose all meaning.

"Thank you for your time," I say. "I'm sure you have a bright future." I look in all directions to find Cliff, but to no avail. Instead, I spot a canvas tucked behind a small wooden table. I point to the obscured picture. "What is that one?"

"Oh that," he says, moving in front of it to further obstruct my view, "it's nothing, nothing at all, just a picture of a man and his dog. One of my lesser works—nothing you'd be interested in."

"No, no," I say, "it's exactly the sort of work I prefer."

The painting is unsophisticated and artless, the composition muddled and unwieldy—but it appeals to me. It's honest and charming, its quality set forth in its simplicity. The painting reminds me of my old dog, Mars, long deceased—a mongrel, part retriever, mostly shepherd—his wiry fur tinted red all over, except for the snout, which was white from age, even when I first met him.

It was ten years ago last April when I first spotted old Marsy boy scavenging the alley behind the apartment building I lived in at the time. I watched him daily go about his business. Then one day I set out half a pastrami sandwich for him, and from then on he became my constant companion, accompanying me everywhere I went. Two years ago, seemingly out of nowhere, the energy just went out of him. I took him to the vet and he said Mars's lungs were filled with cancer. "From secondhand smoke?" I asked. The vet shrugged and said, "It's unlikely but it's impossible to know for sure." A week later my best pal succumbed to the disease. To this day I keep his favorite tennis balls and leash.

"How much for the dog painting?"

The man eyes the painting carefully, perplexed. "Will you give me fifty for it?" he asks.

Without hesitation, I pay the man his fee and collect my bounty. Most pleased with my good fortune, I hold the painting up high in the air, displaying it proudly. Cliff spots me from afar, and makes his way to me.

"You didn't just pay money for that, did you?" Cliff asks.

"A tremendous bargain," I say.

I throw my arms around the artist. "I love it," I say to him. "Thank you for this wonderful piece."

I tuck the painting under my arm and saunter away, rejuvenated and hopeful, my spirits lifted.

"I don't get it," Cliff says.

"Don't get what?"

"The painting, it's awful. Why would you want such a piece of shit?"

Stopping on the path to admire it, I reply, "It's sentimental. It moves me."

"Frannie is never going to let you hang that thing in the house."

"I'm making a stand."

"What stand?"

"Cliff, my good man," I say, patting him on the shoulder, "I'm no longer concerned with style points."

"You're not making any sense."

"I've been leaning on Frannie for too long. I need to see if I can still stand on my own. This painting is a step in the right direction for me."

"I'm telling you, she won't let you in the house with it."

"Maybe I won't bring it to the house."

Cliff places a hand on each of my shoulders. "What are you talking about?"

"Forget it," I say, "it's nothing. Let's get out of here."

"Can you drop me off at the gym? I should probably get another sparring session in today."

Chapter

That afternoon I head back to the motel. Before going up to my room I stop at the front desk. A Pakistani man is running the place. He's watching a soccer match with focused intensity. The volume is turned up all the way, and the announcers are shouting in sophisticated-sounding British accents. I squint to check the score. It's zero-zero, or nil-nil, as the say in *futbol*.

"What are they so excited about?" I ask.

The man turns his head around to take a look at me. "Shoosh," he says. "There is only one minute left in injury time. If Manchester holds on, they win the championship league." The man flings saliva at me as he speaks, and when he's done, he breathes in deep, sucking back all the excess spit collected in his mouth.

"They're going to take the title on a tie?"

I consider the implications of such an unsatisfactory resolution and conclude the following: no matter what people say, this sport will never catch fire in this country. We won't stand for it. Americans like winners and will accept nothing less. It's nearly unfathomable to us how these foreign sportsmen can accept a draw. The only good draw in sports is a race for pistols. No stalemates allowed.

He doesn't bother turning his gaze from the TV to respond. "What do you want?"

"I need a hammer."

"A hammer? What for?"

I lift the painting up and rest it on the desk, facing him.

"I'm going to hang this in my room."

"You can't do that."

"Of course I can, I'll pay you."

The man stands up out of his chair and hunches over the desk to get a better view of the painting. "It's awful."

"The artist assures me that someday he'll be regarded as a magnificent painter."

"And you believe him?"

"Who am I to say?"

The man sits back down. "Fifty dollars."

"I'll give you twenty-five to borrow the hammer, the nail, and for the damage to the wall."

He goes to the utility closet and retrieves my supplies.

In my room I strip down to my underwear, stand on the bed, pull a painting of a sea captain off the wall, and hang my own painting in its place. After a few attempts at making certain it's level, I stand back and admire how it brings the room to life. Although the picture's colors are muted, they seem to radiate positive energy. I lie down on my back, my head toward the foot of the bed, and light a cigarette.

"Marsy boy, what will bring me happiness in this world? What can I do? Isn't there anything left out there that will inspire me?"

Outside my window I hear a school bus's doors open and the sounds of children laughing.

"Tell me, Mars. I need you now more than ever."

Mixed amongst the children's voices, I hear the faint, low, grumbling bark of a lone dog. I go the window, part the curtains, and peer out. There, sitting on a bench, are two young boys dressed in tatters, struggling to read from a book.

"Christ, Mars, are you listening to this? They're hopeless-sounding!"

Another bark comes from the distance.

"You're right, Mars. If the next generation can't read, then my work will be lost to the ages."

Like a lightning bolt from Heaven, it comes to me: volunteer with children!

My rational mind toys with the idea. I'm very suspect of it.

I've never before had a charitable impulse, and I'm untrusting of the prospect. Could the spirit of my deceased dog really be trying to send me a message? It seems like the only possible explanation. After all, as the recipient of my most selfless act on record, he's the only one capable of such influence.

I dial Sebastian's cellphone.

"I've had a great stroke of inspiration."

The voice on the other end of the line sounds unimpressed. "What now, Lou?"

"I need to spend time with the children."

"What children?"

"School kids."

"Is it for the book?"

"I'm sure it'll be good for the writing, but more importantly I feel something deep inside of me. A drive. I need to be with the children. I have so much to give."

"Please, Lou, don't go all Roman Polanski on me. I won't bail you out of jail again, not for this."

Defiantly, I wave my fist at the telephone. "No, you idiot, it's not like that."

"Where is this coming from?"

I reach for a pen off the nightstand and scratch a series of notes across the surface of the sea-captain painting.

"It's from Mars."

"The planet?"

"My dead dog."

"I don't understand."

"I need you to set me up at a school as a volunteer—a really poor school, one with throwaway kids."

"Throwaway kids?"

"Yes, throwaway kids—the little shits nobody wants, the boys destined for prison and the girls who will make all the babies."

"And what do you plan to do with these kids?"

"Teach them, of course, and inspire them, too. Try to make

their lives a bit more tolerable, if I can."

"And what, pray tell, might you teach them."

I read aloud the notes I've scribbled across the face of the sea captain:

1. God, as the Bible presents him, is a vindictive and merciless being whose evil impulses outpace even the worst of mankind.

2. Love and death are biological tragedies.

3. I hate almonds.

I pause to reflect on the logic of my subconscious.

"I haven't worked all that out yet, but it's essential I begin immediately."

The next day I'm on the schedule as a substitute eighth-grade English teacher at Polk Middle School. Classes are set to begin at 8 a.m. Unfortunately, the motel doesn't offer a wakeup-call service, and I'm forced to rely upon my cellphone as an alarm. I set it for 7 a.m. but fail to turn up the volume. By a stroke of good fortune, I'm roused from my slumber by a garbage truck making its collections. By 7:39 I'm out the door and arrive at the school a hair past twenty minutes after the hour.

Once I get past the metal detectors and the pat-down at the school's entrance, I'm escorted through the school's halls by a security guard whose name tag reads, "D'avion." He's a man of about fifty, black, portly, wears a uniform and a badge, no gun, equipped with a nightstick, handcuffs, and a most ponderous keychain dangling from his belt.

"You with social services?" he asks.

"No."

"You a P.O.?"

"Why would you ask that?"

"You're white so you can't be a parent, and I ain't never seen you before. We get a lot of folks from social services and the justice department around here."

"Actually, I'm a volunteer sub."

Opening the door to the reception of the principal's office, he asks, "What do you mean 'volunteer'?"

"What do you mean, what do I mean? I'm here for the kids."

The secretary, a woman whose cheeks are so puffy she looks like she has a mouth full of marbles, intervenes. "D'avion, leave that poor man alone." Then, she smiles at me. "Take a seat—the principal will be with you shortly."

I sit down next to an adolescent Mexican boy with a well-manicured mustache. He's wearing a long, blue L.A. Dodgers T-shirt that would fit a man twice his size. He's picking at a scab on the inside of his wrist. After a concerted dig, he penetrates the wound and the blood flows. He lifts his arm to his mouth and sucks at it. When he finally puts his arm back down, the ends of his mustache hairs are dripping with blood.

"Cut that out," I say, "it's disgusting."

"*Que?*" he says back.

"*Detenerlo!*"

The Mexican boy springs to his feet. "*Vete a la mierda, hijo de puta!*"

"Take it easy, kid."

The principal opens her office door.

"Santiago, sit down, now!" she says.

The boy says nothing but locks his eyes on me in a piercing stare, then sits back down.

"It's nearly eight-thirty, Mr. Brown," the principal says to me.

She's a black woman, middle-aged, hair and nails done, wide as a barn-door, dressed in a power suit, very determined. Her own stare is nearly as penetrating as the boy's.

"I'm late to hundreds of things," I say with a hesitant grin.

"You think I think your act is cute?"

"No, ma'am, I'm sorry."

We head out of the office and through a corridor. A glass trophy-case runs along the length of the hallway. As we walk, I read the inscriptions on the plaques and medals. It seems the school hasn't had a winner since the late '80s.

"You're taking over for Ms. Barajas."

"Is she sick?"

"No, not sick. She quit."

"What happened?"

"They broke her."

"Broke her? Who broke her?"

"These kids have been through three English teachers already this year."

"They're just kids."

"You ever teach middle school before?"

I reach for my cigarettes. "I've never taught a thing."

The principal intercepts the cigarette before I can lift it to my mouth. She looks at me like I'm deranged. "You've never taught a thing?"

"Well, no," I say, "but I've been handling punks all my life."

She flicks the cigarette into a garbage can next to the vending machine. "I don't understand, Mr. Brown. Why are you doing this?"

I think back to the day I left that sandwich out for Mars. I then recall the moment at my motel window, looking out at the illiterate boys on the bus bench.

"All of life's greatest pleasures come from strange and inexplicable beginnings."

She resumes walking, leading me toward my classroom, stopping at a door marked "66" in bold black numbers. Someone has added a third "6" in red marker. I can hear the students' screams and laughter through the wall. "Well, they're yours as long as you want them," she says. "But don't say I didn't warn you." She turns the handle, and the door falls open. In front of me are three-dozen adolescents in various states of disorder— boys slap-boxing each other, girls braiding one another's hair, a couple groping and fondling over the teacher's desk, a game of Cee-lo transpiring in the corner, and a group of students battle-rapping over beats provided from a cellphone by the window. "Everybody sit down! Immediately!" the principal shouts. It doesn't take—hardly anyone even registers our presence. "Hey, I'm talking to you. Everybody sit down," she says again. Her voice is a husky and commanding alto. The students loaf back to their desks. I'm struck by their lack of urgency. We move to the front of the room. Someone has written, "Leonard is a *fagot!*" on the chalkboard.

The principal makes a gesture and I erase the slander. The class breaks out in a fit of laughter.

"You think this is funny? I don't think it's funny," the principal says. "*Faggot* is misspelled." The class's laughter reaches a crescendo. The principal shakes her head in frustration. "This is Mr. Brown." She whirls around to acknowledge me. I put down the eraser and scramble to her side. "He's going to be teaching you for a while. You should all consider yourselves extremely fortunate. Mr. Brown is a very well-respected author."

I stand up a little bit straighter—most pleased with this introduction. However, my debut makes no impression on the students. From the back of the room someone shouts, "He looks like a faggot!"

"Faggot with two *g*s," I say.

The principal shoots me a look. "I'll leave you to it," she says.

She hurries out of the room, slamming the door behind her. The kids all look up at me and I become unnerved. I flee the room, searching out the principal, finding her in the hall reprimanding a young man for playing hooky.

"What the hell am I supposed to do with them?" I ask her.

"It's an English class, teach them English."

She snaps her fingers, turns her back on me, and walks away, the truant by her side.

I hesitantly reenter the classroom. Half of the students are already out of their seats doing other things. The worst offender is a boy standing by the window, stripped down to his underwear, dancing. I'm baffled by how he got his pants off so fast.

"Stop that!" I shout at him.

He's really immersed in his wiggling and my command does not get his attention. Instead, his shaking and shimmying only escalates. The class takes notice, rising to their feet, cheering, and clapping encouragement.

"Stop it, everyone, get back to your seats. Now!" I holler.

No one heeds my order. They're transfixed by the dancing boy's moves. He's an unattractive, chubby thing with bad acne on his face and back. But the kid can really shake it—I have to give him that. I approach him cautiously, frustrated, yet partially enraptured by the spectacle.

"Get away from me," he says. "Can't you see I'm dancing here?'

The rest of the class chants in unison: "Let him dance! Let him dance!"

I fend off their taunts with an ineffectual wave of my arm.

"What the hell do you think you're doing?" I ask him.

The boy locks his hands behind his head and bucks and thrusts his hips in the air. "I'm giving the people what they want," he says. "I'm an entertainer."

"What's your name, kid?"

"Don't call me kid."

"Cut the crap. What's your name?"

"My name is Tony Chikki Garcia."

"And where are your pants, Tony Chikki Garcia?"

He leans out the window, his red and white striped boxer shorts sagging a bit low, exposing two inches of butt crack. The class erupts in uproarious laughter. "They're down there," he says, pointing to a bush below the open window.

I point at a dour-looking girl sitting quietly at her desk, the only one in the class so well-behaved. "You," I say, "please go outside and retrieve Mr. Chikki Garcia's pants."

An embarrassed smile forms on her lips, and she rushes out the door.

The boy licks his lips and grinds his hips against a wall. "My mom's boyfriend works at Chippendale's. He's teaching me how to dance, so one day I can work there too."

I stare at the boy as if he's an animal in a zoo. "It's important to have ambitions."

The boy is feeling all around himself, pinching his love handles, testing the muscles in his arms. "My mom's boyfriend says I need to get a fit body before people will pay to see me dance."

"He told you that?"

"He says I need to lift weights and run."

The boy is staring up at me all longing and hopeful, perhaps waiting for some helpful tips or encouragement. "Please go sit down," I finally say.

The boy returns to his seat, folds his arms in front of himself, and buries his face in them. I give him a small pat on the shoulder as I return to the front of the room.

"I see that some of you have a copy of *Lord of the Flies* on your desk," I say, addressing the entire class. "Who amongst you can tell me a little bit about it?"

There is a loud chatter in the room, all of the students talking at once. I try to make an appeal to control the chaos. "Raise your hands, people. Don't just shout out. We must have some order."

Ten hands go up in the air but the students raising them are all still shouting.

"The whole point of the hand in the air is so that I can call on you. If you don't wait for me to call on you, the raised hand is meaningless."

The word "faggot" is shouted again from the back of the room, but I don't know from whom. The class roars with laughter. This continues for an entire minute. I don't interject. Resistance would be futile. Instead I stand there, my arms crossed in front of me.

Finally the laughter recedes and I try again to impose on them some discussion of the book. One kid shouts out, "They bashed the fat kid's head in with a rock."

"Yes, that's true. They bashed poor Piggy's head in."

Again, the room devolves into an uncontrolled bout of sustained laughter. "But can anyone tell me any of the themes in the book?" I say over the hysterics. But no one hears me.

The quiet dour girl returns with Tony's pants, and he dashes from his seat to her side, takes them from her hands, and swings them over his head like a lasso. A boy shouts out, "*Make money, get cream, the business is pussy and the business is a dream!*" This call incites further provocations, and Tony jumps up on a chair, bends over, touches his toes, and shakes his ass in the air. All the other students join in on the call. "*Make money, get cream, the business is pussy and the business is a dream!*"

"Get off the damn chair!" I holler. "Get off of it now!"

Tony jumps off the chair, lands on the ground, does a combat roll, springs to his feet, and bows. The students all clap their hands in appreciation of his antics. Even the dour girl is impressed. She is clapping along with the group.

I turn to the student closest to me, a skinny black kid with lines shaved into the side of his head. "What the hell does that even mean?"

"That's Thirsty James," he says. "You can't say shit on Thirsty James? Man, you whack!" He throws his arms in the air in a wild salute and sings even louder: "*Make money, get cream, the business is pussy and the business is a dream!*"

"That's enough, thank you," I say to the boy. He continues without pause, and my next command comes in a more critical tone. "I said that's enough."

"You can't tell me that's enough. I decide when I've had enough. You think 'cause I'm black you can tell me what to do?"

I'm fighting the urge to slap the boy. "If you make me tell you again, I promise you'll regret it."

The boy grits his teeth at me and then capitulates.

I refocus my attention on Tony. He's gotten down from the chair, his movements have become sluggish and flat. His hips no longer gyrate with the same unbridled enthusiasm. When he *drops it low*, it's not even that low. I see my window of opportunity.

I shout, once more, over the cacophony of sound. "I'll ask again: what are the main themes of the book?"

Ten different students unleash a barrage of nonsensical answers that I dismiss immediately. I scan the room for a single obedient pupil. One very thin boy with spiky black hair sits in the back with his hand raised.

"You there, in the back, what is your name?"

His reply is too soft to discern.

"Everyone shut-up!" I say to the class. "Once more, what is your name?"

"Marcos," he says.

"Thank you for raising your hand, Marcos. Now, what would you like to say about the themes of the book?"

The classroom noise diminishes to a grievous hum. Marcos speaks in the shy, wavering tone of a non-native speaker. "Well, it's about how people act when there are not good rules in place to make them act right."

I feel an instant kinship with this Marcos. In his face I can see all the hopes and dreams for our country's future. I'm sure he's destined to cure cancer or become President. "That's right on, Marcos," I say. "That's exactly it. It's about the conflict between the human impulse towards savagery and the rules of civilization which are designed to contain and minimize it." He is taking furious notes, inspiring me to continue. "The book is about the end of innocence and the darkness inherent in human nature."

I flash a big smile at Marcos, and he reciprocates with one of his own. It's one of those moments you hear teachers gush on and on about that they say make all the long hours and low pay worthwhile. I get it—I'm only fifteen minutes into my career as an educator and I've got the buzz—I'm hooked, I've found my calling. I can't wait to bestow America's youth with more knowledge. The great savior of education—LOU BROWN!

"Let's talk about some of the characters," I say. "Does anybody have a favorite?"

"Jack's a bad mofo!" someone shouts.

"That's true. Jack is a bad mofo. But next time, please raise your hand."

Another student ignores my request for hands and calls out, "Ralph is the good guy."

"Does anyone know what an allegory is?" I ask.

Marcos raises his hand.

"Yes, Marcos."

"It's a story about one thing but really about something else. Something bigger."

"Marcos, my boy, that's brilliant," I say.

The tension in his face melts away and he smiles a lopsided grin of crooked teeth.

"I'm going to elaborate to make sure everyone understands," I continue. "An allegory is a story that can be interpreted to reveal a hidden meaning. For instance, *Lord of the Flies* is an allegory. Ralph and Jack are not just boys in a story. As Marcos said, they represent something much bigger. Ralph represents *civilization*, and Jack represents *savagery*. This is expressed by each boy's attitude towards authority. While Ralph uses his authority to establish rules, protect the good of the group, and enforce the moral and ethical codes of the English society the boys were raised in, Jack is only interested in gaining power over the other boys to gratify his most primal impulses."

For a third time, the word *faggot* is hurled through the air, followed by a pencil, which strikes me on the left side of the face, an inch below the eye, pointy side first. Half the students fall out of their chairs with laughter. The other half stays seated but laughs nearly as hard. Even my dear sweet Marcos is whooping it up. However, this time I've seen the culprit of this monstrous injustice—shaved head, narrow eyes, low sloping forehead, puffy cheeks, large jaw, third desk from the back, second-to-last row from the right. The boy is wearing a thick gold chain over a replica Kobe Bryant jersey.

"You in the back, get out of my class. You are not welcome here. Get out now."

The perpetrator flexes his arm, and kisses the bicep. "Don't get so worked up, Teach," he says. "I'm only messing around."

"Last chance, Kobe Bryant. Get out of my classroom."

The boy stakes his position, hi-fiving the kid next to him. I make my move toward him. The boy does not follow me with his eyes. He carries on as if I'm of no concern to him—like the death of a stranger in a faraway land or a leaky faucet in another's home. I position myself adjacent to his desk, within striking distance. A single bead of sweat drips from my forehead. The boy remains seemingly composed, awaiting my next move. His recalcitrance is unnerving.

"Get out of my classroom," I say, my voice dropping an octave to a growling baritone.

The class emits a collective deep breath and falls silent.

"Fuck you, old man," the boy says.

I take him by the arm and give a tremendous jerk. He flies from his seat as if slung from a catapult, lands without setting his feet squarely, and tumbles to the floor. The classroom bursts forth with shouts to incite further violence. I look down at the boy and am immediately struck by his lack of stature. He's nearly as tall as a grown man, but lacks in muscle mass, is soft and undefined. He stands up and takes a swing that I easily deflect. I grab him around the chest, lifting him in the air, a tight enough grip that he can barely fill his lungs with air, and carry him from the classroom. The class cheers.

Out in the hall D'avion the security guard is passing by. He stands as still as a statue, silent, eyes bugged. "Please take this kid to the principal's office for me," I say. I let go of my grip on the boy. He falls forward into the security guard's arms. The two of them amble down the hallway together. The boy walks with his head low, his shoulders hunched. The security guard places a tender and sympathetic hand on the boy before looking back over his shoulder at me.

I reenter the classroom. There is a grave and distressing silence about the atmosphere. I press on, undeterred. "I think today's class has been a sterling example of what *Lord of the Flies* teaches us about how people respond differently to the influences of civilization and savagery. For instance, there are people like Piggy, the fat boy in the book who had his head bashed, who have virtually no savage feelings at all. While, on the other hand, there are people like that boy I just escorted out, who seem completely incapable of abiding by the rules of a civilized society. The author, William Golding, implies that the instinct for savagery is far more natural to the human psyche than the instinct for civilization. What do you think? Would you say that moral behavior is something that civilization forces on the individual, rather than a natural expression of one's individuality?"

All the students stare up at me confounded and perplexed.

"Let me put it another way," I continue. "What do you think is the more natural manner for people to behave: wild and crazy or civilized and orderly?"

All the students scream in unison: "Wild and crazy!"

The classroom door opens and a man enters. He's a squirrelly fellow, neatly dressed in slacks, vest and tie. The thick lenses of his glass magnify his eyes, making them look positively cartoonish.

"Mr. Brown," he says. "I'm here to watch your class for you. The principal wants to see you."

I grab a copy of the book and stuff it into the back pocket of my pants. There is a passage I want to find and read to the class upon my return.

In the principal's reception, I give a flirty wink to the secretary and take the same seat I occupied earlier. The bloodsucking boy with the slashed wrists is asleep in his chair, his Dodgers T-shirt spotted with bloodstains. I look down at my own hands, which are now scabbed over, looking rather misshapen and deformed.

The principal's door opens. The boy I kicked out of my class is seated in a chair in her office. The principal asks me to sit down, and I take a seat next to the future felon.

"Mr. Brown," she says, "our students here at Polk Middle School—"

"Listen," I say, interrupting her before she can finish the thought. "It's true this boy is a terrible disruption to the learning process of the other children, and while I understand it's common practice to remove a bad apple before he can spoil the bunch, I'm here to tell you I don't think this boy is hopeless."

"Mr. Brown—" she says.

Again, I interrupt her. "Now, I'm sure you're thinking there's not a teacher alive who can reach this boy, but you're wrong—I'm that teacher. You should've seen me in that classroom. I gave the most erudite and astute lesson on *Lord of the Flies* on record. If you'd like, I can do it again so you can record it, or better yet, I can give a clinic to the rest of the school's teachers."

"Mr. Brown, are you finished?"

I reach out and mess the hair on the boy's head. "I just don't want you to throw him out of school before I have had a chance to reach him."

"Reach him?"

"Yes, ma'am, reach him."

"Mr. Brown, Ignacio has explained to me that he struck you in the face with a pencil, and that you asked him to leave the classroom, and that he refused."

"Yes, that's correct."

She nods and continues. "And that once he refused, you became extremely agitated, and stood next to his desk in a menacing manner."

I turn my head to steal a glance at Ignacio. "I had to let him know who's boss, right? Kids respond to discipline."

The principal's face turns sober and grave. "Ignacio said you told him to—excuse my language—'get the fuck out of your classroom,' and then threw him to the floor when he didn't comply."

"Why are you speaking to me in such a tone?"

"You understand that he's only a child, do you not?"

"Well, yes, of course."

"And you don't deny that you laid your hands on him?"

"I never lie, it's dishonest."

The principal turns her attention to the boy. "Ignacio, you can go back to class now."

As the boy stands up to leave, he imparts on me a mischievous grin.

"Mr. Brown," the principal continues, "you must understand that under no circumstances are you allowed to physically touch a student."

I place my hands on her desk. Under the fluorescent lighting of her office, they look positively heinous—deep-brown reptile-skin scabs and thin, wet, pink albino skin surrounding the affected areas.

"There are exceptions to every rule," I say.

"There is absolutely no chance, under any condition, that I'm sending you back into that classroom."

My hands gesticulate wildly, moving in big circles around my head, like out-of-control helicopter blades. "With all due respect, there isn't another teacher in the school with such a wide breadth of literary knowledge."

She picks up a walkie-talkie and presses the button. "D'avion, please report to my office. I need you to escort Mr. Brown off campus."

D'avion appears out of what seems like nowhere at all.

"You're making a tremendous mistake," I plead.

"Mr. Brown, this discussion is over."

D'avion drags me from the office. I resist him all the way— creating such a ruckus, the boy in the Dodgers T-shirt wakes from his slumber and the secretary ceases her data-entry.

Once outside, I reach for my cigarettes, but it seems I'm out. I peek into a garbage can to see if there are any half-smoked nubs that I might salvage—to no avail. I can't remember where I parked my car and spend ten minutes going up and down the rows of the teacher's lot.

It's ten-year-old Japanese compacts as far as the eye can see.

I spot two boys wearing long hair, dressed in all-black, crouched behind a van. They are puffing away. I make a careful approach. They don't spot me until I'm right up on them.

"Hey, fellas," I say.

One of the boys hops to his feet, picks up his backpack, and makes a run for it. His tight pants encumber his stride and make it unnaturally short. The other boy stands frozen in place, silently watching as his friend disappears into the distance.

"I'm not here to bust you," I say. "I only want to bum a cigarette."

"You want a cigarette?"

"Your principal threw my last one out."

His hand trembles as he reaches into his pack.

"You got a quarter?" the boy asks. "I'm broke."

I hand him my copy of *Lord of the Flies*. "Here, take this instead. It's worth a million bucks."

He holds it in his hand, eyeing it skeptically.

"What am I supposed to do with this?"

"You'll figure it out," I say, spotting my car two rows down. "Thanks for the smoke."

I take one final look back as I drive out of the lot. The boy is sitting on the ground reading the book.

That night I ask Cliff to meet me at a bar. For an hour before meeting him I walk the streets. Passing me on the sidewalk and cozied together at restaurant patio tables are scores of attractive and affluent young lovers. Just by looking at each couple, it's easy to tell which couples are established and which are still fresh. The men in long-standing courtships nearly always lack vitality and vigor. It's in their softened eyes and stooped posture. If a coupled man is walking, his status is immediately apparent by his sluggish gait, while an unattached man always appears hungry and anxious, ready to fight or fuck anything in his path. It strikes me that it's these men who keep society's heart beating, their masculinity not yet extinguished by the demands of contemporary women.

And just as I've nearly convinced myself that I'm in a better place now, a place where I can reclaim my identity as a man, a rogue, a creative force, I see something terribly wicked that shakes my sense of self to the very core. Inside the window of a restaurant is Frannie, and she is with a man. I can't see who. He has his back turned to me. But the woman is Frannie, I am certain.

I recall the first time I laid eyes on her. I had let Sebastian drag me to a dinner party, against my better judgment—a birthday celebration for a writer I'd never read named Bruce Wagner. And to make matters worse, Sebastian had, without my knowing, brought along a date for me. This woman's name was Kimberly or Amy or something along those lines. She had been divorced from a powerful movie producer several years before and according to Sebastian had really been through the wringer. Having not received the millions she believed she was entitled to from the divorce, she had gotten into the real-estate business, and had become quite successful in her own right.

After having known her for only a matter of minutes, I wasn't surprised to hear that she had amassed a good fortune for herself. From the moment we arrived at the party she was working the room, shaking hands, telling jokes, collecting phone numbers that she would later turn into six-figure paychecks for herself. The woman had grit and determination—a go-getter, a hustler, a wheeler and a dealer. Her loud booming voice could be heard clear across the room as she enthralled the other guests with celebrity gossip and tales of Hollywood intrigue.

Halfway through dinner, after several glasses of wine, my date reached under the table and placed her hand atop my pants and tried to give me a rub. Despite her good looks and well-practiced touch, the gesture seemed wretched to me. I'd never before been so turned off by a gorgeous woman. I swatted her hand away multiple times but she was relentless. Eventually I excused myself and went to the bar to avoid her onslaught. It was there, at the bar, where I first saw Frannie. She was on the other side of the restaurant at a table with the man who was then her fiancé, and another couple.

I tried to read her lips as she spoke with her friends, but to no avail. Despite the fact that I had no idea what she was saying, I became convinced that her words were the most impassioned, profound, and meaningful of any ever spoken in the English language. Even though I knew she was with this other man, I was blind to their connection. In fact, his presence made no impression on me at all. If you were to ask me today to pick him out of a lineup of three men, I couldn't. My attention was completely undivided—an instant infatuation. To have and conquer her became my dogged obsession.

I fixed myself to the bar and stared at her, completely impervious to tact or discretion. After several minutes, I caught her stealing glimpses at me, as well. When she excused herself to go to the restroom I made my move and waited for her outside the bathroom door. The moment she exited I grabbed her by the hand

and pulled her into a dark corner. She didn't resist at all. She acted as if she had been expecting it. I told her my name and that my intention was to spend my life worshipping her. She laughed and laughed. My God, how the sound of her laughter filled my heart. I thought my chest might explode from the good feelings I suffered at the expense of that laugh. She explained to me that she was engaged to a nice man, a good and decent man, and that he loved her in a way a man like myself probably wasn't even capable of. I brushed aside her rebuffs. I begged her to meet with me but she refused. I said it would be the biggest regret of both of our lives if she didn't. She scoffed. I told her I might not be able to go on living if she didn't. She told me to stop being so dramatic and then walked away. But as she did she reached out and touched my hand. I felt an electric spark charge through me like a bolt of lightning. I nearly fell over from the impact. Afterward, I went to the bathroom and splashed cold water on my face. When I returned to my dinner party I kept my eyes glued to her. She only looked over one more time, but in that glance I foresaw a future for us.

My dinner party let out before hers and I waited for her outside the restaurant in my car. When she and her fiancé left, I followed them all the way to their place. That night I slept in my car outside of their home. In the morning, her fiancé left for work first. Ten minutes later, she left too, and again I followed her, all the way to Chinatown. She spent her morning inside a garment factory, and I spied in through the window and watched as she sampled and procured different fabrics. She carried herself with such grace and poise—a consummate professional. The jealous feelings I harbored toward the silky textiles she pressed to her cheek to check for texture brought me to the brink of arson. In fact, I forced myself to toss my lighter onto the roof to prevent my urges from getting the best of me.

She spent three hours touring the facility, and I spent every minute of that time tracking her whereabouts. In order to so, I scaled fire escapes, hung from gutters, and balanced on precarious ledges. Anything I had to do to keep her in my sights. When she was finished, I followed her to lunch. There she met with two associates. They chose a restaurant along the water's edge in Venice. I pursued them in and sat down two tables away. I pretended not to see her but I knew she had seen me. When she finally approached, I acted aloof.

"Oh, hello," I said.

"Don't be like that with me," she responded. "You're following me, aren't you?

"You think I'd do that?"

"I don't know what you're capable of."

"Would you like to sit down?"

She looked back over her shoulder at the company she met.

"I'm here with friends."

"Okay," I said. "It was nice running into you."

I then lowered my head and pretended to read a copy of Ken Kesey's *Sometimes a Great Notion* I had carried with me into the restaurant. A couple minutes later, I got up and went to the restroom, and when I came out, this time she was waiting for me.

"You're not like some total psycho who is going to cut me up into little pieces and then feed me to your pet snake, are you?"

"I don't have a snake."

"But you have to admit, it's creepy the way you followed me here."

"I didn't follow you here. I come here all the time. They have terrific lasagna."

"What you're doing is stalking and it's illegal."

"It's just a fortuitous happenstance that we both ended up here today."

"Because of the lasagna—right."

"You don't like lasagna?"

"I don't think so."

"You're missing out."

"We'll see."

She handed me her card, and once again our hands met. A shockwave passed through me. I bit down hard on the inside of my cheek to keep from shouting. She smiled and then walked away. Two days later we had our first date and two days after that she returned her fiancé's engagement ring, moved out of his place and in with me.

I weigh my options. I can't afford another violent, ruinous affair like at the club. The legal ramifications would simply be disastrous. However, the potential for such a run-in is so enticing that I nearly storm the restaurant—fists clenched, fixed in my quest for hell-bent destruction. But then something far more treacherous comes to me.

I pick out a man on the street, the most lecherous one I can find: exotic brown skin, oily hair, embroidered jeans, and a flare for ostentatious jewelry.

"Sir," I say. "I have a proposition for you." I point at Frannie through the restaurant's window. "Do you see that beautiful woman there at the table? The one in the strapless black dress, with the long dark hair."

He peers in through the glass.

"Oh yes," he says. "She is a most beautiful woman." He starts rubbing his hands together, as if to warm them, and then passes his tongue across his lips. "The things I would like to do to her."

"She's my fiancé."

The startled man tries to push past me, but I block his path.

"My fiancé has committed an unforgivable offense against me. I need your help in seeking revenge."

The man takes a step back, aghast. "You want me to murder your fiancé?"

"You'd do that?"

The man fingers the cumbersome gold chain around his neck, checks the time on his jewel-encrusted wristwatch, and adjusts several of the rings on his fingers. "Are you a cop?"

"I don't want you to kill her. I only want you to call her on the phone and tell her you're a nurse at the hospital, and that you're calling because she's been listed as an emergency contact and that her mother's been in an accident."

The man leaps back, as if launched from a cannon. "I'd sleep better if I just killed her!"

"I'll give you a hundred dollars."

The man takes a moment to study Frannie through the restaurant's window. "Cash up-front," he finally says.

"Done deal," I say, reaching for my wallet. "Here's fifty now and you'll get the other half once it's done."

I give the man all the details of what I want said: mugged on the street, possible sexual assault, found in an alley, brought to the hospital by ambulance, in critical condition.

"You're a sick, twisted individual," the man says to me.

I watch through the window as the call is made. It goes flawlessly. Frannie stands up and rushes from the table and out the front door of the restaurant, leaving her date alone, confounded and dismayed. She hails a cab at the corner and it sets off, cutting across three lanes of traffic to make a U-turn, in the direction of the hospital.

I pay my co-conspirator his money, and he goes about his way. I glance back through the window again. Frannie's dinner companion has settled the bill and is coming toward the front door. He doesn't look like much—man of about thirty-five, the sort of bore who is gainfully employed and has conservative views on topics such as money and sex—solidly built, probably an adept athlete or at least an avid fan of sports. He piles into a four-wheel-drive vehicle with a surfboard strapped to the roof, and drives off in the opposite direction.

I take my phone from my pocket, holding it in front of my face. For two minutes I wait for it to ring. When it doesn't, I break down and call Frannie. It goes straight to voicemail. The sound of her voice makes me dizzy. I lean against the window of the restaurant, on the verge of fainting.

A young man in a fedora and skintight jeans stops in front of me.

"You're Lou Brown, aren't you?"

"It's hard to know for sure some days."

"I heard what you did," he says. "I was standing right over there." He points to the newspaper stand next to the front door of the restaurant. "You're despicable. I can't even believe it. You're nothing like the guy in your book. He was full of courage and strength, a hero of the streets."

I bend over, hands on knees, trying to catch my breath. "I'm a man on the decline. It's nothing I feel good about."

"And to think I used to look up to you."

I straighten up, using a parking meter for balance. "You're too damn old to have heroes."

The young man spits on my shoe, then turns and walks off.

"Sometimes you get exactly what you deserve," I say to myself.

Cliff is hunched over the bar, his stool precariously balanced on its front two legs, his cargo pants riding too low, making it plain to see he's not wearing any underwear. As I sit down next to him, he looks over the top of his dark sunglasses at me. He then picks up his drink and brings it to his lips. All the ice cubes come undone by gravity and rush towards the rim of the cup and spill out from the corners of his mouth, running down his face and across the front of his shirt.

"You look like you're in good form," I say.

"Get on your feet," he says. "I want to show you something."

I stand up and push in my barstool. "What now?"

"I want you to try and hit me."

I assume a fighter's stance, and start to circle him. Cliff bobs and weaves from side to side. He's got his hands up in front of his face.

"No way," I say, "I don't want to get punched."

"I'm not going to hit you back," he replies. "Just throw some punches already."

I try to stick him with a short jab that he slaps away with an open hand.

"Go on," he says, "really try to hit me."

I fire off my best combination. Cliff slips the left with subtle head movement and ducks under my right hook, the whole time demonstrating ideal poise and balance, not taking his eyes off me for a second. I go for the body and he sidesteps my attack. I throw a left cross and hit nothing but air. Several of the bar's other patrons are laughing at me. I make a final charge, hurling haymaker after haymaker at Cliff's head. Each one misses worse than the last.

I stumble back to my bar stool and order a whiskey on ice.

"I met with the promoter today," Cliff says. "If I win I should make enough to pay off my child support."

"What if you don't?"

"My ex and her new husband have already filed for full custody."

"They can do that?"

"Judge says if I don't pay in full this time, I'll lose all rights to the boy."

The bartender asks Cliff if he wants another round.

"Better make it a water," Cliff says.

"So what's going on with that little Mexican girl of yours?"

"Adrianna..." he says. "Don't get me started on that. Things have really taken a turn."

"A turn?"

Cliff shakes his head despondently. "She's moved herself into my apartment."

"That's insane."

"She pawned my Golden Glove trophy."

"Impossible."

"She said it was tacky."

"I'd kill her."

"She wields her sex like a weapon. I'm totally defenseless."

"You have to get your trophy back."

"She bought an iPhone with the money."

"Sacrilege."

"I should get out of here," Cliff says. "Adrianna is making spaghetti, and I have an early-morning session."

I refocus my attention on the drink in front of me. I power through it and manage several more in the same fashion. Every ten minutes I try to reach Frannie by phone, but only get her voicemail. With each failed attempt I turn my phone off and promise myself I won't make another call. After an hour, my battery dies, technology helping me accomplish what willpower alone cannot.

I feel a set of animal eyes on me. They're burning a hole in me. Every time I look up, there they are, just like laser beams. It's a stare like I've never encountered. It's not playful, it's not sweet, there's no hint of vulnerability to it.

The woman has deep red hair and a strong, almost masculine face with high, high cheekbones and a well-defined chin. She's thin, almost a waif, but her arms are well-toned. Her top is tight around her smallish breasts and her hard nipples poke through the fabric of her blouse.

I stand up and walk toward her, taking great effort to appear loose and casual. She watches me all the way. No false pretenses, no modesty, all intention the whole way through. I take a seat.

"I'm Lou," I say.

"What took you so long?"

She's not smiling as she says this. It's like she genuinely feels like I've been wasting her time, and I'm in need of reprimanding.

"I've been busy with other things."

"I was just getting ready to leave."

"What's your name?"

"I'm Tessa."

I notice she has a smattering of freckles on her nose and cheeks.

"I like your freckles," I say.

"I like your mouth," she replies. She reaches out and touches her finger to my lips.

I feel myself blush, and I take my drink and press it against my hot cheek.

"You come here alone?" I ask.

"Did you?"

"I met a friend here, earlier"

She removes an olive from her drink, opens her mouth very wide, and slowly bites down on it, cutting it in half. "And how is your friend?"

"Rough shape I'm afraid."

"Oh?"

"He's in jeopardy of losing his son." Her expression doesn't alter, unaffected by the news. Confused by this reaction, I explain further. "He owes child support."

"I'm going to have a cigarette," she says.

She stands up, the bottom of her dress catching on the seat. I'm treated to a flash of the curve of her ass, and a glimpse at her lacy black thong. I take a deep breath to compose myself. Outside on the patio she takes a cigarette from her pack, and I take one from mine. I light hers first and then my own.

"You want to know something?" she asks.

"I do."

"I was fired from my job today."

"What line of work were you in?"

"I was a model."

"Why did they fire you?"

"My agency said I needed to lose ten pounds."

"I don't think you have it to give."

"Not for a lack of trying," she says, stomping out the remains of her first cigarette, now reaching for another. "I nearly died of starvation trying to make those pricks happy."

"You're probably better off."

"But I'm afraid I don't know what I'm going to do now. I don't have much of what you'd call a skillset."

"I fully understand and sympathize."

I go to light her cigarette but she turns away from the flame, digs into her bag, and pulls out her own lighter. "Sure you do."

"What's wrong now?"

"I just find it ridiculous that you presume to know my mind."

"I think you'd be surprised."

"Anyone who presumes such a thing about anyone they've just met is a fool." Her eyes turn prideful and combative. "If you can relate to my troubles so well, tell me: what is it you're afraid of?"

I stomp out my cigarette and light a second. "I'm like a little baby bird struggling to get out of its egg."

She sighs loudly. "Don't be vague with me. I can't stand it."

"The egg is my world. If I ever want to really live again, I must first destroy it."

"I'm cold," she says.

She stretches my arms around her body and presses herself against me. I seize hold of her waist and pull her in closer. Her hair brushes up against my nose and mouth, and I inhale deeply. The scent is not that of a sweet rose or a lily, but of a woman.

"There was a time once," I continue, "when I had it all figured out."

"How's that?"

"This may sound counterintuitive, but I only came into myself when I abandoned all concern for being a productive member of society. That was the only way the world was going to get any value out of me."

"So what are you going to do?"

"I need to start training—try to get back to that place where I can become myself again. I need to start eating less, sleeping less, owning less. I need to just *be*."

"You sound like a kook."

I push her toward the bar's exit. She doesn't put up a hint of struggle. But once we hit the street she removes her high-heeled shoes, and runs off in the opposite direction. I give chase, catching up to her a half-block down. I secure her by the shoulders and pin her against the wall of a bus-stop terminal.

"What is wrong with you?" I ask.

"I can't stop thinking about my friend Carolina."

"What about her?"

"She had a condition where she always thought she had spiders crawling on her body."

"Yeah? So?"

"She shaved off all her hair and carried around a comb and a wooden spoon."

"Did she see a doctor?"

"They put her on anti-psychotics."

"And did it work?"

She slaps me across the face. "She hanged herself with a bed sheet."

I restrain her from slapping me again. A passer-by involves himself, asking her if she's all right. She nods her head in the affirmative. "Are you sure?" he asks, carefully sizing us up. She nods again. The man reluctantly moves on, looking back over his shoulder to check on her.

Behind her, embedded in the fiberglass wall of the bus-stop, is a poster for a movie starring Jennifer Aniston about a happy love story touting nonsensical romantic ideals. I brush the hair out of Tessa's face, tucking it behind her ear.

She clings to me tightly, weeping openly and without restraint. I hold on tighter, uncertain what else to do. Her sobs are shrill and grating, and I'm growing more uncomfortable the longer it continues. Her wet tears soak through my shirt. At one point she opens her mouth so wide to moan that her jaw pops violently and I have to wonder whether her face is still intact.

Without warning, the crying comes to a halt and she seizes my face in her hands and kisses me. Her tongue moves like an airplane propeller through my mouth—up and down and all around, stretching and reaching every corner and crevice. I can scarcely breathe as she greedily chews away at my lips. I reach down and slide my hand up the backside of her dress and cup her ass-cheek.

"Touch me!" she groans into my ear.

I push her underwear to the side and slide two digits into her sopping-wet cunt. She chokes and sputters and bites down hard on my bottom lip. It takes all my restraint not to smack her in the face.

The shining streetlight overhead beats down on us.

"Let's go somewhere," I say.

"There's no time," she insists.

I gather myself and look all around. To my right there is a prematurely bald man in a business suit and a woman whose sleeveless dress exposes her flabby and loose upper arms. They are scowling at us. In the opposite direction a group of drunken college students is headed our way, pointing and ogling, watching in heated passion to see how far this spectacle will go.

"Come with me," I say to Tessa.

We pass the restaurant where earlier in the night I witnessed Frannie's most recent betrayal. I scarcely give it a moment's consideration. Upon reaching my car, I open the passenger-side door. I push Tessa inside and race around to the other side and get in. In my pants I can feel my cock swollen to its maximum capacity. In a jiffy Tessa opens my fly and has my cock out, stuffing it into her mouth like a hungry animal. Taking the whole damn thing in, she makes gagging noises. When she can no longer breathe at all she comes up for air, spits on it, and then gives it a tug with her hand. Her eyes are all watery and it looks as if she might faint. I climb into the backseat. She follows right behind me. I bend her over and slide her underwear down her legs, and push it into her from the rear. She goes off like a bitch in heat, panting, gasping—wiggling around like a worm on a hook. I cover her mouth with my hand to stifle her screams, and she bites down hard on my palm.

"What's a girl got to do to get her hair pulled around here?" she bellows.

I grab a fistful by the roots and yank back hard, extending her head back as far as the neck will allow.

"Fuck me harder!" she calls repeatedly, and then, "Faster, faster!"

I put everything I have into it, thrusting wildly, tugging on her hair for extra leverage, digging my fingers into her ass. Finally her breathing becomes short and she hollers, "I'm coming, I'm coming!"

And just as I hear that, I reply, "I'm gonna come too!"

And with that I do, collapsing on top of her, my dick still hard as a hammer inside of her. We lie there panting, sticky, dripping with sweat. I remove my dick from her and a river of semen oozes out of her. She tells me not to worry, that she's on the pill. I cheerfully bend her over and bite down on her ass, leaving a red imprint of my teeth.

"I need a cigarette," she says.

I zip up my pants and attempt to look out the window, but we're totally steamed in. The air is thick and viscous and stifling to breathe. I reach out the palm of my hand and wipe away a small circle in the condensation. From my vantage, the coast looks to be clear. I pop the door open and breathe the cool night air. As it fills my lungs, I look up to the night sky above. The city lights shield the stars and all that is visible is a shroud of brown fog. I turn around to check on Tessa's status, and she's splayed out across the backseat already smoking.

"Come out here," I say. "It's so much nicer."

The two of us sit down on the curb and smoke our cigarettes. She begins mouthing numbers and counting on her fingers.

"What are you doing?" I ask.

She stops counting and returns her hands to her sides. "I'm not doing anything."

"Yes you were. You were counting. What were you counting?"

"You don't want to know."

"I don't want to play games."

She shrugs and takes a long pull from her cigarette, and then pushes her hair back behind her ears. "A big part of my eating-disorder issue is the need to control my surroundings and emotions." She pauses to take another drag from the cigarette. "I have all sorts of unusual behaviors. That's what they call them in rehab: 'behaviors.' For instance, I used to count my daily chews."

"What do you mean, your daily chews?"

She opens and shuts her jaws repeatedly, demonstrating the act of mastication. "You know, like you put food in your mouth and you *chew* it before you swallow. Like, one day I would allow myself one hundred chews. And then the next day I would try and beat that and only do ninety-nine chews. It was a way of controlling my food intake without having to actually be cognizant of just how little food I was consuming."

"I've never heard of anything like that."

"It gets worse, I assure you."

"Well, you're not eating now, so what were you counting?"

She strikes a defensive posture. "I've sort of replaced my food compulsions with something else."

I finish one cigarette and go for another. "Oh Jesus, don't tell me. Are you like some sort of sex fiend now?"

"Goddamn it, Lou, don't say it like that! I have real issues. It's not funny."

I stand up and pace back and forth between the five feet of

space separating the back bumper of my car and the car parked behind it. "How bad is it?"

"I just got out of rehab a month ago. I'm still adjusting."

I stop pacing and stare right down at her. "It seems to me like you were doing a lot of counting. Just how many guys have you been with in the last month?"

She wears the shamed face of a culpable child.

"Go on," I say, "out with the number."

Her voice is almost soundless. "Maybe around fourteen."

My voice explodes. "Maybe around fourteen! What the hell is wrong with you?"

"You said you weren't going to judge me."

I flick my cigarette to the ground. "I didn't expect it to be so many. I thought you were going stay three or four, five at most. I hope you didn't give me anything."

The tears she's been fighting hard to hold back break free and begin to flow. "I shouldn't have told you. You have every right to react like that."

She stands up and falls into my arms. I run my fingers through her hair and caress her shoulders and back. A river of black mascara runs down her cheeks. When she tries to speak, she gets all choked up and has to wipe her nose.

"Do you want to come back to my place?" I offer.

"Really?"

I kiss her forehead. "Why not."

We climb back inside the vehicle and I steer it towards the Frontier Motel. Several more of the lights in the sign have gone out, and now it simply reads: F t M t. Emma, the prostitute, is out front haggling with two men. One is shirtless and well-muscled with cornrows for hair. The other is tall and thin, his baggy clothing hanging off of him like a king-sized blanket thrown over a twin bed. They are all sharing a bag of potato chips. As soon as Emma sees my vehicle, she dismisses the men and starts toward us. Her stride is uneven, staggering from side to side, holding out her arms for balance, as if negotiating a tightrope. Her face is one of complete concentration. I turn to look at Tessa and her smile is glowing.

The more muscular guy shouts, "Get that money, Marigold!"

"They call you Marigold?" I ask her. "I like that."

"No, honey, you don't mind them. You call me Emma."

She places one hand on the hood of my car for support and pivots back toward the two men, shooing them off with her free hand, nearly falling over in the process.

Emma looks Tessa up and down, her bug eyes bulging and her lips pursed, making a careful study of Tessa's form. "Who's this trick?" she says. "I thought you said you were off pussy."

"Emma, this is Tessa," I say. "Tessa, meet my friend Emma."

The two women share a vigorous handshake.

"Has Lou told you about my gymnastics?" Emma asks Tessa.

Tessa glances at me and then fixes her gaze back on Emma. "No, he didn't mention it, but I'd love to see it. You have a tremendous physique—such strong arms and a rock-solid core."

My eyes drift down to Emma's midsection. She's got a crop-top on, and her stretch marks and belly fat are on full display.

"I'm confused," I say. "Was it gymnastics or ballet you prefer?"

"Oh, honey, I do them both in equal measure." She performs a short plié and her thighs wobble and knees nearly buckle.

Tessa claps her hands in appreciation of the effort, and Emma takes a small curtsey.

"It was so nice seeing you again, Emma," I say, "but Tessa and I must get going."

Emma's face turns sour, exhibiting the full range of emotions concerning female pettiness. "So that's it? No more time for your dear friend Emma now that you've made a new friend."

"You're welcome to join us, if you'd like," Tessa says.

The two women exchange amiable smiles.

"Are you sure?" I whisper to Tessa.

"Of course, I'm sure," she says, loud enough for Emma to hear.

Once inside, first thing, I check the status of the trashcan. It's nearly half full with leaky ceiling water. I take the can to the bathtub and drain it of its contents. Emma has already poured drinks for us upon my return to the bedroom.

"I love the new addition," Emma says, pointing to the painting of the man and his dog.

The three of us turn our attention to the work of art. "Thank you," I say. "I bought it yesterday in the park from a painter who assures me he's uniquely talented."

"It's fabulous!" Tessa says.

"Everyone in this world possesses a single, unique talent," Emma says. "I've always thought so."

"I disagree entirely," I say.

"Oh, honey, you don't know the first thing about people. Everybody has something that makes them special. Tell me, Tessa, what's your talent?"

"My talent? I'm not sure I have any."

"Oh come on, everyone has a talent. For instance, Lou is a writer. Did you know that about him? I looked it up. Apparently he's quite successful at it." Tessa stares at me puzzled, and I shrug and pour myself another drink of whiskey. "But I have a much more useful talent than that," Emma continues. "I'm the world's greatest lover." I roll my eyes and Tessa fights to hamper her laughter. "Stop it, you two. I'm not talking about sex. I'm talking about real love.

"I had a husband once, the most wonderful man in the world. It was a long time ago, but I remember every moment of our time together like it was yesterday. We met when I was only sixteen, still living in my parents' home in the small village where I was born. After only two months of knowing each other I became pregnant. We had a child—a baby girl. We moved into a small apartment together and were very poor. I wanted to work but my husband wouldn't allow it. He was a proud man, and wanted to provide for his family. He'd work two or sometimes three jobs at a time, but often there was still not enough to eat. I begged him to let me work. But he insisted I stay at home with the child.

"Every morning he'd wake up and I'd make him toast and tea and I'd serve it to him at the table like it was a great feast, and I would kiss him on the face and tell him that I love him, and that he was the greatest man in the world. And I meant it, too.

"In my line of work, you hear a lot of talk about disaffected lovers, people unhappy or unfulfilled in their relationships. But I was never like that. Each day I loved my husband more and more, no matter how hard things got. Every day, year after year, I made new and exciting discoveries about his character, found fresh reasons to love him."

Emma stops her story and turns her back to Tessa and me. She begins to breathe in short staccato breaths, on the verge of hyperventilating, and then blows her nose vigorously, many times in succession. This act produces one of the harshest, most discordant noises I've ever heard.

"I'm sorry," she says, "I haven't told this story in a long time."

"It's a lovely story," Tessa says.

"If it's okay, I'd like to continue."

"Please," Tessa assures her.

Emma's words come tumbling out like an avalanche coming down a mountain, making them difficult to discern. I tilt my head toward her to better make out what she's saying.

"Well, one day my husband came home from the job he held at a local factory and told me that there was no more work for him there. He promised me that it was not so bad, that he would find something else. And every day he went out and looked for a new job, but there was nothing for him. After one month we had nothing left, no food to eat and nothing to pay the rent with. Still, his spirits remained high. He said, 'Please do not worry. We will not starve, I will see to it.' But I was scared and for the first time I did not believe him. I had a child to feed, after all. The next day, when he went out looking for work, I left our daughter with a friend and went out myself. I had heard stories of women making good money visiting the fisherman at the docks, so I took a one-hour bus ride to the coast. There I sold my body for the very first time. Five different men paid me for my services. They smelled terribly of fish but I did it and it was okay because I understood that my family needed the money. That night I returned home with lots of food for us to eat. My husband was waiting there for me. He was smiling when I walked in the door, but then he saw what I had brought home and he stopped smiling. 'Where did you get that?' he asked. At first I tried to lie. I told him that I had found the money. But he did not believe it. Then I lied further and said that the money was given to me by a kind stranger. This, too, he did not believe. After all, he knew me so well, and could tell the difference between when I was telling the truth and when I was telling lies. Finally, I confessed to him that I had slept with different men for money."

Her voice drops to a slow whisper, like her words are moving through honey.

"And do you know what?" she finally says. "The day I had sold my body was the day he actually found a job. That is why he was smiling when I came in."

"Where is your husband now?" Tessa asks.

The room fills with the sound of Emma's hysterical crying. I remain seated in my chair, powerless to help. But Tessa takes to her like a mother would a fallen child, holding her tightly, soothing her, caressing the pain away.

"I can't believe I allowed myself to go on and on like that," Emma finally says after regaining her composure. "My true intention was to learn about you." She grins generously and strokes Tessa's cheek with the palm of her hand.

"That's okay," Tessa says. "Another time."

The conversation veers to my writing career and I dismiss it entirely. Instead I tell them about my new aspiration as an educator. I spare no detail explaining my day working as a volunteer instructing an eighth-grade English class in the finer points of *Lord of the Flies*. Both women remain as still as bears in winter as they listen to my tale, mesmerized by the passion with which I speak. When I tell how I was unfairly ousted from my position after just one half of a single class, Emma springs from the bed to her feet and throws her arms up in protest. "What a terrible injustice!" she says. "We must organize a rally and march on the school grounds. We'll shut the place down until they reinstate you."

Her enthusiasm inflames in me an unbridled rush of emotion. In an instant I make a hundred different plans to exact my revenge against the school's principal. I decide I will turn the whole thing into a media circus. I'll start with an investigation into the principal's own conduct. Once I dig up the dirt, I'll blackmail her until she abdicates her position, at which time I'll be installed as principal. The reforms I'll make as a school administrator will be unprecedented. The whole system will get shaken from its roots, flipped upside down, and turned inside out. My throwaway kids will test off the charts and then storm the Ivy League, where they'll make breakthroughs in the fields of physics and chemistry—resulting in a succession of prestigious awards including the Nobel Prize. Due to my successes, there will be tremendous demand for me to move up the bureaucratic ladder, and within a handful of years I'll be elected superintendent of the Los Angeles Unified School District. From there, the sky is the limit: mayor, senator, governor, President!

"We should begin immediately. There are so many preparations to be made. Where is my phone? I must get my agent on the line!"

I scour the room, clearing the clutter from the table with one fell swoop of my arm, checking underneath the bed, behind the curtains, inside the shower.

"Try your pocket," Emma says. I do, and lo and behold it's there.

I dial immediately.

"Sebastian, it's me, Lou. There's been a development and I need your help."

"You've written something. That's tremendous."

"Written something? No, that's all in the past. I'm onto something much bigger now. Today I was fired from the volunteer teaching gig you got me. I want to organize a protest and have the principal removed from her position, and have me installed in her place!"

"Fired?" he shouts. "You were only there for a day."

"Actually," I concede, "I didn't even make it through a single class. I was terminated halfway through. But that's not the point. I had a breakthrough—an epiphany, if you will. But I need your help. I'm at the Frontier Motel. Come here, immediately, so we can discuss the future. I have big plans, and I see you having a place in the mix."

Sebastian takes off on a rant, and I lay the phone down on the table until his shouting has ceased.

"Calm down, you're hysterical, it's not as bad as all that," I say. "Why don't we discuss this in the morning? I'll meet you at the Grove for breakfast at 10:30."

"You're ruining yourself. You understand that, don't you?"

"There's always that chance."

Sebastian hangs up the phone.

"So, is he on board?" Emma asks.

I sit down in a chair and pour another drink. "Sebastian's not a visionary: he's a details guy. But he'll come around."

"I'd like to make a toast," Emma says, holding her glass high. "To Lou Brown and his 'throwaway kids.' The future is bright!"

"Here here," Tessa says, clinking glasses with Emma and myself.

"I'm feeling too good," I say. "I can't waste all this energy. We must go out and celebrate."

"What do you propose?" Tessa asks.

Standing in front of the window, I light a cigarette, neglecting to take care to blow the smoke outside, and watch as a silver cloud passes in front of the yellow sliver of moon.

"I've got it," I say. "Let's all go have a swim. If I remember correctly, there is a YMCA no more than two miles from here."

"It's 11:30 at night," Tessa says. "It must be closed."

"That's no problem at all," I say. "I'm sure there is a way in."

"Wonderful idea!" Emma says.

"And there is still time to stop for provisions," I say.

For the duration of the car ride to the grocery store, Tessa is telling Emma all about her most recent tarot-card reading. The fortune teller, Tessa explains, is a former civil servant. The woman had been carrying mail for over twenty years. Then, one day along her route, she opened the lid of a mailbox and found that a swarm of bees had built a hive inside. Being terribly allergic, she panicked and dropped the stack of coupon books and catalogues she was holding onto the nest, agitating the bees. She ran down the sidewalk in a frenzy, leaving a trail of bills and other important correspondence in her wake. The bees gave chase and overwhelmed her, stinging her dozens of times on the face, neck, and arms. The postwoman went into anaphylactic shock and fell to the ground, striking her head on the bumper of a Japanese compact car on the way down, knocking her unconscious. When she awoke, the effects of the bees' poison had exacted a severe toll. Her hands were swollen into useless clubs, her eyelids had ballooned up, compromising her vision, and her tongue was in paralysis, making it impossible to speak. For an hour she lay there and no one came to her aid. Yet she was not afraid—she knew she would survive this harrowing ordeal, for something else had occurred, something magical. The postwoman wasn't sure if it had come from the blow to the head or the toxins in the bee stings, but she could now see into the future. And her death would not occur for many years to come, when, deep in sleep, she would pass peacefully from this world and into the next.

Emma is deeply interested, asking more and more questions about this postwoman-turned-clairvoyant, and about the occult in general. And Tessa is more than happy to oblige, sharing with Emma what this woman told her about her own future. She goes on to explain that she received the 9 of Swords card, a card which most often relates to anxiety and fear. Emma, so enraptured by this moving tale, is having trouble maintaining composure, bouncing up and down in her seat, holding her breath until she turns white, pulling out chunks of her own hair.

"My worst fear," Tessa states, "is that when life offers me a great chance, I will be too cowardly or indecisive to seize it, and that life will take away the good card I've been dealt."

"And what did this fortune teller say about that?" Emma asks.

"She said that if my heart is open, there will always be another chance to return to whatever happiness I might have missed before."

"Oh, honey, that's very good. I like it very much," Emma says.

The two women share a deep hug, and I think to myself that this fortune teller is telling lies—that in life, if there is a moment for doing things that can bring true happiness, it is imperative that one act immediately, because once it passes the opportunity is squandered.

I run into the grocery store by myself, leaving the women to continue their emotional bonding. I collect only the essentials (bottle of Jack Daniels, package of beef jerky, and cigarettes) and proceed to the checkout line. The clerk has a square, heavy face, and is wearing a red vest with a nametag that reads: Brian.

"Are you a club member, sir?"

"No."

"Would you like to be?"

"No."

"If you sign up today, you'll get four dollars off this whiskey."

"There's no time for that now. I'm taking my friends swimming."

He scans the items in quiet disbelief, and I pay the bill. As I go out the door I turn around and witness him punching numbers into the machine, then taking four dollars from the register and stuffing it into his pocket.

"Very resourceful," I say to myself.

We park three blocks from the YMCA in a deserted alley. The sound of police sirens can be heard in the distance. Overhead, a helicopter circles the surrounding area, a bright beam of light shining down. The temperature outside is still hot, and there are deep sweat stains in the armpits and back of my shirt. Emma complains about the bunions on her feet and takes off her high heels. She attempts walking on her toes over the broken glass and assorted trash covering the street. I pick her up and carry her piggy-back. Tessa, meanwhile, spots a grey kitten with a white stripe down its chest, peeking its head out from under a dumpster. When she gets near the cat, it crawls out, revealing itself. The poor thing has a wounded paw. Tessa sweeps it up into her arms, stroking its head and belly, as the cat gently purrs.

An American flag hangs limply from the top of a flagpole in front of the one-story YMCA building. The path to the front door is flanked by half-dead, brown grass, and a hedge that needs trimming. Under the cover of darkness, I creep up to the window. Inside is a total blackout, not a single security light in operation. I signal for the girls to stay put while I investigate further, although they hardly need coaxing. They've busied themselves playing pouncing games with the cat. Tessa has tied a knot around a tube of chapstick with a long piece of dental floss, the cat giving chase while they run in circles.

There is a six-foot-tall, cement wall surrounding the backside of the building. It takes me two attempts to pull myself up, my arms no longer having the strength in them they once did. In the doing, I tear a hole in the knee of my pants and receive a scrape on my forehead. Having scaled the wall, I find exactly what I had hoped for: a competition-sized swimming pool, its wrinkled surface shimmering in the moonlight. I lower myself down off the wall, unlock the gate, and let in Tessa, Emma, and the cat.

We undress by the pool's edge and on the count of three dive in. I feel the air leave my lungs as my body constricts upon penetrating the chilly surface. Breathless, I swim to the bottom, and sit Indian-style on the pool's floor. Tiny air bubbles float all around me, illuminated by the moon's light. The realization strikes me that one day I will die, and somehow this epiphany makes me feel most alive. It's almost as if I have the perception of having entered an alternate reality, one in which the problems of any past life can do me no harm. After a few moments of ecstatic bliss, I swim back to the top.

"Good to see you again," Tessa says. "We thought you might be trying to drown yourself."

"Just the opposite," I say. "I'm having the best time of any I can remember."

Tessa swims over and presses herself against me. I can feel her heart beating against my chest and the side of her foot stroking the inside of my calf. We share a kiss before being interrupted by the splashing water of thrashing arms and legs. Emma is struggling to swim. Her stroke is pure self-preservation, no hint of technique or knowhow. When she finishes, she sidles up next to us, exhausted, panting hard, her face serenely lit up like a nighttime city skyline.

"I love a good bit of exercise," Emma says. "It's so life-affirming."

"It's important to test one's physical limits," I say.

"I can't imagine you as an athlete," Tessa says.

"That's where you're wrong. It's my competitive spirit that sets me apart from my contemporaries."

"Now you're just being silly," Tessa replies.

"No, I'm dead serious. In fact, it's the desire to find out what I'm truly made of that makes me regret not having ever seen a war."

"That sort of talk is no good," Emma says, shaking her head in disapproval.

"I want to prove my mettle. Give me a challenge."

The girls conspire in secret negotiations while I climb out of the water, sip on the whiskey, chew a handful of beef jerky, and pet the kitten. When they're ready, they issue their test.

"We bet that you can't swim underwater from one end of the pool to the other on a single breath."

I study the length of the pool, formulating a strategy, weighing my options. Twenty-five meters has never looked more daunting. The starting blocks on the far side of the water's edge appear a million miles off, like a distant snowcapped peak in the horizon. It seems to me a heavy challenge, perhaps even beyond my reach.

"That's all?" I ask, mockingly. "I thought you'd propose a true feat of strength."

"Okay," Emma says. "Make it up and back, then."

I immediately regret my swaggering display of false bravado, but it's too late to back down now.

I light up a cigarette and take big, heaving drags. "Give me a moment to prepare myself," I say. "The smoke helps me to expand my lungs, improving airflow." By the time the cigarette has been smoked down to a nub, I'm on the verge of breaking out in anxious hysterics. Reentering the pool, my arms and legs are trembling, and my lips and eyelids, quivering. "This will be a piece of cake," I manage to say.

I stand against the edge of the pool, my hand bracing the wall. The girls are having a wonderful time of shouting taunts and insults at me. I attempt to recall inspirational mantras from long-deceased heroes of a bygone eras, but none come to mind.

Finally, I make my move, sucking in a big gasp of air and pushing hard off the wall with my legs, reaching my arms far out in front of me and then pulling them back toward my body in a fluid and dynamic motion. My body cuts through the water with great precision, and I glide like the wing of a bird riding an updraft high above a desert canyon floor. Having completed the first half of my first length, I'm amazed at what an easy time I'm having of it. This is no problem at all, I think. Nothing could be simpler. I release a small amount of air, and continue on.

By the time the far wall comes into reach, I'm beginning to feel the strain: the lungs are tight and I'm no longer gliding effortlessly, rather my movements have devolved into short, choppy strokes. However, there is still gas in the tank, and my confidence is high. But when I make my push off the wall for the second half of the challenge, I overexert myself and allow too much of my breath to escape. The deprivation of oxygen to my brain is starting to have its effects: tiny flickers of blinding light flashing in my eyes, followed by inky black spots that are clouding my underwater vision. At the halfway mark of my second length, I'm suffering hallucinations: An older gentleman with a long white beard, dressed in silky white robes, descends from the sky and implores me to give up my struggle. He assures me that if I allow myself to sink peacefully to the bottom of the pool, he will resurrect me to enjoy an eternity of celestial riches. The temptation is too much to resist. My arms and legs simultaneously quit, my eyes shut, and I float to the pool's floor.

Lying prostrate, five feet below the water's surface, tiny bits of debris and pebbles pressing into my back, a second vision comes to me. It's of a lush pasture resting in a valley of golden hills. Plants of all variety sprout from fertile soil. Grass as high as my knee. Patches of yellow and white blossoms bloomed from wild growing bushes. A cold mountain stream meandering its way across the valley floor. A bird of prey soaring effortlessly high up in the sky, making large circles over the land on its hunt.

There is a white stallion tethered to the trunk of a lone, leafy oak tree. Next to the horse is a man with a round, austere face, dressed in black coat and pants. His entire mouth is concealed behind a grotesque mustache. He is grooming the animal's coat with a wire brush and speaking to it in an affectionate yet somber German accent. I pick myself up and make a slow approach. The horse's black eyes detect me in its vicinity and he rears up on hind legs and makes a terrible neighing cry. The man, now alert to my presence, attempts to soothe the animal, patting its shoulder, speaking gently to it. When the horse calms, the man turns to me.

"There is something I'd like to show you," he says.

The man takes the horse's reins in his hand and leads us to the stream's edge. There is the sound of the slow-moving water gently lapping against the banks. A light breeze blows the heads of the reeds lining the shore. Under our feet are a bed of smooth round stones fixed in the hardened mud.

We walk for an hour and hardly a word is exchanged between myself and this man. Instead he speaks only to the horse in a resolute and bleak voice. He refers to a particular star tucked into the corner of a twinkling solar system, upon which there were clever beasts who invented knowing. There is great scorn and derision in his tone, practically spitting his words as he speaks about the aimlessness and arbitrariness of human intellect. This man really has it in for these cretins who think themselves the center of all creation. There is a quality to his speech so unique to him that it's impossible not to imagine his influence affecting all of mankind.

I'm so engrossed in his story, I barely notice that the ground we walk on is growing steeper and more treacherous, and that the river has narrowed into a funnel of white water, thrashing and breaking over the boulders that dare stand in its way. The horse's alarmed whinnies break me out of my ecstatic state.

We find ourselves standing at the top of a majestic waterfall, where the ground gives way and Earth simply ceases to exist. The tumbling fall's bottom is obscured by a thick cloud of white mist rising up from the infinitude of the unknown.

"Do you know why you find yourself here today?" the man asks.

I inch toward the edge of the waterfall and peer over. There is nothing that I can see beyond the wall of vapor. The sound of the pouring water smashing against the ground below seems a hundred miles off.

"A man in white robes insisted I trust him and give myself over to him. He assured me that if I did so, I would be rewarded beyond my wildest dreams."

"And you simply went without any further inquiry or investigation?"

"To be saved would be divine."

"If it's only peace of soul you're after, then believe. However, if it's truth you seek, you'll have to keep striving."

"Do you think a man can be loved, not in spite of his flaws but because of them?"

Before the man can answer, I am seized around the waist by a most powerful force and dragged upwards. *So long, world — the grouchy German was wrong,* I think to myself. *I'm being whisked off to a better place now.*

But instead of arriving at Heaven's door, I'm splayed poolside. Tessa's hands are stacked on top of each other, delivering crushing blows to my chest, each new compression forcing my body to pop and recoil. There is the sound of counting in the air, and then Emma presses her mouth to mine, her hot breath breathing new life into my languished body. From my lungs, a geyser of water rises up and sprays out my mouth. My violent coughing returns me to a state of awareness.

"I guess I'm not as strong a swimmer as I thought I was," I say.

"I'm in no mood for your jokes," Tessa says. "You nearly got yourself killed."

"He almost made it," Emma says, "a damn good effort!"

"Where'd you learn CPR?" I ask.

"I once volunteered on the front lines as a nurse for the army," Emma says.

"You did?" Tessa asks.

"I've been so many things in this life."

The two women help me into the seated position, and the kitten jumps into my lap, thirstily lapping up the pools of water collected on my boxer shorts. Emma and Tessa both light cigarettes but refuse to offer me one. There is a distinct ringing in my ears, sounding like mariachi horns. I wonder if that will be a permanent condition. *What can't be cured must be endured,* I say to myself.

Tessa drives and Emma sits shotgun on the ride back to the motel. The two women have been exchanging non-stop compliments about each other's bravery and coolness under pressure. This spectacle of female friendship is a rarity in my experience and wonderful to see.

I lie across the backseat with the cat sleeping on my chest. I attempt to recall the details of my near-death experience, but it's a total blank. The transition from life to death is an impossible thing to understand. I've never been less accepting of the prospect of my own mortality at any point in my life.

Emma and Tessa ease me up the steps to my room. The three of us take each other in a long and tender embrace, as if we were kin. There is the sensation of a gentle caress on my cock, and I look down and Emma is messing with the zipper of my pants.

"Another time perhaps," I say.

"That's okay," she says, "I really should get going. I haven't earned a penny all night."

Emma opens the door and goes out. She sings a tune as she descends the stairs. Her voice is a shrill warble, full of trills, quavers, and melodic embellishments.

"She's the most wonderful woman I've ever met," Tessa

confesses.

I reach for my package of cigarettes and light one for each of us. Tessa places it in her mouth and takes small, delicate puffs. I kiss her on the cheek and she rubs my leg affectionately.

"That was some night," I say.

She takes another drag off her cigarette and answers softly, "I feel much better now."

"Me too."

She clings to me even tighter, and I feel her body shivering. I kiss her resplendently white, freckled shoulder.

Chapter

Sebastian is sitting outside at a table on the restaurant's patio. The weather outside is already a balmy seventy-five, but he's wearing a heavy blue sweater and a scarf draped around his neck. The table is littered with half-drunk glasses of coffee, orange juice, water, grapefruit juice, and some green substance that looks and smells like lawn clippings.

I point to the green drink. "What is that?"

He picks it up and takes it back like a better man would tequila or whiskey.

"It's wheatgrass. My acupuncturist says it prevents cancer."

I pick up the empty glass and sniff it. "Your acupuncturist told you that?"

"She's a world-renowned expert on Eastern medicine."

"Is that right?" I say. "What's her name?"

"Her name is Dr. Ashley Stephenson."

I laugh heartily. "Your doctor of Eastern medicine is named Ashley Stephenson? That's the WASPiest name I've ever heard. Where did she study?"

He gives me a withering look. "She's from Kentucky. Are you happy now?"

I reach out and give a tug on the end of his scarf. "It's summer. What's with the après-ski attire?"

He readjusts the scarf. "I'm suffering from a cold. The sweater and scarf keep my core temperature up, which stimulates the immune system."

The waitress arrives and I place an order for a breakfast burrito, a coffee, and a Budweiser. Sebastian requests an egg-white omelet with mushrooms, tomatoes, and feta cheese.

"You know, Lou, alcohol leads to psychic and physical exhaustion."

"I feel fine."

"You're infuriating," he says. "Don't you want to make use of your talent?"

"I'm awful at everything that matters."

Sebastian slams his fist into the table, knocking over his grapefruit juice. "Goddamn it, stop making fucking excuses for yourself."

I bring the palms of my hands to my eyes and rub them in a circular motion, causing me to see what look like exploding stars. When my vision clears, I look out into the parking lot. There are three Italian sports cars parked in a row. "The words just don't come like they used to."

"Well, they better *start* coming."

"I can't seem to commit to a path."

"You never had any trouble making decisions before."

"Making decisions was easier before I knew what it was to live with the consequences of bad ones."

"Speaking of poor decisions, I checked your accounts this morning. You're nearly broke."

"You're exaggerating."

"Do you know what your fiancé is spending each month?"

"How am I supposed to know something like that?"

"Take a guess."

I close my eyes and work some facts and figures in my head. "Two thousand dollars?"

Sebastian bursts into mocking laughter. "She spent fourteen thousand last month. Twelve the month before."

I pull at my hair. "Dear God! How is that possible?"

"What you need to understand is this: A beautiful woman coming from a wealthy family like that needs a special kind of treatment. Maybe you don't know what I'm talking about because you grew up poor, but now I'm going to tell you. You see—society conditions rich, beautiful women differently than everyone else. Women like that, from the moment they are first recognized as beautiful—usually around three years old—are catered to in a manner that the rest of us can't possibly fathom. Every whim, desire, and impulse, no matter how outlandish, is realized on their behalf. And if they don't get what they believe they're entitled to at all times, then they'll seek it elsewhere."

My temper blazes at this gross affront. "Quit your tedious moralizing, Sebastian! You don't know what you're saying."

"Ah, but you're wrong. I do know what I'm saying. I'm absolutely correct."

"Do you realize there was a time when I wanted nothing more than to spend all my hours adoring her, worshipping at her feet, caressing her with exotic lotions, cooking her favorite meals. I loved her all the way. I would've gladly given up all other claims on my life. I would've done anything for her. I would've slit your throat from ear to ear if she had asked me to."

Sebastian tightens his lips and squints his eyes in frustration. "You know, Lou, you're going to die one day and the only thing that will be left is the work you leave behind."

"But perhaps you're wrong. Maybe I am capable of living a whole different life. Perhaps I'm capable of being an instrument of good in the world. Perhaps it's not all about my own body of work. Maybe I can do something more selfless than write books. Who does that help, anyway? Why can't I be an educator, a husband, an altruist? I've been an agitator, an instigator, and a subversive all my life. What good is it? Isn't it better to build something up rather than tear it all down?"

"Where's this coming from?"

"I nearly drowned in a swimming accident. It's got me thinking, that's all."

Sebastian shovels a fork full of egg-white into his mouth, then wipes his lips with a napkin. "We all have our place in the world. It's up to you whether you exploit that or not. No one can really be anything in this world until he accepts who he truly is."

"People can change, you know. One doesn't have to be stagnant—a person can transform himself, be anything he can imagine."

"You don't really believe that, do you?" Sebastian asks.

"If you commit yourself to it, I do. No halfway measures, that's what I say. If you're willing to burn all bridges to the past, you can accomplish anything."

"Is that what you're doing here—burning your bridges?"

I cast him a melting look.

After breakfast I take a ride out to see Frannie. Over the past couple of days she's left countless messages I haven't returned. Pulling up to the driveway of my house, I'm a tourist in a faraway land. I wonder if Sebastian is right. Can a man never really reinvent himself?

Frannie is standing in the foyer, just inside the front door, as I enter the house. Her hair is pulled back into a tight ponytail and she's without make-up. She's wearing black stretch yoga pants and there is a ring of sweat around the crack of her perfectly round, bubble-shaped ass. Her navy-blue sports bra is darkened by a layer of sweat, and the beads of moisture that have collected on her arms and stomach sparkle like tiny diamonds.

"What are you doing here?" she asks.

"Christ, Frannie, I own the house. I can come and go as I please."

It occurs to me that no matter how familiar you are to the sight or touch of a particular body, once the owner of it has perceivably denied you access to it, that body becomes irresistible. That said, the fact that she's been touched, caressed, fucked, and sullied by another man makes her mysterious and alluring to me in a way she never was when in my possession.

"I'm ready to talk to you," I say, reaching out and touching her arm, cupping it just above the elbow.

She yanks her arm away, leaving me with a handful of her sweat. It stirs in me a tumult of commotion and zeal. When she looks away, I bring my hand to my mouth and taste the salty residue on my fingers.

"Well, go on," she says in a harsh, discordant tone, "say what you've come to say. I'm listening."

My steely demeanor betrays me completely and I reach out and grab her, pulling her into me, my right hand burying itself deep into the crevice of her ass, and my left hand sliding up her neck, holding her by the base of the skull. I press my lips into hers and her mouth is hot and sticky, and her tongue swollen and pulsing.

"What do you think you're doing?" she says.

I continue with renewed vigor, forcing myself on her. This time she cedes to my power and kisses back with feverish intensity. My hand moves from her butt to inside her pants and finds her slit. It's open like a blooming flower and my fingers slide effortlessly into it. I suck and bite on her neck and she undoes my belt and my pants' button and zipper. She takes ahold of it with a firm grip around the head and the thing is standing straighter and taller than a flagpole. I flatten her down onto her back and seize her yoga pants by the waist and yank them down. Being too eager and forceful, I rip them. Frannie says, "Doesn't matter, just get them off!" Normally Frannie would never go for this sort of thing—sex just after exercising. She'd insist on a shower and the requisite soaps, lotions, and perfumes. But sexual niceties don't seem to be a concern at the moment, and I'm most thankful for it. Her natural scent is pure bliss to me. If she'd let me, I'd bottle it and splash it over my top lip to sniff all day long. I notice she's grown a bit of hair down there. She has it trimmed into the shape of a landing strip. Unable to delay any longer, I dive into her.

"Play with me," she says.

I reach around and find her ass. With my finger in there up to the second knuckle I can feel my dick pressing against it from the other side of the vaginal wall. "Get behind me, get behind me!" she insists. From behind her I run my hand across her back. It's all red and irritated from the coarse fiber of the carpet. From between her legs appears a hand, which reaches up and cradles my balls, giving them light squeezes and tugs.

"You're going to make me come!" she hollers in a hoarse shout.

"Do it, I want you to come!" I respond.

"I am, I am," she says, "I want you to come with me! Do it now!"

I come with everything I have and then collapse on top of her, dick still planted firmly inside.

The two of us lay together in silence. I try to run my fingers through her hair but it's too sweaty and tangled. Instead, I brush it all across one shoulder and plant small kisses behind her ear and down her neck. She traces her hand from my pubic region, across my stomach and chest, up to my shoulders, where she gently kneads the muscles until they loosen.

"I didn't expect all that this morning," she says.

"It wasn't exactly what I had in mind either."

"No?"

"Are you kidding?" I say. "I'm furious with you."

I finally withdraw my dick from her. It hangs all long and soft and glistening against the inside of my thigh. I set my elbow into the floor and prop my head up with my hand, rolling onto my side.

She emits a loud sigh that sounds almost like a grunt. "Darling, you can't still be upset about what happened at the club. Is it a crime for someone to have fun dancing with her friends?"

"I certainly don't dance like that with *my* friends."

She places her hand on my chest and caresses the bump in my collarbone where I broke it as a teenager. "Darling, you don't dance at all."

"Tough guys don't dance. Norman Mailer said that."

"Who?"

"The point is, I can't trust you."

"Darling, I'm completely committed to you. Just the same as you are to me. And you would never cheat on me, would you?"

My words sputter out of me: "I would never cheat on you."

"Of course you wouldn't, darling. And neither would I."

I study her eyes for misgiving, but it's no use. No man can match a woman in the art of deception. There's not a woman alive who isn't skilled at telling lies.

She sits up and leans back against the base of the staircase. Her eyes take on a new shrewdness, like a hawk hunting prey. "Someone called me last night and pretended to be from the hospital. They said that my mother had been in an accident. Can you believe that?"

"Your mom was in an accident?"

"She wasn't, but somebody called and said she was—to scare me."

"That's terrible!"

"An awful thing to do."

"So did you go to the hospital?"

"I did."

"But she wasn't there?"

"Are you telling me it wasn't you who orchestrated this?"

I feel a sharp cramp in my stomach. "I was out with Cliff last night," I say. "Where were you when you got the call?"

She takes my hand in hers and interlocks our fingers. "I was at home, alone."

"You were all by yourself? Nobody else around, at all?"

"Yes, all alone." She lifts our adjoined hands to her mouth and plants a kiss just below my scabby knuckles. "So what does your visit here today mean? Are you moving back in?"

My heart starts beating fast and I become nauseous, so much so that I fear I will throw-up. "Is that what you want?"

"Well," she says hesitantly, "I have something else I need to tell you."

I sit there patiently, not saying a thing, waiting for her to continue.

"I'm pregnant."

My eyesight fails me and the world goes black, my ears fill with a thumping ominous drone, sweat secretes from every pore in my body, and my mouth goes completely dry. I rock back and forth like a monk in deep hypnotic prayer, oblivious to my surroundings, entering a new plane of consciousness. "Pregnant? That's not possible."

"Not possible?" she says. "It happens all the time."

"But what about your precautions?"

"You mean birth control? Birth control isn't surefire."

"And you're sure it's mine?"

She strikes me with a sharp blow to the face, her finger catching me in the eye. "You fucking asshole!" she says. "Who else's would it be?"

The impulse to shout out that I know she lied about her whereabouts when she received the hoax phone call pours through me, but I resist. "I'm sorry, Frannie. I just always figured that life ended with me."

"Your own self-importance always did mean more to you than any other person ever could."

I place a tender hand on her leg and she shrugs it off.

"And you're completely certain?"

"A woman knows these things about her body."

Frannie gazes intently at me. Her eyes are filled with a haunting light. In her face I envision a future full of structure and mutual dependability, healthy home-cooked meals, bedtime stories, kids' soccer, car pools, an indefinite journey into the heart of the bourgeoisie. "So what do you want to do about it?"

"What do I want to do about it? Are you serious?"

"I only meant…"

She cuts me off. "I know what you meant."

"I was only…"

"You have this endless dissatisfaction, this yearning for something more that is missing, and now that you may finally have something to fill that gap, you're shrinking from it."

I ponder her words. It occurs to me that this missing-something is just an illusion. As soon as one need is filled, a new one will always promptly rise up in its place.

"It's a big shock, that's all. Especially considering the circumstances."

"What circumstances?"

"Come on, Frannie, our relationship isn't exactly on sure footing."

"Certainly not after this conversation."

I mumble to myself: *"What about the guy at the restaurant?"*

"What?"

"What about my work?" I ask in a panic to recover.

She laughs stridently. "Your work? Is that a joke? God damn it, you really are lacking in depth."

"You're right, I'm sorry."

"You know, Lou, in the past I put up with a lot of bullshit from you because at least you never bored me. But now that's just what you are, a bore, a big fucking bore, and have been for some time."

"I can't handle this sort of abuse right now."

Frannie stands up and makes her way to the stairs. Halfway up, she stops and turns to me. "Don't even worry about it," she says. "You'd be a lousy father, anyway."

Chapter

I commit myself to a day of hiking the trails around Malibu. Having left the house in a hurry after my fight with Frannie, I am ill-prepared for it. Instead of hiking boots and shorts, I'm attired in a button-down long-sleeved shirt and tight-fitting jeans. Twenty minutes into my drive, I consider going back to change clothes, but the comfort of my air-conditioned car convinces me I'll manage fine. I smoke cigarettes and sing along to Television's *Marquee Moon* the whole ride out. I pay the ranger five dollars to access the park and he warns me that temperatures will reach the 90s today. The parking lot is full of loose dirt that gets kicked up by the breeze and blown into my eyes. A husband, a wife, their two fair-skinned children, and a golden retriever get out of a Toyota. The wife applies sunscreen to both kids' faces while the father opens the back hatch of the car and retrieves a backpack. The dog is not on a leash but is well-behaved and does not run off. The children both have hiking sticks and they use them as swords against each other when their parents aren't looking. I'm already sweating in the heat and the denim material in my pants is making my crotch chaff. Between two pine trees is a map of the surrounding area, and to its left, a water fountain. I search my car for something to drink out of, and in the backseat I find a Budweiser bottle. I fill it to the top and drink the whole thing, and then fill it again. I consult the map but it makes little sense to me. It's full of topographical lines and hard-to-decipher keys and symbols. After a minute of studying, I give up and put all faith in my instincts.

There are two trailheads in front of me. The one to the right is well-worn and its final destination, a rocky hill sparsely covered in brown shrubs, is visible in the far-off distance. *Why bother taking the journey if you already know how it's going to end?* I ask myself. The trail to the left is overgrown with brush and narrow and the ground is uneven with jagged rocks and other treacherous obstacles. Not more than two hundred yards down the path it bends around a dry creekbed before disappearing around a sheer sandstone cliff. An orange butterfly with black-tipped wings flutters over my head and I chase after it. It leads me off the trail, through a field of tall grass, and up a steep hill with rocky outcroppings. I climb and climb, always keeping the butterfly in my line of sight. I come over a bluff and into a patch of purple and yellow desert flowers. The butterfly stops to rest and I do the same, sitting down atop the flattest stone I can find, drinking water from my Budweiser bottle. A fly hovers around my face and I swat at it with no luck and then it lands on my neck and bites me. In the horizon I spot a red, dome-shaped rock as big as a house balancing precariously atop a much smaller rock. When I stand up again I'm made so uncomfortable from my jeans rubbing my thighs raw that I take them off, sling them over my shoulder, and then press on in my underwear. The trail meanders in a way that makes no sense to me and I decide to bushwhack it, eventually finding myself at the base of a steep rock formation. I finish what is left of my water and then set the bottle down and begin my ascent. Hand over hand I pick my way up the technical climb as if I'd been raised in the valley of the Swiss Alps. When I reach the top, I look down at my legs and they are covered in scratches and bleeding in several spots. I stand at the edge of the cliff and take a piss off the precipice, admiring the expansive views of the Santa Monica Mountains.

On my way back down the mountain, I pass a Cub Scout troop. Their leader, a man who sports short khaki shorts and wears his mustache long and bushy, instructs the kids not to speak to the man not wearing any pants. By the time I reach the parking lot I am badly dehydrated and famished from having spent six hours on the mountain in the high heat without proper preparation. I light a cigarette and collapse in the front seat of my car to nap.

When I wake, it is already nighttime. There are no other cars at the trailhead. A furry spider is crawling across the windshield of my car. All eight of his eyes are staring at me. I start the car and turn the windshield wipers on and he disappears into the desert night. Even late into the evening, the traffic along the Pacific Coast Highway is bad. The shoulder of the street is lined with cars. From the road I can see the beach is peppered with the orange flame of bonfires. At a crosswalk, a drunk guy with no shirt on and an acoustic guitar strapped across his back falls off his skateboard and two of his buddies rush out into traffic to aid him. The rescue has traffic backed up for a mile. It takes me over an hour to get back home.

Before I go in, I sit for a time in my car, parked on the street in front of the house. I know Frannie is home because her metallic-silver Mercedes SUV is parked in the driveway, and I can see through the window the lights of the television flashing all different colors against the back wall of the bedroom.

I feel lost in an utter state of confusion, unable to discern any distinction between hopes and regrets, stuck in an indefinite twilight period where I no longer feel the joys of youth, but have yet to be beset by old age. The clock on my car dashboard reads midnight. I consider driving to Tessa's and then reconsider and contemplate returning to the motel. *But what about the child?* I ask myself. After smoking three cigarettes in succession, I make my move toward the house. There is a note waiting for me on the front door. It reads: "Sleep on the sofa!"

There is a neatly folded blanket and pillow for me on the couch. I lift the pillow to my face and give it a sniff. Remnants of Frannie's vanilla-scented shampoo cling to its case. A wave of gut-wrenching emotion passes through me and I stand there crippled by a combination of tenderness and confusion. I walk from the living room to the kitchen in a daze. It's a struggle just to place one foot in front of the other. I pour myself a whiskey and drink it down. It doesn't feel sufficient, so I pour another and then another and another and so on.

I awake in the morning with Frannie standing over me. She's speaking to me, but I do not understand any of her words. My head is dull and pulsing, and my body is shaking violently. There is a small puddle of blood all around me, and the ground is littered with flower petals. I wonder what has happened: *Am I injured? Is Frannie trying to kill me? Did I attempt suicide?*

I struggle to my feet. Every glass, vase, bottle, and shoe in the house is spread out across the kitchen, overflowing with haphazardly arranged bouquets of both exotic and regional flowers. I turn myself around in a circle to take in the sight. It's the single greatest bounty of pinks and reds and blues and yellows I've ever seen.

"Is this your idea of an apology?" Frannie asks.

"Do you love it?"

"You're impossible," she says, pointing her finger toward the front door. "You need to go outside. The police are waiting to speak to you."

"The police?" I ask. "What for?"

"Go find out for yourself," she says.

It's a terrible struggle to walk. My limbs aren't under the control of my central nervous system. The legs keep splaying out to the side, and I can't manage to coordinate which arm is supposed to swing forward with each step. I stumble from one support object to another. At the front door I'm greeted by two lawmen. One is old and grey and grossly pot-bellied. The other is fresh-faced, with very closely cropped hair and an imperious look in his eyes.

"Good morning, officers. What can I do for you today?"

"You the home owner, sir?" the fresh-faced cop says.

"Yes, officer."

The older cop looks at me questioningly. "We've had complaints from several of your neighbors that their gardens were ransacked during the night. We came out to investigate, and it seems every house within a half-mile radius has been affected but yours. You know why that might be?"

I glance over my shoulder, back into the house. There are several conspicuously ill-placed flower adornments positioned on the ground in the foyer. I step outside and close the door.

"I don't know anything about that. That certainly is odd, though."

"Come see for yourself," the younger officer says, holding his hand over his eyes to shield the sun, looking out toward the closest neighbors' front yard. "The Millers' prize rose bushes are in ruins."

"Hmm..." is all I manage.

"And over there," he says, pointing in the opposite direction. "The MacGregors are devastated over the loss of their hydrangeas."

"They had quite the botanical wonderland over there."

"So you don't have any theories on why someone would destroy all the gardens of all the homes around you, but spare yours?"

An intense bout of nauseas strikes me, and I vomit at everyone's feet. The fresh-faced cop reaches for his gun and the fat cop rushes between us. "Take a walk," he says to the younger cop.

"I'm sorry, officer..." I squint to read the fat cop's nametag, "...Boyles. I've been sick as a dog all morning."

"You mind if we take a look inside?"

"In my house?" I say. "Of course I mind!"

The cop moves closer to the front door. "Sir, if you have nothing to hide, there shouldn't be any reason for you not to let us in."

I move between the door and the cop. "I know my rights," I say. "Now if you'll excuse me, I have a very busy day ahead of me."

"This isn't over. Someone must be held accountable for the

damages."

I open the door enough to slip inside and then poke my head back out. "I hope you catch your crook, gentlemen, but I really must be going."

I move from window to window inside the house, drawing the curtains shut. Peering out, I can see the two men arguing. There is a lot of gesticulation with the hands, culminating in the fatter cop reaching out and removing the gun from the fresh-faced cop's holster. Finally they get back in their squad car and leave the premises.

Frannie is waiting for me in the kitchen. She's got the sternest of faces on. I'm feeling positively jubilant about my victory over the police.

"You don't really think you're going to get away with this?" she says.

I plant a kiss on her mouth, and she bristles. "Those guys aren't going to do anything."

I keep attempting to get close to her but she rebuffs my advances, using the classic football stiff-arm technique. "You really think you outsmarted them?"

"If those men had any intelligence at all, they wouldn't be police officers."

Frannie's face softens and then in an empty, hollow voice she says, "You're already in enough trouble. Why would you do something so foolish?"

"You don't think it was a romantic gesture?"

"You destroyed thousands of dollars' worth of people's property."

"I did it for you."

"You need to get rid of all these flowers."

"Get rid of them?"

She picks up a wine bottle I've stuffed with tulips. "Have you noticed all the bees flying around the house?"

I listen carefully and my ears detect the ominous drone of

buzzing. "You don't know when you have it so well," I say.

She walks out of the kitchen, and I pursue her to the stairs in the living room. She climbs halfway up, looks back over her shoulder, and says, "Olivia is on her way over. We're going to Pilates. I don't want her to see this mess. It's embarrassing."

"Who's Olivia?"

"You can't be serious. We went out to dinner with her and her husband, Doug, at Chaya Venice just a few nights ago. You told them you were 'taking up arms with the Jews against the Arabs.'"

"I don't think I would've said that. Are you sure I didn't say I was going to join the Arabs?"

Her eyes flutter with frustration. "I can't believe you don't remember my friend. You don't make any effort at all."

I stride up the stairs after her, leaping two steps at a time. "What do you call all these flowers? I must've been up all night putting this together."

"You call this an effort?" she sweeps her arm in front of her. "This isn't a man trying to make amends. It's the work of a lunatic! Try taking an interest in my life. That you can't remember my best friend doesn't bode well for us."

"Like you make such an effort? What about *my* best friend?"

She utters an abrupt stiff laugh. "You mean Cliff? Don't you dare compare Olivia to Cliff. Olivia is a sweet person, a good person—a loyal friend. Cliff is an animal."

"You think I give a shit about good hearts and generosity? That's not what interests me in a friend. I'll tell you what I look for: someone who can say something that makes my hair stand on edge, someone who can think something new and different."

"And who does that?"

"Well," I say, "just the other day I met a prostitute who suggested I organize a rally to have an unfit principal removed from her school."

She laughs viciously. "You, an organizer?"

"I could start a revolution."

Her eyes glisten with tears. "Is that where you've been these last few days, shacked up with some prostitute?"

"Don't be so dramatic, Frannie," I say. "I've actually made several friends these last few days."

"Like who?"

"I met a man called Vic. He lost his legs to diabetes, but he tells everyone that they got blown off in Iraq. He wears all these medals and ribbons pinned to his shirt to better solicit money."

"He's in a wheelchair?"

"No. He pushes himself along on a skateboard."

"And what did you and this legless skateboarder do together?"

"For one thing, he unburdened himself about a murder he committed. He also taught me all about how the soul can get separated from the body in death, and how when that happens, both parts are fated to wander alone for eternity."

Frannie's face contorts itself into a sickly expression of revulsion.

"He killed someone?"

"He said he did."

"And you call this man your friend? What's wrong with you?"

"There are certain men for whom any behavior is justified. Vic is such a man. You'd be wrong to consider what he did a crime."

"Do you even hear what you're saying?"

"Frannie, the man has no legs. You can't fathom the hardships he's suffered. Where's your compassion?"

The doorbell chimes.

"That's Olivia. I'm running late, thanks to you," Frannie says. "Go let her in."

I open the door, and Olivia is standing there in full workout attire. I now recall her from the restaurant. She's lost some of the luster I previously associated with her. While her body is impossibly tight and toned, her green eyes look dull and lifeless.

"All ready to go work on your fitness?" I ask.

She smiles and in doing so I can see all the cracks in her heavily applied make-up.

"I'm training for a competition."

"What sort?"

"A bikini contest."

"Oh," I say, holding the door open for her to enter. "That's interesting."

"It's the hardest thing I've ever done. I'm training six days a week, several hours a day."

"I thought Frannie said you were a lawyer."

"Yes, I am. But the new trainer I've hired has me seeing everything in a new light. I'm thinking of going part-time at the office to make more time for other things. Besides, Doug makes enough money for the two of us." She lines herself up in front of the mirror and strikes pose after pose, pursing her lips, popping out her buttocks, pressing her tits forward. She goes through the entire series of positions completely unashamed or self-conscious. "It's really all about self-improvement. I'm trying to be the best version of myself, and that starts with the physical."

"I see your point."

She places her hands under her tits and lifts them toward her chin. "Do you think I would look better with bigger breasts?"

"Bigger breasts?"

"Doug says I'd look better with a D-cup."

I take a pen off the coffee table and write on the inside of my arm: *Even the most successful woman can't be happy with herself unless she's first objectified as a sex object. Being worshipped by men will forever be a woman's most paramount priority, regardless of all else.*

"It's something to consider," I say.

Olivia continues admiring herself in the mirror while I fix myself a drink. Frannie comes down the stairs dressed in her own workout get-up, and the two of them exit out the front door without saying goodbye.

I decide to attempt some writing. The idea of sitting down with my computer and my thoughts is enough to give me a case of the meltdowns. My stomach turns rotten, and I break out in a cold sweat. I return to the whiskey to ease my panic-stricken nerves. I don't bother with a glass, instead taking long pulls straight from the bottle—the whiskey's warm sting soothing my upset stomach. After what must be twelve ounces of whiskey, with my nerves calmed, I seek out my laptop, finding it in the bathroom, under the sink, below a twelve-pack of toilet paper. I go out onto my bedroom's balcony, stand on the railing, sling my laptop onto the roof, and then pull myself up.

The sky directly overhead is a shining blue but there is a cloud of brown hovering over the tops of the buildings downtown, only miles away. I take off my shirt and allow the sun's rays to beat down on my chest. The heat fills my body with a life-affirming energy.

I consider climbing back down into the house to grab a chair, but ultimately decide it would be too much of a struggle to get it onto the roof, and I don't want to waste another moment. Too much time has been wasted already. I sit with my legs dangling off the edge of the roof, the ground below a nearly thirty-foot drop onto rocks and cacti.

Unperturbed by the possibility of death, I open my laptop and find the document labeled, 'book 2.' I read what I've written so far: *God and everything was overthrown—everyone raging in a wild, deranged dance of life.* With such a magnificent first sentence to work from, the possibilities of where my creative genius will lead me are endless. I close my eyes and clear my mind of all distractions, allowing my sub-conscious to take the wheel and steer my ship. In my mind an image comes into focus. It's of a man who finds himself in an exotic and remote land. He's brand-new to this place—his first day, even. He has arrived by prop-plane—a four-seater. This foreign locale is tropical and his clothes are soaked through with sweat. The natives are brown-skinned and scantily clad in brightly colored fabrics. They talk in what vaguely sounds like a derivation of French. Hovering in the air are winged insects, nearly as big as a man's fist. It is clear this man has come for an adventure. Perhaps he's a geologist, a mercenary, or a criminal.

With my eyes closed, I press my fingers to the keyboard. Instinctively, they start to dance. One sentence after another comes pouring out. It's like a dam has been released, and the impending flood is consuming everything in its path. I'm not even remotely aware of what cosmic force is guiding me—no control at all—I'm simply a vessel. My job is simply to hold on and allow this higher power to use me to do its bidding. After an indefinite amount of time, perhaps a minute or an hour or even three hours, my fingers are cramping so badly I am physically unable to continue. Without looking at the screen, I place the computer on the stretch of roof next to me and stand up. The sensation of doing the work you were put on this Earth to do is fulfilling like nothing else. With so much electric energy buzzing through my body, I decide to perform a small exercise routine: twenty jumping jacks, ten lunges on each side, and push-ups till my arms collapse. I fall prostrate to the ground. Lying there, I'm nearly bursting with pride and relief.

It's over, I say to myself, *the writer's block is gone.* I can finally put all this angst and worry behind me, because there are brighter days ahead. Now that I've been blessed once more with my gift, all the secrets of the universe will reveal themselves to me in due time. What to do about Frannie, the baby, and even Tessa no longer seem like problems but welcome challenges that I will face with courage and wisdom.

I open my eyes, sit up, and reach for the computer. The screen is black. I squint. *Perhaps it's just too bright out here,* I tell myself. I pick up the machine and bring it to within inches of my face. No, it's not the contrast of light or the sun's glare—the screen is black. I begin pressing keys indiscriminately, hoping the machine will come alive again. Nothing works. Finally, I try the power button but it too fails to bring my computer to life. I grab the dead object and hop to my feet. I do not bother to climb down from the roof to the patio. Rather, I make the eight-foot descent in a single leap. I race to find an electrical outlet and plug in. The seconds it takes for the computer to restart feel like hours. I scream at the machine as it loads: "Hurry, goddamnit!"

When I finally get the document open I can scarcely stand to look—for I already know what awaits me. Nothing I wrote has been saved. I typed the whole damn thing on a battery-dead computer. I fling the machine across the room and it slams against the wall. The screen comes unhinged from the keyboard and the two computer pieces separate and sail off in opposite directions. I let out a demonic howl of anguish and then sob like an orphaned child.

Amidst all my weeping, a new line of prose comes to me: *I am nature's failed attempt at creating a human being.* I mull it over in my head. It's got a good rhythm and cadence. I say it out loud, first very quietly, and again with more vigor. Soon I'm shouting it at the top of my lungs. I search out a marker and scrawl the words onto the kitchen wall in broken cursive, then step back to admire the view. I sigh deeply in recognition that I must begin anew, once more.

Today's lost efforts have taken a heavy toll on my psyche, and I'm now even suffering physical symptoms. For instance, my mouth is completely dry—sun-bleached, bone-in-the-desert dry. I put my head under the sink and drink from the tap, but the moment I swallow, the mouth is once again made scorched and barren. Furthermore, my left eye seems to have developed a strange malady. Every couple of minutes the lid goes into spasm and opens and shuts repeatedly at fantastic speeds. I go to the mirror and stand there, watching this glitch in human biology repeat itself over and over, each time bringing me to a new and heightened level of neurosis. After several minutes, my state worsens to the point where I'm suffering hallucinations. My image in the glass appears distorted and wavy, as if I were standing in front of a funhouse mirror.

The delusions I'm suffering take me back to the beginning days of my sophomore year in high school. It was an Indian summer, and I had no interest in attending classes. Instead my girlfriend and I would choose a new destination each day and play tourist all over L.A. In the first week of school alone we hit the Getty Museum, Hermosa Beach, West Hollywood, and a Dodgers game. Regardless of whatever else we did in the midst of our blossoming love, nothing made quite the lasting impression as the day we took LSD and attended the Los Angeles County Fair.

This girlfriend of mine was active in the school's theatre department. She did set-design and had keys to the wardrobe closet. On this day we decided to partake in some role-playing for the day's venture. The production they were working on at the time was a stage adaptation of the movie *King Kong*. Once I laid eyes on that monkey suit, there was no taking it away from me. I stripped down right there in the Performing Arts Center, put on the costume, tossed my clothes into a trashcan, and assumed the identity of Hollywood's most infamous primate.

The forty-minute car ride out to Pomona was a treacherous one. The costume's head allowed for no peripheral vision, and the thick padded monkey feet made it difficult to get a good feel for the pedals. The drugs kicked in ten minutes into the drive and I no longer recognized I was operating an actual two-ton steel death machine. Instead, I felt convinced I was a character in a video game. The roadway transformed into the plains of the Serengeti, and the other cars were lions. The object of the game was to make it past all the lions without getting eaten.

While most of that day's activities are now fuzzy in memory, the day's conclusion was unforgettable. It was evening and we were waiting in line for a ride when I got the undeniable impulse to scale the Ferris wheel. Abandoning my girlfriend, I ran from the line, hopped over a metal barrier, and began my ascent. No one noticed at first, as there was fair-chaos all around us. But once I got about thirty feet off the ground I heard screams and shouts. I looked down to see the commotion below. A crowd of hundreds had gathered to witness the scene. I continued to climb up and up. Three quarters of the way to the top the operators stopped the ride. Dozens of people stuck suspended in mid-air due to my stunt. As I passed each Ferris-wheel basket, I let go of my grip with one hand, pounded on my chest, and let out a mighty jungle roar. When I reached the summit I stood atop the ride and reenacted the film's tragic ending for the collection of news-team cameras sent in to document the spectacle. It took the fire department over an hour to rescue me.

The desire to revisit the location of this great triumph is resolute and unwavering. The loss of my day's work seems but a faint, distant memory. I race to my car and take off, dialing Cliff on the phone as I drive. I tell him my plan.

"The fair?" he says. "But I hate clowns!"

"What clowns? There are no clowns at the fair. You're thinking of the circus."

"Are you sure?"

"Nearly positive."

"We need to make a stop on the way. I have a package I need to mail."

From a block away from Cliff's home, I can hear a woman's scream ringing in the air. It sounds as if her very life is at stake. Pulling up to the curb, I see Cliff running down the sidewalk with a package under his arm. He is being chased by a woman wielding a baseball bat. If this is Adrianna, she looks nothing like Cliff described her to me. She is as wide as she is tall, an acne-riddled face, and an awkward stride as bow-legged as a cowboy's.

Cliff sees me and makes a direct line for my car. I open the passenger door and he jumps in just as this crazed woman closes in on him. As we speed off, she throws the bat, striking the back end of the car, smashing a taillight. In the rearview mirror, I watch her as she continues to give chase. She's surprisingly quick for a woman of her size. I blow through the next stop sign to escape her.

"A bit of domestic strife?" I ask.

"We're through."

"What happened?"

"I told her you and I were going out."

"Yeah, so?"

"She overheard me on the phone. She knew it was the fair."

"And..."

"She loves the fair. It's her favorite place in all the world. But I wasn't going to let her come. Out of the question."

"I appreciate that."

"She didn't take it well."

"No?"

"She smashed out the windows of my bedroom with my World Series bat."

"But you realize she's surely in your apartment now. She's going to destroy the place."

"Should I call the cops?"

"It's a thought."

"Forget it."

Cliff busies himself trying to flatten-out the crumpled edges of the package resting in his lap.

"What do you got there?" I ask.

"It's a telescope for my boy," he responds, beaming proudly. "I took Adrianna's iPhone to the pawn shop to try and get back my trophy but they didn't have it so I got this instead."

I park in the post-office lot. A man wearing a letter-carrier's blue outfit exits the store and locks the door behind him. There is a sign in the window that lists the location's hours. It's says they close at six on Wednesdays. The BMW's clock reads 6:04.

"Don't worry about it," Cliff says. "I'll drop it off tomorrow."

The highway is an endless sea of cars stretching out in all directions, every vehicle occupied by only a lone commuter, each driver lost in his own private world of cellphone communication, talk radio, or top 40.

It takes us over forty minutes to reach the fairground. By the time we arrive the air temperature has dropped from a stifling ninety degrees to a most pleasant seventy-five. Soft white clouds blow in the breeze. The sun has nearly completed its steady descent in the west.

We stand at the back of the line to buy our tickets. We're the only grown men without children. All the families look indigent yet well-fed, obese beyond reason. From the oldest grandfather down to the smallest infant, the fair is one enormous fat-farm. My sympathies for the common man come into question. Having always been a staunch social progressive and champion of liberal values, I find myself wondering why I suddenly feel so much contempt for the proletariat. *Look at these folks,* I say to myself, *where is their sense of dignity and self-respect?* A whole class of people devoid of any spark or purpose, mindlessly ambling their way from cradle to grave.

After paying the price of admission, we head directly to a ride called Drop Zone. It's a fairly simple concept: you sit in a chair, get harnessed in, the ride takes you up twenty stories, and then you go into a free-fall death-spiral until a hydraulic marvel of modern technology stops you only inches before hitting the ground and exploding into a thousand pieces.

At the last possible moment before getting tethered to the death machine, Cliff has second thoughts.

"Look at the guy operating the ride," he says.

I observe the man carefully: mid-fifties, nearly toothless, bald on top, scraggily long hair on the sides and back of his head, scabs on his face, and the emaciated figure of a meth junkie.

"Yeah, so?" I reply.

"I guarantee you he's the guy that constructed this ride."

"Have some faith." I strain my eyes to read the junkie's nametag. "I'm sure Val is very competent."

"I'm out," Cliff says, and exits the line.

When it's my turn, the nearly toothless meth junkie sits me next to a girl of about twelve. Her stomach is so large it overflows past the boundaries of the harness. I look down at the excess of fat. The skin is covered in dimples and small brown hairs. I raise my gaze to her face. It's the very image of terror.

"You ever done this before?" I ask.

From her heavy breathing and trembling lips, it's obvious she is teetering on the edge of a breakdown.

"Who are you here with?" I ask.

"Nobody would do the ride with me."

She reaches out her hand and I stare at it, blankly.

"Will you hold it?" she asks.

"Your hand?"

"Please!" she shrieks.

As the machine lifts us toward the heavens, I take her sweaty little paw in mine. My ears fill with the ominous sound of the machine's grinding gears. The view at the top—millions upon millions of twinkling city lights—is the same one I remember from my time spent in the monkey suit atop the Ferris wheel, twenty years before.

"Are we going to die?" the girl asks.

"There's a chance, but it's small," I reply.

She squeezes my hand with a strength that belies her corpulent stature. The pain distracts me from the nervous, sick feeling in my stomach. A quarter falls out of my pocket and I start to count the seconds it takes for it to reach the ground. I don't get to *three* before gravity takes over and we race toward impending death. I open my mouth to scream but the gravitational force on my lungs prevents any sound from escaping.

When we touch down gently, the meth addict unfastens us, and we struggle to stand. The girl collapses into my arms. She reeks of corn dogs and Dr Pepper.

"We're alive!" she says.

A man I take to be her father is giving me the most alarming scowl from the other side of the metal barrier surrounding the ride.

"Yes, we're alive," I say to the girl, "now run along."

She takes off at a brisk waddle, through the gate, and to her father's side. He's a hulking man, heavily mustached and tattooed, with a shaved head and lots of wrinkles and creases down his neck. It's clear he's waiting for me, so I linger back a bit, asking the meth addict inane questions about the ride's thermo-dynamics. But, no, the girl's father is a man of some patience and is waiting me out. As I pass through the turnstile, the man nudges his daughter out of the way and approaches me with a head full of steam.

"Hey, pervert," he shouts at me.

"Pervert?" I say with forced bravado and courage.

"What kind of man goes around hugging little girls?"

He gets right up in my face. So close I can see bits of fried turkey leg in his mustache. I feel that surge of adrenaline one always gets before being punched or punching someone. I squeeze my hands into fists. "What kind of man is so cowardly he makes his little girl ride the Drop Zone by herself?"

The man cocks back to take a swing. Anticipating the punch, I duck. However, I badly mistime my preemption and his fist catches me on the top of the head on my way back up. I fall to the ground, stung but not hurt. The little girl jumps in the way, shielding me from her father's next attack. I scramble to my feet and launch a haphazard punch of my own that is absorbed by the man's swollen abdomen. His little girl screams in protest. The man emits a battle cry, and charges forward. But before he can fire off another shot, Cliff appears from the crowd. The man recognizes him straightaway, abandons his hostility towards me, and gushes all over Cliff. You would've thought this man was meeting the Pope for the reverence he showed him. Cliff signs an autograph and poses for a picture, and we all shake hands and say goodbye like old friends.

"I could've taken that guy," I say to Cliff.

"Whatever you say, Lou. Whatever you say," he says, throwing his arm around my shoulder.

I reach for my cigarettes and say, "I need a beer."

"I can't have one, but I'll hang while you do," Cliff says. "I got the fight tomorrow."

"You're really taking this serious."

"I got no choice. I have to get my kid back."

Inside the beer tent I purchase a cold one, and we sit down on a picnic table. We're surrounded by men with ponytails and no sleeves on their shirts, and women with permed hair and bedazzled jeans.

"I'm proud of you, pal," I say. "I didn't know you had it in you."

"I'm not sure being willing to take a beating is such an admirable thing."

"You're a better man than I."

"I'm just trying to be a father, the only way I can."

"I'm not sure I'll be able to handle it."

"What are you talking about?"

"Frannie thinks she's pregnant."

"Fucking hell, Lou, that's great. Congratulations!"

I take a long drag off my cigarette and watch a man eating a funnel cake pop open his belt buckle and undo the button of his jeans to make more room.

"Yeah, we'll see," I say.

"You're a fool."

"How's that?"

"You think happiness comes from freedom, but you're wrong."

A family of five walks past. The father's arms are filled with carnival-game stuffed-animal prizes. The mother is castigating him for having spent too much money on frivolous activities. Their son, a boy with chubby red cheeks and blond hair, is in hysterics about God knows what. He drops to the ground crying and screaming, kicking his legs, thrashing his arms. The two daughters make repeated calls for more ice cream.

"More than anyone I know, I've resisted the trappings of the adult world: marriage, children, work, taxes, bills, and now you're going to tell me my whole worldview is without merit."

"For as smart as you are, you sure are dumb."

I snuff out my cigarette and finish my beer. "You're being ridiculous. It's so stupid how miserable people always insist on having children. I mean, they hate their lives, so why do they think life will work out any better for their kids?"

"I can't explain. It's just the way it is."

I walk around in circles, making odd guttural noises, smacking my lips, mumbling odd phrases and platitudes to myself, as if I have gone mad. "You're going to feed me this line of bullshit after what you've been through because of your wife and kid?"

"I'd give anything for a chance to start over and do it again."

"Marriage and children?" I scream at Cliff. Everyone in the beer garden stops to witness the spectacle I've become. "I can't sign up for that. You belong to me, and I belong to you? It's bullshit! Nobody belongs to anybody!"

Cliff yanks me by the collar and drags me from the beer garden. The onlookers let out a collective "Boo!" in protest, and I raise my arms in triumph and shout, "Fuck forever!" A smattering of claps and cheers erupts.

"You got it all wrong" Cliff says to me. "You think that marriage-and-kids is like some sort of copout but it ain't. For the more steadfast and righteous, a family is the greatest blessing that can be bestowed upon a man."

"Get the hell away from me!" I shout at him.

Cliff shoves me up against the chain-link fence that surrounds the perimeter of the merry-go-round, puts his hand to my throat, and presses tightly.

"Listen to me," he says. "If Frannie is having your child, you have to make that work. You understand? I lost my boy and you see what it's done to me. You'll never forgive yourself. It's the worst thing that can happen to a man."

"I can't fucking breathe," I say in a strangled whisper.

Cliff lets go of his death grip, turns his back to me, and mumbles something to himself. When he turns back around he says, "Give me a fucking cigarette."

I take out two, hand him one, light his, then mine, and we walk aimlessly. We don't say a word to each other for the longest time. When Cliff finishes his cigarette he flicks it to the ground. "I wasn't going to smoke until after the fight," he says. "But you had to go and get me all worked up."

I finish my smoke and light up another one. "You're the fourth person to try and kill me this week."

"That should tell you something."

I keep walking, finally finding myself in front of the Test Your Strength game. The operator shouts at us, "Step right up! Let's see what you're made of! Who are the men and who are the boys?"

I hand the operator three dollars, place the cigarette between my teeth, pick up the mallet, and strike the machine with everything I can muster. The puck climbs up the length of the tower and stops inches from hitting the bell.

The operator says, "A good try it was, but not good enough. C'mon and try it again. Prove your strength and win a prize!"

I hand the man three more dollars and try again, this time not hitting the lever squarely, and fail to improve on my first attempt. I silently curse myself and hand the mallet back to the operator.

"No stamina at all!" the man says.

Cliff looks at me like he thinks I'm utterly hopeless.

I snatch the mallet out of the operator's hands and slam it down one last time, striking the machine just right, ringing the bell.

"You didn't pay for that!" the operator says. "Cough it up, buddy!"

I take the cigarette from between my teeth and blow out a billowing cloud of smoke, flip the mallet to the ground, and walk away.

I drop Cliff at his apartment and weigh my options: Flophouse or Frannie's? This exercise in decision-making is too taxing to do in my head, so I pull into an Arby's parking lot, get out a pen and paper, and make a pros-and-cons list. There is much to be said on each side of the argument, and I go through three pieces of paper in a matter of minutes. After my list is made I assign a numerical value to each item based on a complicated algorithm I've designed. The results of the experiment are astonishingly improbable—a dead tie! I decide to start a new list with a couple minor tweaks to the formula. Forty-five minutes into the exercise, I stop for a break and go inside and purchase a #3 Combo Meal: Roast-beef and cheddar sandwich, curly fries, Mountain Dew. I sit at a table near the back of the restaurant and continue to scribble equations while eating my dinner.

A boy with a flat nose and foggy black eyes sits down with his mother at the table next to mine. The woman's got floppy, greying locks of hair, crinkled eyes and thin, tight lips. She closes her eyes and holds the boy's hand and declares her gratitude to Jesus. Halfway through her blessing, I finish counting up my new tally and it's another tie. I scream out, "You rat bastard!"

The woman scowls at me before going back to her *amens*. The boy intently watches me. When his mother finishes, he addresses me directly: "Mister, what are you scribbling?"

"I'm trying to make a big decision."

"But what are you deciding?"

"The fate of the world, of course."

The boy takes a bite of his sandwich and bits of roast beef fall out of his mouth. "You get to decide the fate of the world?"

"Of course. We all do, each and every one of us."

"I don't understand," he says. "There is only one world and each of us is so small."

I look up from my work and lock eyes with the boy. He's holding his pointer-finger and thumb very close together.

"You're wrong," I say. "Each of us is the center of our own universe. And without *us* calling the shots, everything would cease to exist. It's a privilege and a tremendous responsibility."

The boy's mother turns to face me. She appears disheveled, nearly broken. "Sir, my son is only a child. Please refrain from filling his head with such ideas. What happens to each of us in this life is God's will."

When the mother returns to her food the boy steals a last glance at me. His mouth is ajar and his eyes are wide and burning. I wink at him, and he smiles in return.

My phone rings. The display reads: "Tessa (recovering model)."

"Hello, lovely," I say.

"Come pick me up. I have a surprise for you."

"Last time someone said that to me, I ended up at church."

"Please, please, please," she says.

I check my "Flophouse or Frannie" list one more time, and a heavy burden settles into the pit of my stomach. I crumple the paper into a little ball and, like morning dew in midday sun, the burden evaporates.

"I'm on my way," I say, and hang up the phone.

I arrive at her apartment and ring the bell. A skinny black man with a neatly groomed mustache, dressed in short denim shorts and a brightly colored vest with no shirt underneath, answers the door.

I check the address again. "I'm looking for Tessa," I say.

The man gestures for me to come in with a facial tic that looks like Tourette's.

Tessa is sitting on a couch with her kitten perched on one knee. Next to her is a chubby, pale fellow with shoulder-length, thinning blond hair. The man is making adjustments to a video camera he is holding in his lap. Tessa jumps up, throws her arms around me, and kisses me on the mouth. She tastes like peppermint gum and vodka.

"What's going on?" I ask her. "It looks like you're setting up for a porno shoot."

She throws her head back and laughs. "You're not a prude, are you, Lou?"

Uncertain of her true intentions, I begin to take off my shirt.

"Jesus, Lou, I'm only kidding," she says. "This is my friend Norman." She reaches over and touches on the arm the guy with the camera. "And over there is Legz." The tall black man bares his teeth at me and makes an uneasy growling sound.

"Norman and Legz?"

"Legz is a painter," Tessa says. "He's got his first big gallery show tomorrow."

"Is that right?" I say. "Good for you, Legz."

"Legz wants to make some last-minute changes to his exhibit," Tessa says. "You mind driving us over there?" She pats me on the leg and kisses me on the cheek. "It'll be great—I promise you'll love it."

Tessa puts out a bowl of milk for the kitten and locks the apartment door behind us. The four of us climb into the BMW— Tessa up front and the two fellows in back. Sitting at a stoplight,

I sense something distinctly sour and rotten in the air. My eyes water and my nose runs. I open the window but it offers no relief.

"What the fuck is that?" I ask.

Tessa sniffs around and says, "It smells like a combination of dead fish and feet."

"But where is it coming from?"

I check my rearview mirror. Legz and Norman have both popped the tops off of Tupperware containers full of kimchee.

"Are you guys fucking insane?" I shout at them.

Neither acknowledges my plea. Instead they continue shoveling days-old stink cabbage into their mouths. I reach back and snatch the chopsticks out of Norman's hand and throw them out the window.

His eyes radiate with the pain of injustice. "What gives?"

"You can't eat that shit in my car."

"Why the hell not?"

I turn to Tessa. "Do I really need to be driving these assholes around?"

Norman sticks his fingers into the container and lifts a handful into his open mouth. "Why don't you try showing a little bit of respect for five thousand years of Korean culture," he says.

At the next light I engage in a tug-of-war match with Norman for the Tupperware container. When the light turns green, I'm still half in the backseat. The cars behind me commence with a symphony of horn-honking.

"Just drive the car!" Tessa shouts.

"Yeah, just drive the car, you nut!" Norman says.

I climb back into the front seat and continue to tool the car down the road.

"Some authorities credit Kimchi with helping stop the spread of disease," Tess says, "including SARS."

I bang on the steering wheel with my fists. "Fuck all of you!" I say.

My childlike temper tantrum incites Tessa and Norman into a

fit of laughter. Legz doesn't express any recognition of anything happening around him. Instead he stares blankly at the seat in front of him.

"Hey, Legz," I call to him. "You still with us?"

He doesn't stir.

"What's with him?" I ask Tessa.

Her mouth twists into a lopsided frown. "He's pretty far-on-the-spectrum, anti-social, you know."

My gaze drifts back to the rearview mirror to take another look. He's got his eyes rolled back into his head, and he's chewing ferociously on his lips.

We park in front of the gallery and Norman readies his video camera. Legz surreptitiously loads a few items into a bag, and throws it over his shoulder. The gallery owner greets us at the entrance. She plants a kiss on each of Legz's cheeks, and he stands there, still as a statue.

"Legz wanted to come down and see how everything is going," Tessa says. "He's so excited!"

"Yes. Please come in," the owner says. "Have a look around."

Legz forces something halfway between a smirk and the wounded countenance of a man who a great crime has been committed against.

The gallery is alive with workers preparing for the show. Everywhere I turn, there is a guy on a ladder making adjustments to a light installation, or a woman repositioning a sculpture. They all appear very serious about the work, as if they were curing cancer or fighting a war. The gallery owner links arms with Legz and gives us the tour. Tessa and I trail close behind, and Norman brings up the rear, filming us.

A man, as small as a child, dressed in head-to-toe black couture, races over and whispers something into the gallery-owner's ear. She pinches the bridge of her nose like she's warding off a headache. The man whispers to her again, and this time she unleashes a barrage of obscenities at him. He skulks off after receiving his comeuppance.

"It's so hard to find good people," the gallery owner says. "I'm so sorry, but do you mind if I leave you to it?"

Legz grunts, and the woman takes off after her assistant. Legz pushes ahead with absolute purpose, and we follow him like the disciples of a new messiah. He stops in front of a series of three grand canvases—abstract portraits composed of thick and colorful diffuse lines.

"These are Legz's," Tessa says, beaming like a proud mamma. "He's redefining what new-wave contemporary painting is all about."

I scratch my head. "Uh-huh," I say.

"Tell me what you think of them."

Norman is filming me, and Legz is staring intently at the paintings. There are small tears rolling down his cheeks.

"I like the colors," I say hesitantly, feeling wholly stupid.

Tessa scratches her chin while thinking carefully. After a minute of consideration, she says, "I think the mish-mash conglomeration of figureheads and mixed-signal facial features exude a most concrete sense of self and introspection."

"You do?" I ask.

She holds onto my elbow and leads me up to the painting.

"See this here?" she says. She points to a rough part on one of the canvasses that has been sanded down to give it a certain tactile quality. I press up real close to the painting, and then reach out my hand and touch the work. The paint is thick and soft and gives way under my touch. I leave a fingerprint on the portrait's chin. Out of the corner of my eye I look to see if Tessa has noticed, but she hasn't. Her gaze is fixed, like the painting has the gravitational pull of the sun. I exhale a deep breath, thinking I've gotten away with it.

A hand seizes me by the shoulder and yanks me backwards. I stumble over my own feet and hit the floor. I look up and Legz is attacking his paintings with a can of black spraypaint in each hand. For two minutes he sprays, covering every square inch of the canvas under a blanket of black. Nobody tries to stop him. We stay exactly where we are, as if rooted to the ground. When he finishes his destruction, he takes three steps back, turns around, and collapses onto the ground next to me. Norman stands over us pointing his video camera into our faces. I stand up and scurry away to get out of the shot. Legz assumes the fetal position and weeps with the savage intensity of a grieving widow. The magnitude of Legz's violent act has swallowed all the air in the room, making it nearly impossible to breathe. Tessa bends down and puts a comforting hand on Legz's head and strokes his hair.

"It's okay, honey," she says. "It's going to be all right."

He lets loose a maddened and abrupt shriek. It fills the museum's halls, escalating the tension. She continues to rub his head, back, and shoulders.

"You've done a wonderful thing. You're a genius," she says.

There is drool running down his face and off his chin. It collects in a puddle on the collar of his shirt. He makes primal grunting noises. Norman stands over him with the camera, documenting the whole thing.

I approach one of the paintings. The black paint is wet, and smells of noxious chemicals. I touch it again. The tip of my finger turns black. I turn around and hold the finger in the air. Norman points the camera at me. There are no words. It's like walking amongst the rubble in the aftermath of a tornado.

The gallery owner approaches with her mouth wide open, her eyes bugged, and her head twitching involuntarily. She walks right past Norman, Tessa, and Legz, and goes straight for the paintings. Her body convulses and trembles. It appears she's going to shriek but not a sound escapes her.

She points an accusatory finger at Legz. "You're a monster! Do you understand me? You've ruined yourself, and you've cost me a fortune!"

Legz smiles a big hokey grin. Tessa's face illuminates like a thousand rays of light. Norman is still filming.

"These paintings were to be auctioned tomorrow," the gallery owner continues. "Based on interest we've already received for the work, we were estimating to get between twenty to thirty thousand dollars apiece for these paintings."

"Holy shit!" Norman mumbles from behind his camera.

The gallery owner gets in Legz's face. "This stunt is going to cost me big-time," she says. "How are we going to recoup my costs? And be certain: you *will* help me recoup my costs—you're under goddamn contract!"

"Don't' you get it?" Tessa asks the gallery owner. "We have this whole thing on video. It's conceptual art. We can project the film onto a screen next to the paintings during the show tomorrow. It'll shake the art world to its very core."

The gallery owner holds her hands up in front of her face, creating a frame through which to view the destroyed pictures. "You'd better be right, or I'll come after all of you. You're all accomplices—all culpable."

The gallery owner slaps Legz's face as she walks past him.

"We did it!" Tessa shouts.

Legz sits Indian-style on the ground, removes a red marker from his pocket, and sketches a picture of a dinosaur in a spacesuit on the gallery's floor.

An hour later Tessa and I sit outside her apartment in my car. It's my first time to Silverlake in many years. In my twenties I used to go there to buy cocaine from Mexican gang members. Most of the pawnshops that used to line her block are now closed. In their place are hipster dive bars and boutique clothing stores. Only one of the taco shops in the area has survived. A group of white college-aged kids dressed like they play in rock bands stand out front eating burritos and nachos.

My mind is overflowing with things I'd like to say: confessions, promises, passions, fears. But I remain reticent, not sure of the right course of action. One false move and I might lose it all.

Every man has a buried nature that life tries to whip and tame away until it is all but dead. Yet if people are lucky and brave, sometimes they meet another who has a similar nature, and that gives them a chance to be happy and strong. Being with this woman I've only just met, I feel my life entangled with hers, a desire to take her in my arms and pour myself out to her. I'm nearly certain I once harbored similar feelings for Frannie, but the memory of that connection is so distant I can't even form the image of it in my head. It's like waking in the morning with the sense that deep in sleep you had a most wonderful dream, but for all your efforts you can't conjure a single detail of it.

I close my eyes and concentrate on memorizing the following sentence: *Guilt, a most horrible burden, but perhaps one's last connection to a lost humanity.*

When I open my eyes, Tessa is staring at me all tender and hopeful. To me it sounds as though there are notes of piano music floating through the air. Afraid I'll say something ill-conceived, souring things between us so completely that I'll never see her again, I remain silent. Instead I make a mental rendering of her blistering swirls of disheveled red hair, her heavy-lidded green eyes that make her appear half asleep, and the light dusting of freckles across her delicate nose. I want to be able to recall her appearance in perfect specificity for as long as I live.

"Did you enjoy yourself tonight?" she asks.

I compel myself to smile, not wanting to admit I'm already harboring feelings of love for her.

"I was thinking about Legz destroying his paintings," I say.

"Cheap stunt or bold artistic statement?"

My first instinct is to err on the side of cheap stunt. It was a cowardly move. Legz didn't have the faith or confidence to stand up to the scrutiny of critics. Myself, I have no idea whether his work is any good. As my affinity for the painting of the master and his dog proves, my predilections when it comes to visual art tend toward the sentimental and obvious. However, I'm sure Legz *does* know if his work is any good, and his actions demonstrate an overarching insecurity about his talents. But before I voice this opinion, I reconsider. Perhaps it's not at all cowardly—rather the opposite: the boldest, most courageous act on record. A man willing to completely break ties with everything he's worked for. What could be more gallant? I wonder whether I could potentially find a similar strength in myself. The audacity it must take to wipe all slates clean and begin anew is inspiring.

"Legz may be the most noble and exalted individual I've ever come across."

"I'm glad you think so," she says.

"I'm not sure I do, but he may be."

"I'm afraid I may have ruined him."

"So that was your idea?"

"People have been making paintings for thousands of years. They're dull. I wanted to try something new."

"You're insane," I say. "Tell me something more about yourself."

"I'd prefer to stay on more useful subjects."

"You never answered Emma's question about your unique talent."

"I was telling the truth when I said I didn't have one."

"What is it that you've loved more dearly than anything else in this world?"

"There is one thing," she says. "When I was a small child my mother enrolled my older sister and me in piano lessons. My sister hated it more than anything. She had to be bribed with treats in order to get her to practice. But I loved it—couldn't get enough. Every free moment, I'd spend at the piano—morning, noon, and night. I drove the rest of the family crazy with my playing. There was no escaping it in our house.

"The first three years of my playing were pure magic. Nothing made me happier, and as I improved, the enjoyment I received from my efforts only increased. And since I was only a child, I received nothing but encouragement from my instructor. But perhaps the best part about it was that I was so much *better* than my sister. You wouldn't know it now, but I used to possess a real competitive streak. I was obsessed with being the best. And since the only person I had to compare myself to was my sister, I was dead-certain I was on my way to becoming a master—a real virtuoso!

"However, the good feelings were fleeting. When I turned thirteen I convinced my parents to send me to a sleepover piano camp for a month during the summer. There I met kids with real talent—prodigies, if you will. At first I was devastated, couldn't believe how much better they were than me. But then I decided that if I worked hard enough I could catch up, that I could be as good as anyone. So that's what I did. I spent my thirteenth year on this planet completely devoted to piano. I was entirely determined to show up at camp that next summer and blow everyone away. Well, guess what happened when I went back? Even for all the gains that I had made, the other kids had made even bigger gains. Not only was I not the best, I was now one of the *worst* kids in the group. After that experience, I gave it up completely."

"That's horrible!" I say. "I'm so sorry."

"Don't feel bad. I've made my peace with it. That said, I think I still do have a bit of an obsession with greatness. Perhaps that's why I'm so attracted to people like you and Legz. It's not nice to say, but I find ordinary people terribly boring."

Tessa still seems to be in good cheer despite the tragic nature of her story.

"So, tell me the truth," she continues. "Why are you really staying in that motel?"

"It's complicated."

"Are you happy?"

"I'm not sure I've ever been happy," I reply. "I think the best I've ever been was half-happy—like I was on the road to happy, and got lost along the way. I've never been able to figure out what that missing something is." My mind wanders momentarily, finding itself fixated on the prospect of my impending child. And then before I can stop myself, I ask, "What do you think of kids? Do you think you want them?"

I feel my face blush in response to this ill-timed question.

"Well, yeah, I think so. I suppose I always figured I'd end up having children. I think I'd be a good mom." She smiles faintly. "What about you?"

"I didn't used to think I ever wanted kids. My father was a piece of shit and I figured it was just as well if his bloodline ended with me." Seeing the saddened look on her face, I feel a mandate to repudiate my statement. "But now, who knows?" Even as the words are escaping my mouth, I'm aware of just how awful a person I am, yet I can't manage to bring myself to stop. "It might do me some good to put something or someone in front of myself."

Tessa smiles coyly and reaches for the handle of the passenger door.

"Come on, let's go inside," she says.

"Wait," I say. "It's not a good night for me."

"Are you sure?" she asks, looking equal parts confused and injured.

"Yes, I'm very sorry. We'll talk soon, okay?"

She leaves me without a kiss or a hug.

My conversations with Cliff and Tessa about children have left me feeling wretched. I decide it's time I head home and face my responsibilities. As I drive, I give myself a pep-talk: "Cliff is right. Frannie is to be my wife and together we will raise a child. If it's a boy we will call him Henry, and if it's a girl, Aida." This revelation sits heavy in the pit of my stomach, and I feel a desperate urge for a drink. I drive to the nearest gas station, go inside, purchase a tall can of beer, and sit in my car and drink it.

I remember the painting I left at the motel and turn around for it. Fifteen minutes later I'm back, deep in the ghetto. The motel's sign has been knocked down by a runaway Oldsmobile. The driver has abandoned the car on the sidewalk, its front end crumpled from the impact. The pole hoisting the sign is angled at forty-five degrees, leaning against the side of the motel, fifteen feet above the ground. A teenage girl watches with nervous anticipation as her boyfriend traverses the sign like a tightrope. When he reaches the top she claps her hands and cheers gleefully. I stroll across the parking lot, kicking a malt-liquor bottle, wondering if there is any bravery left in me.

The Pakistani man is not at the desk. I ring the bell. Nothing. The TV is turned on to soccer again, this time to one of the Mexican-league games. It's the sixtieth minute, neither team has scored, but the commentators are shouting with wild, agitated voices. I lean over the desk and turn off the television. Without the background noise of the game, I can hear the choked whimpering of a small child. I cup my hand over my ear to get a better listen. I'm nearly certain I've never heard a more tragic cry, and I feel compelled to check on the wellbeing of whatever it is that is making the noise.

I slink past the swinging partition next to the desk and creep my way toward the motel's back office. The closer I get to the noise, the more anguished the sound becomes. I prepare myself for a terrible, treacherous scene—images of an emaciated and beaten, naked child, shackled and caged, dance through my head.

I peek around the doorway. The Pakistani has his head thrown back in tantric ecstasy, sweating profusely. His pants are down around his ankles, and his legs are covered in thick black, curly hairs. Emma is between his legs, on her knees, with her mouth full of his cock. Her head bobs up and down with the weight of the man's heavy belly resting on the top of her skull.

"My God!" I shout, covering my eyes with my hands. "I'm sorry, I'm so sorry!"

The startled man bucks his hips into Emma's face and she falls over backwards with her legs in the air, exposing her full bush.

"Get out, get out now!" the man shouts at me.

I dart from the room, seeking sanctuary on the far side of the lobby's front desk. A minute later, the man appears. He is panting hard and is red-faced. "What the hell do you want?" he says to me.

"I want to check out," I say.

Emma is still adjusting the shoulder straps of her dress as she enters the room. Her hair and make-up are a mess.

The man runs my credit card.

"Here, sign this, and then go!"

I pick up a pen, chained to the desk. "I still need to retrieve my things."

"Fine," the man says. "Hurry up and get them, then get out."

I sign the receipt, push it across the desk to him, and then go for the exit. Emma follows close behind.

Out in the parking lot, she takes a bottle of mouthwash from her purse and rinses vigorously before spitting up on the ground. She then retrieves a container of baby wipes, reaches up under her skirt, and cleans the affected areas.

"There—all better, good as new," she says. "So you're leaving this dump?"

I smile and nod and she interlocks her arm around mine, and we continue up to my room. She sets her purse on the table and pours two whiskeys. She hands me one and we clink cups.

"Upward and onward," she says.

"Hear hear," I reply. I tip my head back, letting all the whiskey drain down my throat in one long go.

I pour myself another and hold the bottle out to Emma, but she declines. Instead she takes out her make-up and mirror and does touchup work to her face. She has a badly battered and swollen eye.

"What happened there?"

She finishes her maintenance and snaps the compact shut. "It's nothing, an occupational hazard. The important thing is I look beautiful again."

"You certainly do," I say, raising my cup to salute her.

"I'm sorry you had to witness that back there."

"I've seen worse."

"It's not so bad. He lets me stay here and do my business."

I nod along, as if what she is saying is all commonplace and not at all upsetting. "If you ever need anything, I mean anything at all, please don't hesitate to call."

"Sure, honey, it's okay."

"No, I'm serious," I say. "Put my number in your phone."

She finishes her drink and pours another. "I don't want to make my troubles your troubles."

I snatch her purse off the bed and start digging. Inside I find booze, condoms, panties, mints, cigarettes, mace, a dildo, and finally her cell. It's of the flip-phone variety and there is a unicorn sticker pasted to its exterior. I pop it open but the battery is dead.

I take the pen from the nightstand and hunt for a piece of paper.

"You really mean it that I can call you?" she asks.

"Help me find something to write on."

She opens up the drawer of the nightstand, picks up the Bible, and tears out a sheet of scripture.

"Here," she says.

The page is from Romans 12:2. *Do not conform to the pattern of this world, but be transformed by the renewing of your mind. Then you will be able to test and approve what God's will is—his good, pleasing and perfect will.*

I scribble my name and number and hand it back to her. She

reads the passage, folds up the paper, and places it in her bag.

"Where's Tessa?" she asks.

I go to the window, open it slightly, and light a cigarette. "I'm not sure I'll see her again."

She joins me at the window. I take out a second cigarette and hand it to her. When she presses it between her lips, I light it. "I think that would be a big mistake. You seemed so much happier when you were with her than when I met you the first time."

I gaze fixedly at the sky. "Yes, that's true."

"You shouldn't be so serious. You need to learn to see the humor in things. Being able to laugh at life can sustain you for years."

"I don't think humor has ever saved anyone," I say.

"You're wrong. There's only two things you need to possess to succeed in this life: bravery and knowing how to laugh."

"Perhaps."

When she speaks again, there is no trace of the arcane foreign accent she's always previously spoken with. Instead, she sounds like a girl from the valley. "Save all the self-pity. Things aren't so bad. Look out there." She points through the window. "Those are palm trees. How can anyone be upset when there are palm trees around? When I was a kid, my daddy taught me how to climb them. It was my favorite thing we did together. The way you do it is you hop up the tree like a frog. The trick is to get your legs perpendicular to your body so you're crouched down real low and you jump up and grab the tree with your hands and feet at the same time."

"What are you talking about? I thought you were from—"

"Don't interrupt me, honey, I haven't gotten to the important part yet. What I'm trying to say is there is goodness all around you."

"How can you say that?"

"Oh, you stop that talk. There were times in my life that I thought that way. In fact, there have been times when I thought all the happiness in the world was gone forever. But I'm way past that now. Now I can see goodness everywhere."

"Everywhere?"

"I recognize it in everything."

I can feel the warmth radiating from her. In her presence all the problems of the world seem to disappear.

"I'm confused. Did you really lose your husband?"

Her accent reappears.

"Of course, honey."

"And the dancing?"

"It's all true. I'm a wonderful dancer. You've seen it yourself, and I have the world's most beautiful body, too."

She breaks out into loud squealing laughter, the type that can't be stopped, and causes one to lose one's breath. She hunches over and places her head between her legs, in order to recover.

The front door swings open and the Pakistani man who runs the place is standing in the doorway with his arms folded. "You said you needed to collect your things. Get them and get out," he says with heavy, thick veins throbbing from his forehead and throat.

I take my painting off the wall, put it under my arm, take a swig from the whiskey bottle, and pick up my suitcase.

"I'll see you around, honey," Emma says to me.

The man moves out of the doorway and lets me pass. I make my way to the car. The sounds of Emma and the hotel proprietor screaming at each other fills the air.

Chapter

Frannie's silhouette is illuminated in the upstairs window before the lights go out. I park the car and then lug my suitcase and painting into the house, up the stairs, and into the bedroom. I lay them on the floor, next to the bed. Frannie rolls onto her side, facing away from me, pretending to be asleep. I decide to play along with her charade. As quietly and gently as I can manage I crawl into the bed next to her.

I whisper to her. "Frannie, baby, I'm home."

No response. She continues to feign sleep, but she's no good at it. Her breathing is far too quick and labored for a sleeping person. I peek under the covers and see that she is wearing the slightest of garments—a white, silk sleeping shirt. I delicately run my hand from her bare shoulder, down her side, slowing my pace around the curve of her breast and then continue down to the small of her back, where my fingers lightly trace the contour of her bowing body. She arches forward and gasps for breath, before I proceed south on my journey, only stopping once I've finally reach naked flesh again, at that mystical intersection where ass meets leg. There I pause and give the area a few sweet pets, exploring the terrain. Frannie pushes her backside into me, as she parts her legs enough for me to slide my hand between. Atop her underwear, I run my fingers over her, periodically stopping to apply pressure in a circular, swooping motion. I do this process very slowly, so as to continue the farce that she is asleep. But her breathing continues to become heavier and more urgent. When she reaches the point where she can no longer pretend to be unaware of what's going on, I relent, simply resting my hand over her soaked-through panties. She begins to stir, rocking uneasily, applying more pressure on my hand so that it pushes harder against her. I slip off my pants and underwear and press my cock against her. She rolls over slightly and spreads her legs like the hands of a clock, all the while keeping her eyes tightly closed. I push her underwear to the side and slide two fingers inside. She emits a low, throaty sigh, and I wriggle her underwear down her legs. She lifts her hips to aid me in my endeavor. I slide the panties off of one leg, leaving them dangling around the ankle of the other, and then push her legs further apart and enter her.

She opens her eyes lethargically, in a state of pretend drowsiness.

"What are you doing?" she says. "I'm trying to sleep."

I ignore her question and increase my pace.

"I don't want to do this right now," she says between moans.

A passion best described as a complete surrendering of control enthralls me.

"I told you I don't want to do this right now," she says, taking my fingers and placing them into her mouth—sucking away at them. "Please, Lou, we shouldn't."

I ignore her pleas, stabbing her again and again.

In between carnal, lascivious cries, she's now almost begging, "We can't, we really shouldn't. I hate you, Lou, I hate you!"

I fold her right leg back so that her foot is over and behind her head and press myself flat against her, thrusting with all the force I can summon. She abandons her objections and calls out: "Don't stop, please, don't stop, I'm coming, oh God, I'm coming!" And when her supplications slow, I allow myself to release, and everything I have stored inside of me flows out the end of my cock and into her.

We lie there covered in sweat, silent, except for the sounds of our heavy breathing. My dick is still three-quarters hard when I pull out of her and roll over onto my back.

"Go get me a towel," she says.

"Give me a second to cool down."

She gives me a fierce shove and I roll off the bed.

"I want the towel now," she says. She is so angry, she is

shaking.

I get up and fetch a hand towel from the bathroom and bring it back to the bedroom. She snatches it from me and places it between her legs, then stands up and walks to the bathroom. I lie on my back and listen as she runs the shower. There is the faint sound of weeping. She stays in there for a long time, and I have to make a concerted effort not to fall asleep. When she comes out of the bathroom I ask her why she is so angry. She says, "Not now, I'm tired." She climbs under the covers and moves to the far side of the bed. I try to spoon her but she brushes my arm away. I'm too tired to press the issue and fall asleep.

When I wake, it's already morning and she has gone to work.

Frannie and I talk briefly on the phone as she is driving home from work. She doesn't remember last night's sexual encounter at all like I do. She says I revel in the degradation of women. I tell her she is wrong. She insists I'm an animal. I counter by saying that women find nothing sexier than a man who engages in his own selfish, reckless pleasure. She says she wants us to see a counselor. I agree without thinking it over because I'm running late to Cliff's fight.

Frannie is coming in the front door as I'm heading out. She has a scarf on her head and is wearing oversized sunglasses.

"Where are you going in such a hurry?" she asks.

"Cliff's fight is tonight."

"What fight?"

"I don't have time to explain."

"But we need to talk."

"About what?"

"About what happened last night."

"Can it wait?"

"Can it *wait*?" she says. "You practically raped me, and now you're going to ask me if I can wait to talk about it?"

"Rape?" I say with a laugh. "You've got to be kidding me."

"You started fondling me while I was asleep and then you rammed your prick into me, even though I specifically said no."

I laugh at what I think must be a joke. "You have that wild, tortured look in your eyes."

Frannie is gritting her teeth. "You're a monster, you know that? You just take whatever you want with no thought of how it affects anyone else."

"What's so wrong with a man desiring his fiancé? I mean, Jesus Christ, isn't that why we got together in the first place? You always complained that your ex wasn't sexual enough. That you didn't feel desired. That there was no animalistic longing, and how you wanted to be ravaged, but that he wasn't up for it. That with him, everything was tender and gentle, and how tedious that became for you."

"At least he respected me."

"Is that what you're looking for during sex—respect?"

"I want to at least share in the delight of sex with my partner. I don't want to be attacked like an animal in the Serengeti. Do you even care about my satisfaction?"

"Do I care? Of course I care," I say, almost sputtering.

"You care only as far as it feeds your ego to have a wonderful sexual prowess. Making a woman come is like a badge of honor for you."

I place a hand to her cheek, and she smacks it away.

"You knew who I was when you took up with me," I say. "In fact, you had the benefit of having read my book. If only every person you might get into a relationship with came with such a thing. I can't even imagine. To have a guidebook to the inner workings of your partner's mind—wow, you really are blessed!"

"That was a book. This is real life! Can't you see the difference?"

"It may be a book to you, but that's my life. I've been trying hard to be a good man for you. Can't you see that? But I am who I am. I'm not just some snake who can slither out of his own skin."

She takes off the scarf and sunglasses. Her eyes are red and puffy. "You're a snake, all right," she says.

"I'll go to therapy, whatever you want, but right now I have to leave."

"Do whatever you want. You always do," she says. "It's fine. I'm going out too."

"With who?"

She digs through her purse, retrieves her phone, and types out a text. When finished, she looks up and says, "No one you'd know."

I reach for my cigarettes and light one up. A string of vitriolic insults take form in my mind. But instead of escalating the situation, I open the front door and walk out.

All the cars sharing the freeway are moving at a harmonious eighty miles per hour. The vibrant orange and pink of the toxins in the air make for the best sunsets. I fire up a cigarette and roll down the window. The air pollution makes my cigarette taste funny. Along the 10-freeway, there is a billboard with the faces of two menacing black men on it. It's an advertisement for the main event of tonight's fights. Traffic slows only once, where a car is stalled on the road's shoulder. The marooned vehicle is a classic convertible Jaguar. From its hood, orange flames shoot six feet into the air. A thick cloud of black smoke floats up into the atmosphere. The car's owner paces along the freeway's guardrail, making agitated arm movements as he talks into his cellphone.

Tonight's fight is at the Grand Olympic Auditorium. Back in the '30s, '40s, and '50s the venue hosted the boxing greats of the day, and all the Hollywood stars and starlets would take their seats in the front rows, place their bets, drink their whiskey, and scream their surly taunts at the fighters.

In the '80s, the place fell into disrepair and could no longer attract the premium events. Instead, it hosted weekend professional-wrestling matches and roller derbies. We snuck in once as kids to watch Andre the Giant take on King Kahn the Mongolian Nightmare. We sat high up in the cheap seats smoking cigars we'd stolen from the local convenience store, and cheered for the Giant to take the arms off the foreign invader.

Years ago I heard rumors they were knocking down the old place, but it remains unchanged from my youth: a rectangular, five-story brown building with few windows that looks every bit like a factory or industrial warehouse. The parking lot is less than half full. I park next to a car of young Mexican men. They each have heavily tattooed arms and necks. Loud Tejano music blares from fuzzy-sounding speakers. The men sit on the hood of the car, drinking malt liquor from glass bottles.

"Viva Cliff Adams," I say to them.

"We love Cliff Adams," one of the men says. "But I'm afraid he's in over his head tonight, amigo."

"If I were you, I'd bet it all on him."

"Oh yeah," the man says. "¿Por que?"

"I just got a good feeling about him."

I light a cigarette and walk to the ticket office.

"I'm picking up my ticket," I say to the woman behind the plexi-glass window. "The name is Lou Brown."

She searches through a box, stopping at a manila envelope with my name on it. "May I see some I.D., sir?" she asks.

I show her my driver's license. She eyes it carefully. In person I look a good ten years older than in the picture. "It's me, I swear it."

"Here you go," she says, handing me back the driver's license along with the ticket. "Mr. Adams left a note for you. He wants to see you before his fight."

I enter the auditorium on the ground floor. There are no people in the expensive seats that surround the ring, only people up above in the balcony. A man in a blue shirt and a black cap stands in the ring, using a wrench to make adjustments to the turnstiles and ropes. A team of judges dressed in sharp suits sit at a table ringside, shuffling papers and speaking to each other in self-conscious voices like people on trains and buses do when they know strangers can hear them. A security guard leans against the wall, drinking a soda.

"How do I get to the dressing room?" I ask the security guard.

He points to an unmarked door on the far side of the auditorium. I enter a long white hallway lit up with the wan light of fluorescent tubes. Every sound I make echoes against the cavernous walls of the corridor. There is a black door with a piece of duct tape stuck to it. Cliff's name is spelled out in black marker. I knock once and Cliff opens the door. He wears the look of a gladiator—hard and humorless.

The room only has two items in it: a wood bench and an iron tub. His trainer—an old white man with droopy, wet eyes and a badly wrinkled face—stands in the corner going through his supplies.

"Good to see you, pal," I say to Cliff.

"I don't want to talk," he says. "I just want you to keep me company."

He sits down in a chair in the corner of the room and takes out a Bible. He reads to himself, quietly mumbling the words. The vibe in the air has the same grim quality as that of a hospice. Cliff closes the Bible and sets it in a black duffle bag under his chair.

"I told some guys in the parking lot they should bet the rent on you," I say.

He takes turns punching one hand into the other. "Hopefully you know something I don't."

"I saw you play ball for enough years to know you're tough as hell."

"We'll see," he says.

A man with neatly slicked-back hair dressed in a tuxedo pokes his head in and announces: "Ten minutes." Cliff strips down to his underwear and jockstrap. His back and chest are hairier than those of any other fighter I've ever seen. He removes from his duffel bag a pair of purple trunks with a black, vertical stripe running down each leg, and slides them on. The shorts fit at least a size too small. He sits back down on the bench to lace up his long, white boxing shoes. The trainer kneels down in front of Cliff, wraps his hands in tape, and ties up his gloves.

"You've been training real good, kid," the trainer says to him. "But now you got to execute."

Cliff looks as solemn as a funeral procession.

The trainer works to flatten out the padding in Cliff's gloves. "You want to hit him with the knuckles," the trainer says. He makes a fist and holds it in front of Cliff's face. The old man's knuckles are swollen with arthritis.

"Stand up," the trainer says. "I'm going to scrape the bottoms of your shoes." He brandishes a knife and Cliff lifts each foot for him to roughen the soles. "Now dance around," he says. "Show me your stuff."

Cliff shuffles from one foot to the other, and throws a series of combination punches at the air.

"When do I get paid?" Cliff asks.

The trainer seizes him by the shoulders and gives him a violent shake. "You can't be thinking about that now," he says. "That guy out there is a killer."

"Do me a favor," Cliff says. "Pray with me."

We gather in a circle and bow our heads. Cliff leads us in a quiet prayer. I accidently sneeze halfway through, interrupting the spiritual communion. The trainer and Cliff both look at me as if I've invited the Devil into the room.

"Sorry," I say.

The door flings open and the man with the pomaded hair and slick attire shouts in, "Show time!"

We make our way down the long hallway toward the ring. The four of us are as silent as monks. The gladiator look Cliff wore earlier has hardened even further. He's in a different headspace now—a state of concentration only the most elite athletes know.

Coming out of the tunnel, AC/DC's "Thunderstruck" is booming from the auditorium's speakers. The arena is less than half full. It is not the atmosphere of a championship fight. When a title is on the line the stadium is filled with the casual fan—people who only follow champions. But tonight is for purists only. Every person in attendance looks to be a true aficionado.

A woman wearing a replica of Cliff's Dodger's jersey shouts, "I love you, Cliff."

He doesn't look up.

"This is it, pal," I say to him.

He nods his head.

When we get near ringside, I take the last seat in the second row from the front.

The trainer holds up the middle rope, making a window for Cliff to climb through. The referee approaches and does a quick check of his gloves. Cliff paces back and forth across the ring with his head hung low, only once lifting his arm in acknowledgment of the crowd.

"I can't believe how nervous I am," I say to the stranger sitting next to me.

"This fight's nothing but a cheap publicity stunt," he says in reply. "Cliff Adams is going to get murdered in there."

He laughs a deep belly laugh that shakes the whole row of seats.

The AC/DC song comes to an abrupt stop. A rap song begins in its place. The entire crowd all at once turns its attention from the ring to the tunnel. A small army of men dressed in matching caps and shirts comes into sight. These men walk out in front of their fighter. Only the boxer's head is visible, but he is many inches taller than anyone in his entourage. Like an executioner, he's wearing a black hood that obscures his face.

He enters the ring and makes a lap around its perimeter. The referee meets him at his corner and checks his gloves. The fighter's trainer helps him out of his robe. His skin is the shade of midnight black that every white man of my generation from Jefferson Park grew up fearing. The name Coleman is written in block letters across the belt of his trunks. From Coleman's physique, it is clear he has a tremendous fitness advantage over Cliff. He hardly even looks like a man. More like a lion.

The two fighters meet in the center of the ring. They each wear their fiercest faces, trying to extort fear from the other. Cliff is probably twice his opponent's age—his potbelly in stark contrast to Coleman's rippling abdomen. The referee gives his instruction, and the two fighters return to their corners.

Cliff closes his eyes and makes the sign of the cross. The bell rings. Coleman comes charging across the ring like a bull, his hands held out like horns. He sticks Cliff in the face with a right as straight as a flagpole. Cliff stumbles backward and a wail goes up from the crowd. Coleman moves in again, throwing two left jabs and a right cross that forces Cliff into the corner—the worst place for a fighter. Cliff throws a feeble left that Coleman swats away. He counters with a severe pounding to Cliff's midsection.

"Get out of the corner!" Cliff's trainer screams.

Cliff tries to fight his way out but Coleman is too strong to let him get away. He lifts his arms to cover his face and takes a barrage of punches to the belly. When he lowers his elbows to protect his ribs, Coleman smashes an uppercut through his gloves, catching him on the chin. Cliff's mouthpiece goes flying out. The referee stops the fight and gives Cliff a standing eight-count.

"Come on, you chump," Coleman taunts from the center of the ring. "I thought you might have something for me, but you ain't got shit."

Cliff is dazed but insists he wants to keep fighting. The referee warns him that if he doesn't defend himself, the fight will be stopped. Cliff hits his gloves together, indicating he's ready to fight. The referee gives the signal for the action to continue, and Coleman comes roaring in again, leading with a big right hand. It misses its target, sliding past the ear. Cliff checks him with a series of jabs to the body that inflict no damage. Coleman goes headhunting, throwing two vicious hooks, the second landing with a thud to Cliff's jaw. He staggers backwards on wobbly legs. Coleman moves in again to finish him off, but the bell rings, and the referee gets between them, sparing Cliff from the knockout.

Coleman pumps his arm in the air to inspire heckles from the crowd. They respond with a chorus of boos. Between rounds, he goes to his corner and stands. When his trainer offers him water, he pushes it away. He beats on his chest and glowers across the ring.

Cliff sits on his stool. His face is already swollen and covered in lumps. He takes a long sip of water and spits it out into a bucket. It's as much blood as water. The trainer rubs Cliff's shoulders and chest, working his fingers deep into the fibers of the muscles.

"You got to *move* out there," the trainer says. "You can't just stand there and take punches."

"He's too strong," Cliff says.

"He's strong, but he's got no spirit. He's nothing but a schoolyard bully. If you can wear him down, he's yours."

The bell rings for the second round. Coleman charges out in a rage, leading with his right again—the most dangerous punch to throw—and this time he misses badly, the momentum of the punch knocking him off balance. Cliff connects with a hard right to Coleman's ribs that jolts him. He follows with an accelerating left to the chin that forces Coleman to the ropes. Cliff goes after him, throwing punches to the midsection. Coleman leans in on him, cutting off Cliff's room to punch. Cliff tries to push him away to create space, but Coleman gets his gloves on him and wrestles his head down. The referee comes over and breaks the clinch.

The two fighters circle, come forward, and then back again, each carrying a keen awareness of what the other is capable of. The rest of the round, neither fighter takes any chances, only showing their jabs. The bell rings and the two fighters go back to their corners.

This time Coleman takes his stool. His right eye is puffy and red. His trainer presses a cold compress against it. Coleman's team is giving him instruction, but he is shaking his head in disagreement. He looks confused, as if he has just learned a truth that he previously thought impossible.

On the other side of the ring, Cliff looks to be in great pain as he struggles to breathe. Sweat is pouring off his body, and his nose, lip, and eye are all cut.

I rush from my seat to Cliff's side.

"How many rounds is that?" Cliff asks me.

"Two," I say.

"It feels like a million."

"If you're going through hell, just keep going."

The bell rings for the third and final round. Coleman, again, comes out as the aggressor. He cuts off the ring, driving Cliff to the ropes, forcing him to the corner. He batters Cliff's belly with punches that land like sticks of dynamite. Each time he connects, Cliff shakes like a flag in the wind. The powerful slugger hits him again and again. Cliff leans back, trying to allow the force of the blows to be absorbed by the ropes. The punches come two at a time, four at a time, even six at a time. Coleman punches until he can't even breathe anymore, and he backs off, then comes in again. But each time, the punches grow weaker and weaker, and Cliff finally comes off the ropes, throwing punches of his own. He's like a soldier in the trenches who knows he has only a handful of bullets left and needs to make them count. And he does, each punch connects with its target, first the ribs, then the head, and the ribs again.

Coleman's trainer hollers from the corner: "Hit him back. He's weak. Knock him out!"

Coleman hurls a wild left that grazes Cliff's ear but doesn't hurt him. Cliff counters with a right hook to Coleman's left side-body, and then a lightning-quick flick to his head. Coleman drifts backwards, his feet dragging across the canvas, his movements sluggish and clumsy. Cliff pursues him, moving as slowly as a man climbing up a snowy mountainside. He throws two stiff lefts that catch Coleman on the chin. Coleman waves his arms feebly, more like pushes than punches. Cliff absorbs them with his left forearm and then throws a right hook that whistles as it cuts through the air, connecting with Coleman's jaw. The punch sends Coleman reeling and Cliff hits him two more times. Coleman tumbles in sections, first the head, then the chest, and finally the legs like two big redwoods.

The crowd roars. The referee begins his count. Cliff stands in the center of the ring, swaying from side to side, as if he could go down at any second too. Coleman attempts to climb to his feet. He looks like a drunk trying to rouse himself off the floor to make it to bed. Only a split second after the referee counts to ten, he manages to stand. But it's too late. It's all over.

"Gonna get murdered, huh?" I say to the stranger next to me.

The door to the dressing room is open when I get there. Cliff is sitting on the bench with his hands on his knees. His left eye is swollen nearly shut and his face is covered in red bruises, but that right eye of his is twinkling like a star in the night sky. He's never looked more handsome.

"You fucking did it, pal," I say to him.

A half smile tickles his lips. "I can't believe it."

"You looked like Ali when he fought Foreman out there."

"I'm just glad it's over."

The trainer enters the room with two heavy bags of ice and runs the tub.

"Get in here," he says to Cliff. "You need to soak that body of yours."

Cliff climbs in with his trunks still on.

The trainer stands to Cliff's side and shines a light into each of his eyes. "You took some good shots out there," he says. "I want to make sure your head is clear. Count backwards from a hundred for me."

Cliff starts his count in a calm, quiet voice. The words come out of him slowly, as if he was reading from a foreign text. When he reaches eighty-seven, he stops and says, "Can you believe it, Lou? I'm going to get to see my boy soon." He then continues counting where he left off, speaking in the same demure delivery.

The trainer turns off his light and makes a further inspection of Cliff's injuries. "Well," he says, "you definitely have a concussion, probably some broken ribs. God knows what else is wrong with you."

Cliff splashes some water onto his face. "I'm feeling all right," he says. "In fact, I haven't felt so good in a long time."

The man in the formal wear with the coiffed hair barges into the room. Two men as big as giants, dressed in black T-shirts and black pants and shoes, escort him in. One is black, the other white. Both their faces display the blank expression of robots.

"Cliff Adams, you son of a bitch!" he says in a loud boisterous voice. "You were marvelous out there. Simply marvelous." He turns to one of his bodyguards. "Jerome, wasn't Cliff marvelous?"

Jerome nods his head in agreement.

"You got my money, Hal?" Cliff asks.

"That was the best fight I've seen in years," he says. He reaches into the tub, pulls out Cliff's hand, and shakes it vigorously. "You were all heart out there."

"How about the money?"

"Money, money, money," he says. "After a fight like that, still all you can think about is money. It's a shame, it really is. But if it's business you want to talk, let's talk about your next fight."

"I'm tired, Hal," Cliff says. "Just give me my ten grand and we'll talk about that another time."

Hal snaps his fingers and Jerome lays a briefcase out on the table and opens it. Hal takes out a copy of Cliff's contract and reads it silently to himself. When he's done reading, he places the contract back in the briefcase, reaches into his tuxedo-jacket pocket, and pulls out a checkbook.

"Would you like it made out to Cliff or Clifford," he says.

"I'm too tired for bullshit."

Hal writes out the check and then tears it from the book.

"Here you are," he says, handing the check to Cliff.

Cliff stares at it like he's lost in space.

"What the hell is this?" Cliff finally says. "The contract was for ten grand. This is barely five."

"Yes, of course," Hal says. "The contract was for ten grand, but that's not all for you. Surely you read the fine print."

"The fine print?"

Hal reaches back into the briefcase for the contract. "Here it is," he says. "Fifteen percent of your earnings go to pay for the trainer we provide you."

Everyone in the room turns toward the man with the wet, saggy eyes. The man shrugs his shoulders and says to Cliff, "I got to eat too, you know."

Hal continues, "Twenty-five percent goes for promotion."

"Promotion?" Cliff asks.

"Those seats don't fill themselves. We have to advertise."

"That comes out of my winnings?"

"It's all in the contract."

"What else?" Cliff asks.

Hal reads further down the page. "And of course there are the miscellaneous expenses: the robe, the gloves, the trunks, the shoes. And you don't think this dressing room is free, or the towels you ruined with your blood and sweat all over them, or the stool you sat on between rounds?"

Cliff climbs out of the tub and the two bodyguards step forward, blocking Cliff's access to Hal. Cliff tries to push his way past the two behemoths. "You're a crook!" he shouts. The two men shove him backwards, slamming him into the tub, sending a wave of water crashing onto the floor. Cliff struggles to stay upright, searching around with his hands to find something to stabilize himself on.

I throw my arm around Cliff's shoulder and ease him down onto the bench. His arms and legs are shaking and his good eye is fluttering. When he tries to speak it comes out sounding like a long stream of vowels and grunts.

Hal takes the briefcase from the bench and walks toward the door. Before he exits the room, he turns back and says, "Tell Cliff to call me if he ever wants to fight again." The two thugs laugh at Hal's comment, and then follow him out of the room.

The muscles in Cliff's body all seize up at once. His face is frozen as if carved in a piece of wood. The paralysis lasts only a few seconds. It's followed by a series of full-body convulsions. The trainer snatches a towel off the rim of the tub and shoves it into Cliff's mouth. It takes both of us to keep Cliff from falling to the floor. After thirty seconds of hard shaking, the violence stops, and we lay Cliff onto his back, and place his duffle bag under his head.

The trainer looks into Cliff's good eye. "We need to get him to the hospital," he says.

"Go find the medics," I say. "I'll stay with him."

The trainer stands up and rushes out the door in his old-man limp, left leg dragging behind the right.

"You're going be all right, pal," I say to Cliff in a trembling voice. "You just overexerted yourself. It was a hell of a fight you put on out there."

Two medics storm the dressing room and get straight to work. Cliff's body is completely limp as they fit him with an oxygen mask and take his vitals.

"His heart rate is at thirty-two," one of the medics says.

"Let's get him onto the stretcher," the other replies.

The trainer, the medics, and myself lift Cliff up and set him in place. He's wheeled into the hallway and taken in the direction opposite the ring. The second fight is underway and the crowd's cheers reverberate throughout the tunnel. There is an ambulance waiting behind the building. We load Cliff in, and then the medics and myself board. The trainer stays behind on the dock.

"Aren't you coming?" I ask.

"I still have one more fight tonight," he says. "If I leave, I won't get paid. It's in the contract."

The ambulance doors slam shut and we take off at a fantastic speed, the siren blaring, the driver maneuvering us through traffic with adroit precision and skill. I peek through the window, over the driver's shoulder, to read the dashboard. The needle registers 105 miles per hour, as we pass all the other vehicles in a blur of taillights and exhaust. My pulse accelerates to its maximum capacity and a wave of nausea forces my head between my knees. I concentrate on taking deep breaths to keep from vomiting. I look over at Cliff and his face is nearly unrecognizable behind the bruises, the swelling, and the mask.

"What's wrong with him?" I ask.

"He's had a seizure," the medic says.

We come to a halting stop. A doctor and a team of nurses are waiting to receive the ambulance. Everyone is shouting slews of medical terminology. The only thing I'm certain I understand is that they are taking him directly to surgery. I chase after Cliff's stretcher as the medical team races him down the hospital's hallways. They pass through a door labeled "Operating Room" and then slam it shut behind them.

I place my palms against the closed door and stare at it blankly. My ears are ringing with the ominous sound of silence. The world feels to me as if it has stopped spinning on its axis, or as if there is no more air to breathe.

A woman appears at my side. "Sir," she says, "you can't stand here."

I hear the words she is saying but it doesn't immediately register that she is speaking to me.

"Sir," she says again, "I'm sorry but you can't stand here."

I turn and look at her. She is a soft, doughy young thing with frizzy hair, dressed in a white smock.

"Where would you have me go then?" I ask her.

She leads me around a corner to a waiting room. In it there is a coffee machine, uncomfortable chairs, and a television suspended from the wall that plays Court TV with the sound off. I take a seat across from a black man with a white beard and a cane. He digs through the pockets of his corduroy jacket and finds a piece of gum. It takes him a long time to unwrap it because his hands are unsteady. He looks straight at me. I feel as if I've invaded a private moment. I stand up and go pour myself a cup of coffee. It is very bad coffee—has probably been sitting out for several hours. I sit down in a different seat to drink it.

There is a three-month-old copy of *The New Yorker* under my chair. I pick it up and flip it open to a random page. There is an article about Japanese fertility rates. Apparently, nobody is having babies there, and soon there will be a crisis of not having enough young people to care for a rapidly aging population. The journalist's hypothesis about what is causing this problem is that people in Japan work such long hours that they're too tired to have sex when they get home from work. On the third page of the article, there is a photograph of six thin and attractive Japanese women, all in their mid-twenties to early thirties, looking very dour and sex-starved.

I fall asleep halfway through the article, and am awoken two hours later to my phone vibrating in my pocket. It's Frannie. It's difficult to understand her words because there is a lot of background noise. She keeps interrupting her conversation with me to talk to other people. I ask her where she is and she laughs cruelly.

In response to her laughter, I say, "I probably won't make it home tonight."

"Oh, really?" she says. "Maybe I won't come home tonight either, then."

"You do what you want to do, Frannie."

"You're such an asshole."

"I have to go."

"Do you even care about me at all?"

"Of course I do," I say. "But I have to go check on Cliff."

"Check on Cliff?" she shouts. "I don't care if he's dead, you don't hang up the phone on me."

"I'm at the hospital now. They took him in for surgery."

"That's not funny."

"Not even a little bit."

"Are you serious?"

"Yes."

"Is he okay?"

"I don't know."

"What hospital are you at? I'm coming."

"You don't have to do that."

"Just tell me what hospital already."

"The one on South Grand Avenue."

She says something to someone in the background that I can't make out. She then speaks directly into the phone's receiver, her voice sounding steadier and clearer than before. "I'll be there as fast as I can."

I stand up out of my seat. My legs are stiff and tingly from sitting in the same position too long. The black man with the white beard and the gum is gone, but there are new people in the room. There is a Mexican man with gelled, spiky black hair, wearing Adidas track pants, sitting directly under the television, which now plays a cop drama. And there is a heavyset woman wearing a T-shirt with a picture of Tweety Bird printed on it, napping on his shoulder. Two chubby kids sit on the floor in front of them. One is drawing with markers and the other is playing a game on a cellphone.

The woman with the frizzy hair who showed me to the waiting room is sitting behind a desk. She is digging through a stack of folders when I approach. It takes her several seconds to acknowledge me.

"I'd like to check on my friend," I say. "His name is Cliff Adams."

She looks down at her computer monitor and pounds furiously on the keyboard. "They've just moved him from the recovery room to the intensive-care unit. It's on the third floor." When she lifts her head back up, her tight-lipped mouth forms a frown. "Elevator is that way," she says, pointing in its direction.

Through the gap in the closing elevator door, I spot Frannie entering the reception area. She's in a short, floral-print skirt and high heels. Her hair is up and she's wearing long, dangly feather earrings. I call out to her but she doesn't hear me. I reach for the button to stop the elevator door from closing but can't do so in time because two female nurses are standing in front of the control panel. When the door closes, I press the button for the third floor.

I peek into the doorways of each room in the hall. Some are dark and the only person in them is the patient, hooked up to a series of machines. In other rooms, in addition to the invalid patient, are doctors, nurses, and family members, all standing around dejected and broken, wearing the forlorn faces of people who are in close proximity to death.

Nearing Cliff's room, I hear a deafening scream. I look in all directions to locate its origin. None of the patients, visitors, or hospital staff has taken any notice. It seems the scream has passed directly from nature into my brain. I take two deep breaths, open the door, and go in.

The man in the bed hardly looks like Cliff at all. His face is purple and battered, covered in a mask, his head shaved. He's got a tube protruding from his skull above the right ear and a ventilator in his mouth. He's lying perfectly still, except for his heaving chest, which rises and falls with the rhythms of a machine. I stand by the side of his bed and say his name: "Cliff."

It elicits no response. I reach down and touch his hand, and the fingers are lifeless and cold. I make a lap around his bed. There are machines monitoring all his body's functions and registering their findings on screens. I pull a chair up to his bedside.

Frannie appears in the doorway. She's got a far-off look in her eyes, as if she was counting the clouds in the sky.

"You came," I say.

"Your friend is hurt. You think I'd abandon you?"

I stand up and go to her, unsure of how to respond. I reluctantly place a hand on her elbow, and she reaches out and pulls me into her. I cry softly, and she strokes my head without saying a word.

A doctor enters the room. He's got neatly combed grey hair and small blue saucers for eyes.

"I'm Dr. Durand," he says.

"My name is Lou," I say. "And this is my fiancé Frannie."

As inconspicuously as I can, I wipe away my tears before shaking the doctor's hand. His grip his firm and authoritative. We stay in the shake for what seems like an inordinately long period of time.

"Cliff's seizure was caused by bleeding from the brain due to a traumatic head injury. The tube you see coming out of his skull is helping to release the pressure." The doctor walks to Cliff's bedside and makes an adjustment to the halo-device holding Cliff's head in place. "We have him on a heavy dose of morphine, which should allow him to rest comfortably through the night. In the morning, if his vitals remain stable, we'll remove the ventilator."

I glance down at Cliff and then back up to the doctor.

"So he's going to be okay?" I ask.

"It's hard to predict with brain injuries, but time will tell," the doctor says. "You should go and get some rest."

I check the time on the clock on the wall. It's nearly two in the morning. "Why don't you go home?" I say to Frannie. "You have work in the morning."

"What about you?" she says.

"I'm going to stay."

"You heard the doctor. There's nothing you can do for him now. Come home with me."

I turn to look at the doctor. He's hunched over one of the machines monitoring Cliff's functions. "I can't, Frannie. It wouldn't be right to leave him all alone."

"But I don't want to be by myself tonight."

"You're a big girl," I say. "You'll be all right."

"Please, Lou, I'm begging you."

I lead her to the doorway. "Go home, Frannie. I'll talk to you tomorrow."

Frannie's face turns sour, and without another word, she walks out the door. I watch her make her way down the hall. Her shoulders are stooped and her hips don't shimmy from side to side with their normal seductive swagger. Her high-heel shoes make a clicking that rings out in the quiet hospital halls.

I return to the room. The doctor shakes his head disapprovingly at me.

"I told her I'm going to stay with Cliff," I say to him.

"Are you sure you don't want to go with her?"

"I'm sure."

"I'll have the nurse bring you a blanket and a pillow."

The doctor checks one more monitoring screen, makes a note on Cliff's chart, and leaves the room. I take my place in the chair by Cliff's bedside and stare at his face, struck by the lips. They are chapped, white, and flaky. It's nearly impossible to imagine that it's the same mouth that has delivered to me so many comforting words in the past months.

The nurse slinks into the room. She's got her hair up in a tight bun. She's young, neither pretty nor ugly, has a mole on her neck that is almost concealed by the collar of her uniform. She hands me a coarse wool blanket and a hard pillow. Instead of turning to leave, she stands there looking down on Cliff. Tears fill her eyes and she covers her mouth with her hands, and silently weeps into them.

"It's just so sad," she finally says. "He was a hero, an idol to millions of fans."

"Cliff's gone through worse and come out the other side," I say. "He'll see his way through this."

"My dad used to take us to Dodgers games when I was a kid." She repositions the sheet on Cliff's bed so that it covers his feet. "When you're a kid, you think these famous athletes are invincible," she continues. "I remember when he had that amazing World Series, my dad said he would do anything to trade lives with him. He said that Cliff got lucky to be born who he is."

"Luckiest man in the world until he isn't."

"I guess so."

Every hour throughout the night the nurse comes in to check on Cliff. And each time, it rouses me from my slumber and it takes me a moment to realize where I am. I watch her as she goes about her business, checking this and adjusting that, making notes, ensuring he's resting comfortably—a real nurturer by nature, she is. I think to myself, *Now, there is someone who's making a difference in this life!*

I wake with the sunrise, its morning rays beaming in through the window, casting its light across the room, magnifying the sterile whiteness of the walls. I stand up and raise my arms to the ceiling, and have a stretch. I emit a long, loud yawn.

The nurse comes in to make her rounds. A few strands of hair have come loose from her bun, and the make-up on her cheeks is cracking, revealing tiny bumps and blemishes in the skin. She puckers her lips and blows in an attempt to get the hair out of her eyes and mouth. When that doesn't work, she uses her hand to tuck the hair behind her ear.

"Good morning," she says to me.

Cliff begins to stir—first his arms, then his legs. Soon his face gets twitchy and he strains to turn his head from one side to the other. Finally he stares up at us with savage eyes, like a feral dog cornered by animal control. He automatically goes for the ventilator tube.

She intercepts his hands, and lowers them back to his lap.

"Mr. Adams, please don't do that. You'll hurt yourself. If you remove the tube improperly, you can cause a great deal of damage to your vocal cords." The nurse manages a small flicker of a smile. Cliff goes for the tube again, and she repeats the behavior of grabbing his hands and lowering them back to his lap.

"Can you please restrain him while I page the doctor?" she says to me.

I pin Cliff's hands to his sides, and after a brief struggle he relents.

"That's better, Mr. Adams," the nurse says. "The doctor will be right in to remove that breathing tube. You're going to feel much better."

She runs her hand down the length of Cliff's arm. I'm certain her eyes are turning moist. I lean in to investigate further, but she turns her back and exits the room. *How does one do this type of work every day?* I ask myself.

"Jesus Christ, pal, you gave us quite a fucking scare!" I say to Cliff.

His wet, sad eyes flicker open and shut.

"They're taking real good care of you," I say. "You should be out of here in no time."

The nurse returns with the doctor.

"So, Mr. Adams is awake, is he," the doctor says. "That's a bit of good news."

Cliff reaches out and yanks on the doctor's white coat.

"Okay, Mr. Adams, please give me a moment," the doctor says. "I need to run through my checklist to make sure everything is in order before I remove your breathing tube."

The doctor looks down at his clipboard, then to one of the monitors, back to his clipboard, to a different monitor, and finally he leans over and has a look into Cliff's eyes. Satisfied with his observations, he turns off the machine and removes the tube from Cliff's throat.

"How do you feel, Mr. Adams?" the doctor asks.

Cliff opens and shuts his mouth, stretches his jaw, and kneads his throat with the tips of his fingers.

"I'm sore as hell," he says.

The nurse takes Cliff's hand and holds it between both of hers. "Do you remember anything?" she asks.

"I don't have the money, do I?" he says.

"The money?" the nurse replies.

Cliff rips his hand from her grasp. "Yes, the fucking money."

"Don't worry about the money," I say to him. "We'll get it worked out."

"It's over," Cliff says. "I've lost all claims on my own son."

"What does that mean?" the nurse asks.

"Don't get him all riled up," I say.

"You should've let me die," Cliff says.

"Heavens, no!" the nurse shouts.

The doctor pats the nurse on the shoulder. "Nurse Melissa and I are going to step out to give you some privacy. We'll be back in a couple of minutes."

The nurse reluctantly follows him out into the hall.

"When I do die," Cliff continues, "I want you to make sure I'm cremated, okay? Make sure they burn me up good. I don't want to take any chances that one day science will once again breathe life back into me. An intact dead body is nearly human—I can't risk it."

"I don't want to hear about your future death plans. Not after what you just put me through."

"Look at my life—it's pathetic. There's no use trying to inject any dignity into it. You'd be a liar if you said there was anything tragic in my passing."

"Stop being ridiculous," I say. "It's not dignified."

"At this point, I just want to be left alone," he says. "I don't want to be bothered. Not by you, not by the doctors, not by anyone."

The doctor and nurse reenter the room.

"You gentlemen are going to have to continue this discussion another time," the doctor says.

"Lou was just leaving," Cliff replies.

"We need to run some tests," the doctor continues. "Rule out another epidural hematoma bleed."

"You really want me to go?" I ask.

"Did you not hear me?" Cliff says. "Get the fuck out."

My house is empty when I get home. I call Frannie's cellphone, but she doesn't pick up. I stammer out a message: "Just got home from the hospital. Cliff is out of his stupor, but is now suicidal. He kicked me out of the hospital. Sorry about last night. Call me back when you get this. Love you. Bye."

I fix myself a frozen pepperoni pizza and take a beer from the fridge and spread out across the couch. The Ferris Bueller movie is playing on cable, and I watch it as I eat. I marvel at Ferris's consummate optimism. In real life there would be no stopping a man of such character.

I fall asleep after the hot-tub scene. I have a dream about the actress who plays Ferris's girlfriend. She has gotten the septum of her nose pierced, and I'm castigating her for mutilating her most beautiful face. She is crying and can't understand why I'm so mean. I explain to her that I'm only looking out for her best interests. The idea of desecrating such a work of beauty is beyond reason, but she insists that it's *her* face, and that she likes the piercing and can do what she wants. I never say it directly, but what I'm thinking is that it's *not* her face, that she's my girl, my possession, and therefore the face belongs to me and not her. I proceed with a diatribe about the value of a benevolent dictator, that sometimes all power should be consolidated in a single leader or entity for the greater good, that people need to be protected from themselves.

When I wake up I have a message on my phone from Frannie. It says: "Cliff's got the right idea. I want you out, too. Don't be home when I get off of work."

I go to the kitchen. There are three stacks of mail bundled in rubber bands sitting on the counter. I pick out an envelope at random and open it. It's from the bank. It says I'm three months behind on my mortgage, and that if they don't receive their money by September 1st, foreclosure proceedings will begin. I check the calendar on my phone. It says today is September 7th.

I pour myself two Don Julio shots and take them in succession. I decide a trip is in order, a little me time, a chance to reconnect with yours truly, a reprieve from my troubles. Vegas is out of the question. Nothing good ever comes out of a Vegas trip. The place is toxic, beyond repute. San Francisco is tempting, but I don't feel like negotiating the tribulations of air travel, and the drive is too long. I consider Big Sur, but again, the drive is too much for me. The Mojave Desert, it is! The place with the grotesque-looking, twisted, spiky Dr. Seuss trees. The allure of this prickly oddity fits my mood, and a two-hour drive is perfectly manageable.

I don't bother to pack a bag. What I have on will suffice— jeans, boots, a button-down shirt. I scribble out a short note to Frannie, and stick it to the refrigerator with a magnet: "Off to recalibrate my moral compass." I take another shot of Don Julio, and rip the note off the refrigerator, crumple it in my hand, and toss it in the trash. I jot down another note, and stick it back on the refrigerator: "As you wish."

I stop to fill up on gas and to pick up two packs of smokes. For the past few months I've been smoking lights, but this time I go for my old favorites, Marlboro Reds. I open the first pack and light one as I wait for the Beamer to fill up. A man wearing a T-shirt with a wolf's face printed on the front gets out of a Toyota Prius and is impelled to shake his head at me in disdain.

Back out on the road, I blast *Exile on Main St.* on the car's stereo. Mick and Keith's special brand of spectral alchemy always brings my darkness into the light. The drive is just as serene as I imagined it would be—massive branching yuccas dotting the sandy plains, studded by granite monoliths and rock piles. Staring out the window, I remember reading that Mormon travelers named these iconic trees after the biblical figure Joshua, but for the life of me, I can't remember who Joshua is. I make a mental note to investigate further. Reaching the park's entrance, I lower the window of my car and the desert's dry arid air is an affront to my senses. Instantly my eyes burn and the inside of my nose turns crusty. My car's thermometer is showing it's ninety-seven degrees outside.

A mile down the main drag, I see a sign that reads: "Spin and Margie's Desert Hideaway", and has an arrow signaling to turn right at the stop sign. Five minutes further down the road, the pavement gives way a dirt path and I follow it past an old metal box spring, some rusted-out cans holding willowy desert blooms, and a couple of old neon street signs. At the end of the trail is Spin and Margie's. The place is one part hacienda, two parts cactus garden, and the rest a '50s-era acid flashback.

There is a dirt lot next to a pink, freestanding bungalow. Due to my aggressive braking, a cloud of dust kicks up. A long-bearded hippie in cutoff jean shorts, a tank top, and oversized aviator sunglasses stands at an artist's easel, coughing.

"Who runs this place?" I ask him.

"Thataway," the man says. He points his wiry arm in the direction of a crumbling adobe structure.

Inside, a plump-bodied woman with straw-textured pigtails, clunky silver jewelry adorned in feathers, and a round sun-beaten face is smiling at me from behind a desk.

"You looking for a room?"

I take off my sunglasses and inspect my surroundings. The room is painted all shades of pink, turquoise, and orange, and the walls are lined with framed photographs of desert landscapes and old Indian chiefs and cowboys.

"Yes ma'am."

"Well, you're in luck, because we got one left," she says in a tone of unsullied goodwill. "It's the Mojave Wanderer Suite. It's one of my favorite rooms." The woman stops and gives a throaty smoker's cough. "But then again, they're all my favorite rooms. I designed them."

The woman busies herself with the paperwork and runs my credit card and hands me the key.

"Just go out this door," she says, "turn left around the benches in the rock garden and go past the coyote fencing until you hit the red railroad-style boxcar. That's you."

Once inside the room, I take off my pants and shirt and flip on the swamp cooler. It makes an ominous humming as it takes effect. I pour myself a glass of water from the tap and lie down on the bed. The room's walls are painted lime-green and accented in wood textures, and the floor is a mosaic of multicolored tiles.

From my place on the bed I can see the setting sun through the window. I light a cigarette and head out to the porch in my underwear. My body shivers because the temperature has dipped what feels like forty degrees. I attempt to make my way back inside to put on pants, but the pink-and-orange glow of the sky is just too enticing, and I'm paralyzed by the majesty of it all.

The image of Frannie's betrayal at the restaurant comes into my mind. I recall my face pressed to the glass, watching her: her generous mouth brushed red and opened wide, in what looked like noisy laughter; her hair long and straight, its black lustrous shine is chic and sumptuous—the very embodiment of regal femininity. But it's what she wore to dinner that really irked me: that dress, something we picked out together for a Mexican beach getaway, a black, delicate chiffon, low-cut, strapless number. I'll never forget sliding it off the length of her body on the patio of our cabana in Cabo, the moonlight's blue glow striking her skin in all the right ways, making me believe I had finally attained a love that was boundless and abiding. We made love on the sand that night, her straddling me while I watched the crashing ocean waves behind her. Of all my relationships, seductions, one-night stands, flings, and affairs, that night stands out as the single greatest—my lone sojourn into unassailable idyllic love. It was that night I asked Frannie for her hand in marriage.

Tears spring from my eyes and I'm overwhelmed by euphoria. I fall to my knees and with my heart swelling, I weep softly, in awe of everything. *What is happening to me?* I wonder. *Where is the outrageous cynic, king of whiskey-stained tables, scoffer at all things sentimental?* After a fleeting moment, this departure from character passes and I dry my eyes. Inside I find a pen, unwrap a bar of soap, and write the following on the inside of its wrapper: "There can't be love without some weakness."

As I'm walking to my car I cross paths with the Hideaway's proprietor and ask her where I can get dinner. She advises me to try the Saloon. I set off down the dirt road and before reaching the first stop-sign, a Ford pickup with monster tires and a "Don't Tread on Me" bumpersticker cuts me off on the shoulder, nearly taking out my front end. I slam on the brakes and give the wheel a hard crank to avoid collision, sending my car into a death spin. The act of losing control happens in slow motion. I have time to take notice of my favorite constellation in the night sky: Draco, the Dragon. I recount to myself the myth of Hercules's eleventh labor, in which he was sent to retrieve the golden apples from the Garden of Hera, a wedding gift from Gala. In the tale, Hercules does battle with Draco, who was tasked with guarding the apples. The result was that Hercules slayed Draco, and Hera felt so awful about the dragon's death that she set his image in the stars. After a two-revolution spin, the car ends up in a shallow ravine. The windshield has a small crack in it. I step down hard on the accelerator and my back wheels catch, catapulting me out of the ditch. By the time I reach the restaurant, the bumps and ruts in the road have transformed the crack into an elaborate web of geometrical shapes and patterns.

The Saloon is a wood-cabin throwback to frontier days. Mounted on the second story is a white sign: "Steaks & Burgers." Framing the words on both sides are pictures of red-and-orange flames. Outside the front door is a six-foot-tall cigar-store Indian and next to that, two rocking chairs. A woman with an apron around her waist and a tattoo of a coyote on her neck sits in one of the chairs and rocks back and forth smoking a cigarette.

"Welcome to the Saloon," she says.

She tosses the butt to the ground and stomps it out with her foot. She starts toward the door but then goes back and steps on the cigarette a second time. "Can't be too careful," she says. "It's not just dry—it's a drought!"

"Safety first," I say.

The Saloon's inside is exactly what's to be expected: dark-lit, low ceiling, fat-and-mustached bartender, pool table, and in the corner a man of eighty singing old-time country tunes in a soft wheezing drawl.

"This gonna work for you?" she asks, leading me to a wooden table against the wall, under a yellow and white, neon "Miller High Life" sign.

"Yeah," I softly say.

The woman asks me what I'd like to drink. I tell her to bring me a scotch-and-soda and "one of those." I point to the "High Life" sign above my head. When she returns with my drinks, I put in an order for a ribeye steak. I sit back and listen to the old-man's tunes. In a gentle coo, he sings a barely recognizable cover of "So long, Marianne". Having always been a Leonard Cohen fan, I stand up and drop a ten in his bucket next to the stage.

Midway through my meal, the singer takes a break and comes by my table to thank me, and offers to buy me a drink. I agree and insist he sit and join me. The waitress brings me another scotch-and-soda and him a Gin Rickey.

He holds out his hand for me to shake. It has a slight tremble to it, like the hands of many old-timers.

"What brings you out this way?" the man says.

"Trying to get my head straight, you know?"

"Oh, I know plenty about that, I assure you. Lady troubles? Money?"

"Among other things," I say.

"What sorts of other things?"

"My best pal wants to suicide himself."

"That's a damn shame. Real sorry to hear that."

"What can you do?"

"Not a helluva lot if he's got his mind made up."

"We'll see."

"What else you got?"

"Professional problems."

"What sort of work you do?"

"I guess you could say I'm a writer of sorts."

"They pay you to do that?"

"They did once."

"So what's the problem now?"

"I'm starting to wonder if an artist needs to be alone in the world. When I did my best work I was extremely poor, a terrible failure, and nothing if not alone. But now that I've had some success, I have demands made of me, and obligations kill an artist."

"It's a woman, right?"

"It can't all be her fault."

"Women are a tricky thing. You resent the hell out of them, but maybe it beats being lonely. I can't make up my mind about it."

"If you figure it out, let me know."

"I suppose you got to ask yourself how you felt before you took up with your old lady."

"I know I didn't feel worthless."

"Not even when you were dead-broke?"

"When I was penniless, I never used to worry I was worthless. I only worried that the world underestimated my worth, or that it somehow missed it altogether—like a flower blooming in the desert with no one there to see it."

"You got a good way of putting things," he says. "I agree completely. I've always said that the happiest man is the one with the fewest needs." He laughs and then his laughter devolves into a desperate wheeze, struggling to get oxygen into his lungs. He reaches into his pocket, takes out an inhaler, and gives it a few squeezes into his mouth. "Young fella," he continues. "You got to remember that your allegiance is to yourself, first and foremost. You see, a woman wants the whole man. She won't settle for anything less. Living with a woman will kill something in ya."

"There might be something to that."

"Well, I gotta get back to it. It's been a real pleasure talkin' with you. I hope you get that head of yours sorted out."

He gets up from the table and takes his position in the corner with his guitar and resumes singing in his beaten and weary tenor. I pay my tab to the waitress and then walk over to the bar and negotiate a price for a bottle of whiskey for the road. We settle on fifty dollars for a thirty-dollar bottle.

As Oscar Wilde once said: "They know the price of everything and the value of nothing."

Fifteen minutes later I park my car onto the shoulder of a forgotten desert road. I yank the cork from the whiskey and take a long hit from the bottle. I get out of the car and light a cigarette. The night air is cool and crisp. A big yellow moon hangs heavy in the desert sky. The howl of a lone coyote fills my ears. I set off on foot. A good walk has always been the best solution for overcoming life's troubles. In the old days I could solve all the world's problems with a single good twenty-minute stroll.

I trek for an hour, crossing fractured granite seams, over dry creek beds, around stacks of rocks eroded away by a million years of desert winds. In need of rest, I lie out like a corpse on a slab of stone, and stare up at the moon and wonder about choices. It doesn't seem as if there are any good ones left. Getting old is no good and dying is a pity.

I continue drinking the whiskey until my mind slips into a state of psychosis, sending my thoughts racing back to youth.

I'm a child in the fourth grade and my father has recently left my mother. She has explained to me—a nine-year-old—that his departure was my fault, that I drove him away. This makes perfect sense to me. I'm not a model child. I've been caught stealing at school on many occasions—first a teacher's lunch, then a baseball mitt, and finally the wallet from my principal's purse. These acts of petty larceny have each earned me fierce beatings from my father's belt. The man was a maestro with a leather strap, capable of conducting symphonies of anguish and pain.

He used to announce impending flagellations by folding the belt in half and snapping it as he walked down the hall toward my room, its echo-y boom reverberating off the walls of the narrow hallway. Before the last of the lashings I received at my father's hands, I used his ceremonial belt-snapping bravado as a time to prepare my defense. I snuck a letter opener from my parents' desk and hid it under the bed where my father would put me over his lap and deliver upon me this sadistic act.

Depending on the severity of my crime, I could receive anywhere from two to six lashings.

On this occasion, I was being punished for a playground scuffle I had had at school. I reckoned this would earn me three strikes. I allowed my father the first two in order to build up inside of me a well of rage. But before he could whip me a final time, I grabbed the letter opener and stuck it through his shoe and into the big toe of his foot. Under the force of my stab, the cold steel snapped the toenail and pulverized the bone. The man let out a demonic howl and he fell to the floor in a fit of terror and pain, while I took the opportunity to make my escape. I ran outside and down the block and hid behind the dumpster in the alley, next to the gas station. I stayed there for hours. And then, under the cover of darkness, I ran full-speed to my best friend Travis's house. There I was fed and given clean clothes. But to my dismay, Travis's disloyal mother had informed my parents of my presence, and an hour later the doorbell rang. My father was waiting for me on the front stoop of Travis's house. He had his foot wrapped in a blood-soaked bandage and slipped into a sandal.

Upon returning home, my father exacted his revenge on me with a severe beating that left me with two chipped teeth and a cut under my lip requiring six stitches. Soon after that altercation, he was gone, and my mother and I had a new set of problems.

My meditation shifts to a new scene. Now I find myself in my second-grade classroom. The class is split into groups of eight, seated around large circular tables. The teacher is lecturing us on addition and subtraction, but mathematics is the furthest thing from my mind. I need to pee and it's excruciating, yet I'm unable to work up the courage to ask to be excused or to run to the bathroom without permission. Instead, I sit there for a very long time in agony. My little-boy bladder expanding well past its limits, my eyes welling up with tears. Finally, I can't take it anymore and I pull out my penis under the table and relieve myself. As I'm going, I search the faces of my tablemates for any indication that they are aware of my indiscretion—but none seem to notice. Upon completion, I push my penis back into my pants, zip up, and refocus my energies on solving the equation 6+8. But now the classroom is filled with the stench of urine. The teacher wanders around the room looking for the source, finally locating it when she approaches my table. She tells my table's group to get out of our seats and line up against the wall. I watch her from across the room as she conducts her investigation.

Somehow, I had managed to deliver my stream so that it settled directly under the middle of the table, making it impossible to determine from which seat the pee had come. With the rest of the class excused, the teacher interrogated my tablemates and me. But my resolve was strong and I never admitted a thing, and the deed went unpunished.

I break free from my trance, finding myself shivering from cold in the Joshua Tree desert. My pants are soaked because I've pissed myself—the first time in years. A smile forms on my lips. It is clear to me that I'm capable of anything I can imagine, and that nothing gives me a greater thrill than seeking out trouble and only narrowly escaping its menacing jaws. The closer I get to it, the better I feel. It's my great medicine.

I follow a wash past crisscrossing animal trails. Every rock formation looks the same as the one before it. I've lost my direction. Boulders as big as trucks choke the path. I press myself against the flat edge of a narrow pass in the rocks and walk sideways through a shallow canyon. A flood line stains the red rock walls at nearly chest height. A five-minute effort pushes me through to the other side. The sun is rising in the east. It glows orange and pink. A rattlesnake sits coiled under a rock, its tongue flickering. A pile of broken beer-bottle glass and a condom wrapper lay on the ground near a months-old makeshift camp. I spot my car in the distance. It's a tiny dot in the far-off desert—nothing but sand, stone, and cactus between us. It takes me another twenty minutes to reach it.

I open the door and collapse onto the backseat. My head strikes something pointy and hard. I search around with my hands, brushing aside notebooks full of abandoned ideas for unrealized novels, beer cans, newspapers, and junk-food wrappers. A box is unearthed. I pick it up and place it in my lap. The corner is dented from my head hitting it. The name Charles Adams, followed by an address in Palm Springs, is written in a nearly illegible scrawl across the top. It's the package Cliff and I never mailed on our way to the fair.

I toss the box onto the passenger seat and climb into the driver's seat. I catch my face's reflection in the rearview mirror. The eyes are those of a man marked for death. I scarcely recognize them as my own. I open the door and release a bellyfull of ribeye steak and whiskey onto the cold highway asphalt. I wipe my mouth with the sleeve of my shirt, shut the door, start the car, and race off. A broken yellow line marks the center of the road into the horizon. There is not another car for miles and miles. The rising sun's rays refract off the cracks in the windshield and beams of heavenly light shine in all around me, giving the drive an aura of divine purpose.

It takes less than an hour to reach Palm Springs' city limits. I reach for my phone to GPS the address on the package, but there isn't enough battery for the task. A force that can only be described as celestial implores me that it's not required, and I push on. Five minutes later I find myself in the driveway of a suburban home. The clock on my dashboard informs me it's 7:15 in the morning. I step out of the car with the package in my arms. My shadow stretches out nearly twenty feet. I look in each direction. The homes along the avenue are nearly identical: two-story, beige stucco, white garage doors, red tiled roofs, unnaturally green grass. I stride to the door and push the button. The sound of church bells rings out. I look down at my feet. I'm standing on a welcome mat with the silhouette of a golfer's follow-through stenciled onto it. I wait another moment and then ring the doorbell again. There is the sound of footsteps coming down the stairs from within the house. I press my face to a window but can't see a thing because the curtains are drawn.

A man opens the door in a robe and slippers. He's got a square jaw and a severe look of superiority in his eyes.

"Can I help you?" he says. His voice is deep and rough and irritable.

"Yes, hello," I say. "My name is Lou Brown. I'm a friend of Cliff's. I need to speak to his son Charles."

"You shouldn't be here."

"You don't understand. It's urgent."

The man looks down at the package.

"What is that?"

"It's a gift for Charles from his father."

"If you give it to me, I can make sure he gets it."

He reaches out to take possession of the package, but I turn my body, shielding him from it.

"This isn't about the gift," I say. "I really must speak to Charles. His father is in the hospital."

There is the sound of more footsteps on the stairs. A woman approaches. She's dressed in robe and slippers too. Her blonde hair is flat on the one side of her head from pressing against the pillow, and wild and billowy on the other. The skin under her chin hangs a bit loose, giving her a turkey neck.

"Who is this?" the woman says to the man.

"He says he's a friend of Cliff's."

The woman tries to shut the door in my face but I shove my arm in the way, preventing her from doing so.

"Ma'am," I say. "Can I please explain?"

She applies more pressure to the door, nearly severing my arm at the elbow. "I'm not interested in anything you have to say."

"Cliff's in the hospital. He almost died!" I shout.

The woman stops pressing on the door and I fall backwards, landing on my ass, the package coming free from my hand, landing in the foliage of a potted plant.

"What happened?" she asks.

I stand up, collect the package, and hand it to the man.

"He took a boxing match to raise money for child support and he got his bell rung pretty good. Had a seizure. Lots of swelling in the brain, maybe some bleeding too. They performed a surgery to release the pressure."

"Is he all right?" the man asks.

"He wants to see his boy."

"Not an option," the woman says.

"I don't know a thing about what Cliff was like when the two of you were together. And I'm sure you have your reasons for putting distance between him and his son, but he's trying his best. Charles is the only thing in this world Cliff cares about. If you take that away from him, he's got nothing to live for."

"Good. Let him die," the woman says. "I don't really give a shit."

"Meghan," the man says to her, "try to be reasonable."

"Fuck reasonable," she says.

The man turns to me. "We need a little bit of time to discuss things in private."

"I'll come back in an hour," I say.

"That'll be fine," the man says.

The woman rolls her eyes at her husband, as he shuts the door.

I smoke cigarette after cigarette walking the neighborhood. The roads are all named for desert flora and fauna: Juniper St., Lynx Loop, Marigold Place, Bobcat Way. But there is no real sign of nature within the gates of this private community. No, this place is a symbol of man's victory over nature. What was once a land of red dirt, rock, and cacti is now a bastion of American consumerism. These sidewalks are roamed by young mothers wearing designer yoga pants, pushing five-hundred-dollar strollers, carrying six-dollar lattes in their hands. Many of the houses proudly display campaign signs in their yards for Republican candidates running for Treasurer, City Council, and Sheriff. Inside the homes, children eat sugar cereal while staring mesmerized at Pixar movies played on seventy-two-inch flat-screen televisions, their fathers banished to garages to run on treadmills, silently brooding about debt and fantasizing about fucking their secretaries.

I struggle to express my mind. It's as if I lack the faculties to assign words to my feelings. The only thing I can understand with any amount of assurance is that life lacks structure and aim.

My thoughts drift to an antique bookshelf that Frannie purchased at an auction for an exorbitant sum of money. This piece had once sat in the master bedroom of the Hearst Castle. "But why would you buy this?" I asked her. "We have no use for it." She informed me it was simply too wonderful to pass on, and that it would be a fantastic addition to our home. I did not feel it warranted a fight and so I allowed it, and we brought the bookshelf into our house, where we placed it against the wall of my office, sitting bare and idle for months and months.

"You must fill its shelves," she said.

"With what?" I asked. "I don't have anything to put on them."

"Then you must start collecting things."

"Like what?"

"It really doesn't matter," she said. "What's important is that the shelves will look better when they're full."

So for the next few months we began to fill the shelves with random objects that came to us: books, souvenirs, pictures, candles, crystals, ceramics, knick-knacks.

And now, as I walk back toward Charles's parents' house, I worry that life is nothing more than a bookshelf—something we mindlessly fill with all the random crap that comes to us, in fear of leaving a void.

I ring the doorbell. The man answers the door again. This time he's in blue jeans and a USC T-shirt. His hair is fastidiously combed.

"They're finishing packing now," he says. "I have a round of golf with clients this afternoon and Meghan drives like shit, do you mind if they ride with you? They can catch a flight home once they're done."

"That's fine," I say.

Cliff's boy, Charles, who at fourteen is a full-grown man—and a large one at that—pushes through the doorway, dragging behind him a rollaway suitcase. He has thick stubble on his chin and cheeks, but none where the mustache would be. His Adidas track pants sag low and rest in bunches atop flip-flop sandals, his hairy toes jutting out from under the fabric.

I hold out my hand. "Hello, Charles," I say. "My name is Lou. I'm a pal of your father's."

He shakes my hand limply, his eyes never looking up to meet mine.

The mother, Meghan, appears next. She's transformed herself from what she was only an hour before: freshly manicured nails, heavily caked make-up, cleavage exposed in a tight-fitting blouse, the big blond hair of a Dallas Cowboys cheerleader.

"Do you need to go to the bathroom?" she asks Charles.

He shakes his head no.

"Did you pack your algebra book?"

He nods his head yes.

She says to him, "Take Mommy's bag and load it in the car."

The boy takes his mother's bag and his own and wheels them to the car, loads them into the trunk, and then opens the door to the backseat and gets in.

"I don't know why we have to do this," Meghan says to her husband. "I think it's a mistake."

"Do you want Charles to resent you any more than he already does?" he asks her.

"I beg your pardon," she replies. "My son does not resent me."

The man shrugs his shoulders.

Without a kiss or a hug, she leaves her husband in the doorway and goes to the car, climbing into the front seat.

"Good luck," the man says to me.

"Thank you for making this happen," I say to him.

The man goes back into the house and closes the door behind him.

For the duration of the two-hour drive to L.A., I'm forced to endure all Meghan's nervous hysteria: fidgeting arms and legs, facial tics, constant gum chewing, streams of prolonged, rambling monologues interspersed with poorly formed coordinating conjunctions, including a surfeit of *ums* and *likes*. I've never before encountered an adult with such distaste for silence—every single passing moment is soundtracked by her screeching voice, every single meaningless train of thought or tangent is simply pretext for something new yet equally tedious.

She verbalizes her thoughts and feelings on topics as broad and diverse as her ongoing battle with Charles's schoolboard over whether yoga should be taught in P.E. classes (she's opposed to Eastern philosophy), the summer's best blockbuster movies (she's partial to anything with Vin Diesel), and speculation about her church's pastor's alleged affair with a member of the congregation (she finds it impossible to believe).

Charles has spent the entire drive staring into his lap, playing a video game on his phone. His face is completely expressionless, as stoic as that of any man I've ever seen, let alone a child. He reminds me of a monk or an ascetic.

When Meghan takes a moment to answer a phone call, I seize my opportunity.

"When was the last time you saw your dad?" I say to him.

He looks up only long enough to say, "I'm not supposed to

call him that," before returning to his game.

Meghan covers the phone with her hand. "He's to refer to Cliff as Mr. Adams."

"Excuse me?" I say.

"As far as I'm concerned, Cliff has lost his right to be Charles's father," she says.

"Are you kidding me?"

She shoots me a look of murderous intent.

"Okay, I get it," I say.

She lifts the receiver to her ear and continues talking.

"So when was the last time you saw Mr. Adams?" I say, putting extra emphasis on the words: *Mister Adams.*

"I haven't seen him since we moved to Palm Springs. I guess that was about two years ago."

"Two years?"

"I think so," he replies somberly.

Meghan finishes her conversation and places the phone in her purse.

"We'll need to stop at the hotel first?" she says.

"What hotel?" I ask.

"We're going to need a hotel. And not some cheap dump, either. A nice place."

Meghan decides Charles should work on his studies rather than play video games. "History or science?" she asks him.

"History," he says.

"Give me an example of how the U.S. government has used their influence to help grow the economies of developing nations."

Charles rattles off a thorough defense for the CIA assassinating President Allende in Chile in 1973 and replacing him with General Pinochet. It's clear Meghan has Charles well-versed in neo-conservative politics. The last thing I hear before I tune out is Charles touting Ronald Reagan as the greatest President of post-WWII America.

The traffic is bad when we reach the city. It takes twenty-five minutes to get from North Grand Avenue to Figueroa St, less than two miles away. Meghan stares out the window in reverence of the boutiques and restaurants. She wonders aloud if she'll have time to shop at the Beverly Center. I turn the radio on to drown her out. It's set to the sports station, and the Dodgers game is being broadcast.

"Anything but baseball," she says. "I've wasted enough time on baseball for one lifetime."

We pull up to the hotel. Charles is first out of the car so he can get the door for his mother. Meghan takes his hand and allows him to practically lift her from the vehicle. She kisses him on the cheek, links arms with him, and the two of them proceed into the hotel. A valet goes to the trunk and retrieves the luggage. A second valet comes for the keys.

"Keep it close," I say to him. "I'll be right out."

I walk into the lobby. Meghan is sitting on a sofa, and Charles is fetching her bottled water from the concierge. I go to the front desk and pay for a room. When I return with the keys, Charles is sitting next to his mother. She has a lint brush out and is rolling it across the sleeve of his shirt.

"You woke us up so early this morning," she says to me. "Now I feel wretched. I think I'm going to take a nap."

"I'll take Charles to the hospital while you sleep," I say.

We both turn our attention to Charles.

"Aren't you tired?" she says to him.

"I feel okay," he replies.

She squints at him and says, "Let's get settled in before we make any decisions."

I hand the valet five dollars, and he thanks me and walks away. Charles and I each take one of the bags, and the three of us ride the elevator up to the twentieth floor. Meghan rests her head on Charles's shoulder as we walk the hall to their room. When we get inside, she lies down on the bed and has Charles remove the shoes from her feet.

"I think I'll take a bath," she says.

Charles goes to the bathroom and starts the water.

"Jesus Christ, what have you done to the boy?"

Meghan waves me over with a finger. I take two cautious steps toward the bed. In a whisper, she says, "I won't have you telling my son what to do. I'm his mother—do you understand me? I make the decisions, not you."

I raise my voice to a level that risks Charles hearing me. "I didn't drive all the way out to Palm Springs and bring you back here so you could lounge around a hotel all day."

"I'm against the whole thing. Cliff was a cancer on our family. He was a philanderer and a liar, he took drugs and gambled away all our money."

I holler to Charles in the bathroom: "You ready to go see your dad?"

He comes around the corner into the main room and looks dead-eyed at his mother. "I'm ready," he says. He walks out into the hall. I head for the door, glancing over my shoulder in time to see the TV's remote control hurtling toward me. I duck and it smashes against the wall, shattering into several pieces.

Charles does not acknowledge my presence in the car. Instead he returns to his video game. His gargantuan hands flash across the phone's face in a frenzied blur, and his eyes trace every tiny movement of his avatar's actions. He does not blink for the entire duration of three red-light stops in a row.

"Are you nervous?" I ask him.

"I don't know," he says, not looking up from the game.

I reach over and snatch the machine out of his hands.

"Don't play that damn thing while I'm talking to you."

He fixes his gaze out the window, as if it was his job to count the passing telephone poles.

"You know, your dad talks about you all the time," I say. "He misses you like hell."

The boy's attention to the world outside his window is resolute.

I continue, "Seeing you is going to be a big surprise for him."

"He doesn't know I'm coming?"

"Well, no."

"He didn't ask you to bring me here?"

"He's been trying to see you all this time."

"Then why hasn't he?" His voice is shaky, nearly breaking

"You'll have to ask your mother about that."

Charles is reluctant to get out of the car at the hospital. I stand outside and wait. My hangover from drinking in the desert is setting in. I'm sweating and panting, thirsty, saturated with doom. A woman being pushed in a wheelchair rolls by. There is an oxygen tank strapped to her ride. I light a cigarette and check my phone. No messages. I have the urge to call Frannie but resist it. A bird on a wire overhead shits on the hood of my car.

"That's it," I shout at Charles, "it's time to go! No more fucking around!"

He moves slowly from the car.

"Come on," I say. "Hurry up."

He stares down at his feet the whole walk through the parking lot, past the reception, up the elevator. The door to Cliff's room is shut. We pause.

"Are you ready for this?" I say. "He's in pretty rough shape."

Charles opens the door and steps in.

Cliff is lying flat on his back, asleep. Some of the swelling in his face has gone down. He looks nearly human again. There are four empty pudding cups scattered on a tray next to his bed. I give Cliff a gentle shake.

"Hey, pal," I say.

Cliff's eyes open slowly. He has a strange countenance to his face, as if he's surprised to still be living. He takes ahold of my shirt and pulls me toward him.

"I thought I told you not to come around here," he says.

"I don't listen much to what people tell me."

"Then you'll get to see me off."

"Your death doesn't interest me, pal."

"Then you shouldn't have come."

"Don't talk like that in front of your kid."

Charles approaches the bed.

"Hi," Charles says.

Cliff blinks his eyes repeatedly, and then stares dumbly at the boy.

"Dad, it's me."

Cliff's lips quiver, trying to form his thoughts into words. "Charles?" he finally says in a wheezing half-cry.

"Mr. Brown drove out to Palm Springs and picked me up."

Cliff struggles to sit upright, groaning and wincing. The boy leans down and eases him up. Cliff seizes him in a hug. The boy looks to have been caught off-guard but doesn't resist. Cliff sobs openly.

I sneak out of the room to give them privacy, finding a seat in the lounge at the end of the hall. I find another back-issue of *The New Yorker*. In it there is an article about a strange and mysterious man who for years donated forgeries of famous painters' works to museums. He made all the paintings himself. This in itself is not fascinating; it's been done before. What's most odd is the man's motivation for doing such a thing. Forgers tend to be artists who view themselves as overlooked. They are people who say, "I'm as good as Vermeer! Why can't people see that?" By forging paintings, they can reconcile their lack of recognition by demonstrating just how stupid, blind, and pompous the art world is. Also, many forgers, like most other criminals, commit their crimes to get rich.

But this man had neither of these motivations. First, he hardly fancied himself an artist at all. According to him, he didn't care to be recognized for his work. He went as far as admitting that he greatly preferred mimicry to anything of his own creation—

hadn't done an original work since boyhood. Most of the forgeries he did he whipped out in less than an hour's time with no particular attention to detail, or even pride in what he'd created.

Additionally, he made no money from this illicit undertaking—hundreds of paintings done without collecting a single dollar for his efforts, not so much as a tax credit. So why did he do it? He simply liked the idea of being viewed as a respected member of the community. To him, donating valuable art was a vehicle to be treated with esteem and reverence. The article claimed that, like many people, he has created a present that is designed to compensate for a deficient past. The man's only friend, a prominent woman of wealth in the small Southern town in which he lived, claimed that the happiest she ever saw him was when he read on his hometown's Wikipedia page that he was listed under the category of "Notable Residents," as an art dealer and philanthropist. This friend said the man wept tears of joy.

Strange what different people value in this life, I think to myself. There is Cliff, who only wants to be with his son. There are men like Sebastian, who care only for money. And there are women like Meghan, who require security above all else. There are some amongst us who demand adventure, and others who simply want their privacy.

Before I have a chance to finish the article and learn what became of this fraudulent philanthropist artist, Charles appears. He's wearing a wide smile that seems foreign or at least long-misplaced from his face.

"You look well," I say.

The boy holds out his hand for me to shake, and when I do he grips it tightly. "Thank you, Mr. Brown. You've done a wonderful thing for my dad and me."

I feel my heart swell in my chest, and a lump form in my throat. "I'm glad to have done it," I say. "Thank you for coming."

"My dad wants to see you."

I pat the boy on the shoulder.

The blue-black bruising around Cliff's forehead and cheeks is unchanged, and the tube remains connected to his head. His eyes continue to move sluggishly, and the lips are still white and cracked. The voice, a choked whisper. Yet it seems he's undergone a tremendous healing process.

"Who would've thought that you, Lou Brown, would be the Lord's vessel to bring my son and me back together?"

"I can't explain it."

"Maybe there's hope for the future of mankind yet."

"I wouldn't go that far."

"I can never repay you for this."

"It was nothing."

"Listen," Cliff says. "I know you're having a hard time right now, but have faith things will work out." His eyes drift to a cabinet against the wall. "Can you get me a pudding? They're on a shelf in there."

I go to the cabinet, get the pudding, tear the lid off the container, and hand it to him.

"The funny thing is," I say, "in the last few days, I've developed an appreciation for the confusion and the chaos."

"You'll find your salvation yet."

"Here's what I've learned: there's nothing worse than suffering and not knowing the root of it. However, to suffer deliberately in order to better understand yourself and the nature of the world, that's all right."

Cliff spoons pudding into his mouth in a rapturous manner, leaving remnants of chocolate on his lips and chin. "I just know that I'll never again give in to the temptation to abandon hope. I'll cling to it always, no matter what."

"So things with the boy are good?"

"I made a lot of mistakes in my past and I don't blame Meghan for taking Charles away from me. But now I'm ready to commit myself to being a father. Charles and I talked about me moving closer to Palm Springs. The Padres have their Single-A affiliate in Lake Elsinore. I have some friends in the organization, maybe they'll give me a job."

"You think Meghan will allow it? I met her today. She's..."

"She's a good person. It'll take time, but she'll come around."

"I'm real happy for you, pal."

"Thanks, buddy," he says. "Now do me a favor and send my son back in here."

When I find Charles, he's on the phone with his mother, explaining to her the reconciliation that has occurred. She is screaming so loud Charles has to hold the phone three feet from his head. The entire waiting room full of people bend their ears to better hear the drama.

When he hangs up, I say, "She didn't take it so well?"

"Better than expected. She didn't officially disown me."

"Your dad wants to see you again. Do you want me to wait?"

"No, it's okay. You can go. I'm going to hang out for a while."

"You want some cab money?"

"I have money," he says. "Thank you again."

The sun beats down overhead from its zenith on the car ride home, its magnificent stature in the sky a reminder of just how small and insignificant we are. Far too often I've made the mistake of putting myself at the center of things, attaching too much importance to my being, like an infant expecting the world to work for my service and benefit. Perhaps now is the time for a maturation, a graduation, an evolution—to put behind me my petty, selfish neuroses, disavow my insistence on freedom, my aversion to binding ties. The opportunity has presented itself for me to work toward something grander—something beyond the bounds of my corporeal being: A family!

I consider my own father—a beast of a man—who never embraced the tenants of fatherhood and responsibility. He suffered nothing but ill feelings and fear, a man crippled and broken by the weight of obligation. And for that he is a non-entity in this world, a nothing, a less-than-nothing. How could I even consider repeating the mistakes of an injustice bestowed upon me? The cycle of neglect and abuse need not continue.

Basking in the light of my grand revelation, shrouded in my commitment to play my part in the continuation of the species, my contribution to humanity, I'm left whirling and spinning. *Divine entropy, be damned—I am not your slave, a casualty of inertia, a victim of fate. That's not my worldview. As a believer in and proponent of free will, I assert my right to change course, to steer my own ship, to choose my own guiding light.*

"Thank you, Cliff," I say to myself. "You're an inspiration!"

There is a U-Haul truck in the driveway. A team of men run back and forth, to and fro, arms full of worldly possessions collected by Frannie and me during our cohabitation. Out of nowhere the sky opens up and rain comes down in heavy, wet drops that explode against the windshield of my car. They sound like an invading army trying to beat down the walls of my fortress of resolve. *My first test*, I think to myself.

I sprint from my car to the house, running as if propelled by a celestial motor catapulting me to speeds never before reached by man or beast. "Put that back," I shout at the men as I run past. "Nothing leaves this house!"

Frannie is standing inside the main foyer, directing this insubordination against my heart's desire.

"What are you doing?" I ask.

"I'm leaving you, Lou. It's over."

Two men carrying the disassembled pieces of our bedframe walk in-between Frannie and me.

"Your plan was to leave without even discussing it with me?"

"Why would I need to discuss it with you? It's not a negotiation."

"We're engaged to be married, we have a baby on the way, we're starting a family."

She waits for the men carrying the bedframe to step outside. "I'm sorry but it's not true."

I grip my hands over her shoulders. I'm breathing heavily, fighting to maintain composure. "What's not true?"

"The baby. It's not true. It never was. We're not having a baby."

My hands clamp down harder around her arms. I can feel the bones and muscles bend under the pressure.

"What the hell are you talking about—no baby?"

She rips herself free from my grasp.

"Just what I said. There is no baby. It was a test."

"A test?" I say. "What kind of sick bitch tells a man he's going to be a father when it's not true?"

She slaps me hard across the face—the impact of her open palm meeting my cheek sounds like the crack of thunder. I raise my own hand in retaliation, and she closes her eyes and recoils. I instead lower my hand, turn away from her, pick up a lamp, and fire it across the room, where it smashes against the wall, exploding into a thousand pieces.

One of the movers runs back into the house.

"Is everything okay?" he asks.

"It's fine," Frannie says, "it was an accident. Please go take a break. Mr. Brown and I need a little time." She smiles, but her eyes belie the calmness of her words. The mover stands in the doorway, confused about the right course of action. "It's okay," Frannie insists. "Everything is fine. Come back in thirty minutes."

The man nods and shuts the door behind him.

"I'm sorry," she says, "but it was the only way for me to know where you stood."

"Stood with what?"

An ocean of tears forms in her eyes. "With me, with us, with this relationship."

I go to her, try to throw my arms around her, but she retreats to the far side of the room.

"I don't understand," I say. "What are you talking about?"

"It has to do with that phony phone call I received the other night about my mother being in the hospital."

"I already told you it wasn't me."

"When I told you about it, you asked if I was alone when I got the call, and I said yes, but that wasn't true. I was with someone."

"Really?" I ask, trying to feign surprise.

"I was with my ex—Seth."

"What the fuck, Frannie?"

"It's not what you think. I'm not sleeping with him. It's not like that."

"So why don't you try telling me how it is, then."

"He had been begging me to meet with him for a long time. I told him no a thousand times, but he kept calling."

"So what? Now you're going back to him?"

"I don't know what I'm doing. He just got me thinking, that's all."

"Thinking what?"

"He told me he loves me and that he wants me back. He wants to start a family. I told him I was with you now, that we are in love, but he wouldn't let up. He asked me if you wanted to have a family. I told him I didn't know. Then he asked if I wanted a family and I told him that I think so—*someday*. But that night, when I left the restaurant to race to the hospital to see my mother, I was in a panic and it occurred to me just how important family is, how it's the only thing that really matters in this life, and that I really want to start a family of my own. And when you came home the next day and we had sex, I couldn't help myself and blurted out that I was pregnant to see how you would react, and you blew it. You really blew it!"

I throw my arms around her once more. This time she allows it. We stay locked in an embrace, her red teary face pressed against my chest, my stroking her hair, and kissing her forehead and cheeks. "Frannie, please give me another chance," I say. "I'm ready for it. I can handle a family."

"You're not. You're not even close."

"You have to forgive me."

"I have," she says. "I'm not angry with you. But we can't be together."

I wouldn't usually take such a threat seriously. In moments of heated emotion, women often say things they don't mean. But the look on her face is calm and steady, unwavering in its resolve. That's because a woman's loyalty is not like a man's. It's entirely conditional. A man can sleep around and do all types of awful things to a woman, but if he truly loves her he will never leave her. But a woman is more fickle. She can love with all her being but she's capable of losing that love, and once the change in her has occurred, there is no going back. After that, she'd just as well spit on her ex-lover if she saw him dying in a gutter.

"Where are you going to go?" I ask.

"I rented an apartment in Malibu," she says, with a newfound world-weariness in her voice.

"Can I call you?"

"There's nothing left to say."

I drive to a bar, go inside, and order a whiskey. Then I order several more. I sing a song of heartbreak in a loud, bellowing voice. The bartender says to me, "Why don't you practice a little bit of moderation and good sense, buddy?" His eyes have a deadened glaze about them.

"Because I find those things inhibitory," I say. I get up and walk outside. I call the Frontier Motel and the owner picks up. He sounds horribly out of breath, as if he's carried something heavy up a tall flight of stairs. I ask if Emma is around, and he grunts unintelligibly at me. I wait for a few moments and as I'm about to hang-up, Emma gets on the line. I explain to her that my house is being foreclosed on, but that it will take a few months for the banks to complete the paperwork, and that I'm going on a trip and don't know when I'll be back. I ask her if she'll stay in the house and see to the details in my absence.

"How's Tessa?" she asks.

"Give her a call. I'm sure she'd be happy to hear from you." I give Emma Tessa's phone number and my address. "Feel free to invite her to stay with you up at the house."

We agree to meet in two hours so I can give her a key and any pertinent instructions. When we hang-up, I book a one-way flight to Mexico City leaving the next day. On the walk back to my car I take out my driver's license and two hundred dollars in twenties from my wallet, and then throw the wallet, my watch, and my car keys into the sewer. I exchange with a bum one of the twenties for two dollars in quarters, and then catch a bus home to pack.

At Roundfire we publish great stories. We lean towards the spiritual and thought-provoking. But whether it's literary or popular, a gentle tale or a pulsating thriller, the connecting theme in all Roundfire fiction titles is that once you pick them up you won't want to put them down.